Spare Parts

SPARE PARTS

by
Rick Hanson

KENSINGTON BOOKS

For Emma Katherine Hanson.
Your courage, wit and unconditional love hath preserved me whole.
Thanks, Mom.

Spare Parts

Chapter One

Never *disembowel yourself with a claw hammer and never speak to Margot before noon.* These were the rules I lived by. And I would happily break the former as a means to avoid breaking the latter.

By coincidence, I actually had the claw hammer in my hand when the phone in my studio clicked onto the answering machine and I heard her deceptively cordial voice. "Adam, it's me. I have to talk to you right now."

I wasn't fooled. Margot McCleet-Zarabi-Hammerschmidt-Luciano-Stang never called just to say hi. She always had a problem. To say that she had a lot of problems would be like calling the Grand Canyon a bit of erosion. Price-Waterhouse couldn't keep track of Margot's problems, and she seemed to think it was my duty, as her brother, to solve them.

"Adam, you big shit. Answer the phone." Her momentary sweetness became strident. "Can you hear me, Adam? I know you're screening your calls. Don't play games with me, you jerk."

There was no way I was going to get caught up in Margot's tantrum. Today I had problems of my own.

"If you don't pick up right now," she threatened. "I'm coming over."

"Knock yourself out, harpy," I mumbled, as I reached for my navy blazer. "I won't be here. Even if you catch me, I have a claw hammer and I'm not afraid to use it."

I was at the door, only seconds away from a clean getaway when her tone transformed into a whimper. "Please, Adam, I'm scared. Something has happened to Phillip. Please."

There it was, the dreaded sob.

I can't stand to hear a woman cry and Margot knows it. She knows that I once drove my car into a tree to avoid hitting a squirrel. She knows that I wept at the end of *Old Yeller*. She knows that no matter how hard I try to immerse myself in the singularly selfish lifestyle of a semi-successful sculptor who is selling his work for real money, I'm still a sucker who will always root for the underdog and defend the indefensible.

I dragged myself back to the phone, punched the speaker button and dropped onto the sofa like an altar boy about to be reprimanded for touching himself in an impure manner. "It's okay, Margot, I'm here. What's wrong with Phil?"

"You asshole! Why didn't you answer?"

"I just walked in."

"Oh, bullshit. You've been there all along, probably working on one of those pathetic little statues of yours. I hear an echo. You have me on that stupid speaker-phone, don't you? Why do you do that when you know how much I hate it?"

"Because I'm afraid if I get too close to the phone chord I might strangle myself with it. Now, can you set aside the verbal abuse long enough to tell me what's got your panties in such a bunch?"

"Always the gentleman, aren't you?"

If I had been anything less than a gentleman, I would have taken a tenderizing mallet to her skull twenty years ago. That was the first of several times when she showed up on my doorstep with her designer luggage and divorce papers in hand. I had recently returned from Vietnam, and Margot made post-traumatic stress disorder seem like a trip to Disney World.

"Margot, what did you mean when you said you were afraid something's happened to Phil?"

"Since you asked, he's supposed to be at an orthodontists' convention in Seattle, and you know how good he is about checking in with me. He was to call me at eight this morning and now it's almost ten."

Phillip Stang, D.D.S., was the courageous little man who swept Margot off her feet and, thank God, out of my house. They met and fell in love when she decided to spend some of the astronomical alimony from ex-husband number three on having her fangs straightened. The braces came off on the day of the wedding.

"Would it be safe to assume that you already tried calling his room?"

"Of course. I made the operator let it ring forty-seven times, and he didn't answer."

"Well," I mused, "maybe Phil just stepped out for the proverbial pack of smokes, got selective amnesia and decided to make a new life for himself in Saskatoon."

"Shut up, Adam. That's stupid. Running away is not Phillip's style. He'd tell me if he was unhappy."

She was right. Aside from his dubious taste in marital partners, Phil was a decent, honest man, and I hated to think something might have happened to him.

While Margot rattled off a detailed schedule of Phil's sojourn in Seattle, I walked to the tall window of my studio and picked up my claw hammer again. I'd built this room myself, added it on to the cottage that clung to the river-front bluff.

From here, I could see the morning fog yielding above the autumn-red leaves of the maples—but not to the blue Portland skies and the golden sunshine, cheerily predicted in the morning edition of the *Oregonian*. Instead, it was raining. The sun only served to backlight an otherwise opaque layer of dark clouds which turned the Willamette River to a gloomy slate gray.

Margot finally paused to draw breath, and I asked, "And what, exactly, do you expect me to do? Run up to Seattle and drag him home for you?"

"Yes."

Her absolute self-centeredness was phenomenal. It never occurred to her that I had a life of my own. "Forget it, Margot."

"You're not going to help me?"

The best help I could have given her was an all-expenses-paid vacation with a crack team of psychotherapists, but I'd actually tried that before, and she wound up marrying the head shrink. "Bye, Margot. I've got to go."

"Before you hang up, there's just one thing I want to say to you, Adam McCleet. Just one thing."

I knew what it was. "Don't start with this. I'm warning you, Margot, I'm not going to fall for it. It's not—"

"Remember when you were nine and I was six and Jamie and Sandy were four? Daddy had been sick for months. You remember, don't you? Daddy couldn't go up and down the stairs any more and so we turned the dining room into a sick room. He knew he wasn't going to get better, and he asked for you, wanted you to stand at his bedside. Do you remember?"

"Vaguely."

"And he told you that you were the man of the family and you were *supposed to take care of Margot.* Isn't that right?"

"I guess. So what?"

"So, you've got to help me."

The statute of limitations on that particular death-bed promise had worn out years ago. Margot was forty-three; she could take care of herself. Nonetheless, I muttered, "I'll do what I can."

"Good. I want you to call your old buds on the police force and get them off their dead asses and out on the streets looking for my Phillip. Is that too much to ask?"

"I'll make some calls, but I'm sure everything is fine. Phil's probably just caught up in the glamour of a dental floss museum or something."

"Don't joke about this, Adam. Just make those calls. Phil's checked in at the Olympic Roosevelt through Sunday morning. Call me as soon as you know something. Can you manage that?"

"Sure, Margot." Perfect, I thought. Since Phil was having too much fun to check in six times a day, I had to do it for him. He'd owe me big for this one.

She said, "Thank you. Bye." Then hung up.

Thank you? Margot hadn't thanked me for anything in years. Niceness was, undoubtedly, some cruel guilt tactic she was testing.

After several minutes of watching the rain and debating whether or not to ignore my sister's ravings, I called Nick Gabreski, one of the few people from my cop days who I stayed in touch with. He now worked, conveniently, in the missing-persons division of the Portland P.D.

I gave Nick the *Reader's Digest* version of Margot's song of woe. After some justifiable complaining, he agreed to call the Seattle P.D. I'd call the hotel.

"I'll be at the Brooks Gallery most of the day," I said. "Thanks, buddy. I owe you lunch."

I got the number of Phil's hotel from information and dialed.

A pleasant female voice answered, "Olympic Roosevelt."

I asked her to ring Phil's room. After ten rings, she came back on the line with the obvious information that he wasn't answering. I asked to talk to house security, got put on hold and listened to a string version of "Achy Breaky Heart."

I picked up my claw hammer and stared across the room at the clay model I'd been working on. The piece was a new style for me with squared-off edges and precisely balanced lines in the shape of a schooner. I hated it.

Finally, the phone made a nasal squawk. "Security. This is Fishman."

"Fishman," I said in my most official voice, the voice they

teach you to use at Police Academy. "This is Special Agent Dullard of the Secret Service. Please listen carefully. This is a matter of life and death."

"Yes, sir."

I could almost hear him snap to attention.

"You have a guest in room 427 who's posing as an orthodontist named Phillip Stang. We have reason to believe he might be plotting an assassination attempt on the life of former Vice President Quayle."

"Oh, my God," Fishman gasped. "What do you want me to do?"

"We know that Stang is currently not in his room. However, it is imperative that we ascertain whether or not he spent last night there. Can you handle it, Fishman?"

"Yes, of course. Do you want me to call you back?"

"Good God, man," I shouted, "there's no time for that. The life of a great American is at stake. Transfer this call back to the operator and have her ring the room until you answer. And you get there as fast as you can. Do it now, Fishman."

I heard a click and seconds later the phone in Phil's hotel room started to ring. I turned on my speaker phone and approached the ridiculous clay thing on my work bench, intending to fulfill the action I'd started before Margot interrupted.

Hefting the hammer like a baseball bat, I took my first swing at the hapless chunk of clay. As I expected, the result was an improvement. I whacked again, reducing my aborted effort to a lump of squished gray matter. When something turns sour, it's better to end it quickly and cut your losses.

There was a smile on my face when the security guard answered again. He was panting like a Fishman out of water. "Agent Dullard, he's not here."

"We know that, Fishman. But did he spend the night there?"

"Negative, sir. One of the housekeepers is cleaning the room right now. She said that when she came in, the bed was made and the mints were still on the pillows."

"Good job, Fishman. It's men like you who make this country what it is. I expect the former Vice President will want to shake your hand."

"Yes, sir, thank you, sir. The name is Roy. Roy Fishman."

"One more thing, Roy. The events which have transpired this morning must remain secret. You are to tell absolutely no one. If Stang returns, you will not approach him. You will not attempt to apprehend him. You will call Detective Nick Gabreski of the Portland P.D. at once. Is that understood?"

"Yes, sir."

I gave him Nick's number and hung up.

I thought about Phil on my way to the gallery. For a lot of men, being absent at an out-of-town convention was no big deal, but Phil was different. He was anything but a womanizer. As for partying, I'd never seen him drink more than a single glass of wine. The fact that Phil had apparently not spent the night in his room was cause for concern. He was a creature of habit, the kind of guy who might be tempted to make his own bed at a hotel, but I doubted that even Phil would put mints on his own pillow. Damn it. I absolutely hated it when Margot was right.

Chapter
Two

The Brooks Gallery was one of the most prestigious in Portland's upscale Pearl district. It was uncluttered, warmly lit,
elegant but unpretentious. The owner, Alison Brooks,
knew her business as well as anyone and better than most. My
statues were displayed throughout, in such a way as to allow the
viewers' own curiosity to lead them, casually, from one room to
the next until the entire gallery had been explored.

None of the staff noticed my arrival, and I wandered about,
playing fly on the wall, listening to how people reacted to my
work. Since today was the First Thursday Opening of October,
when viewing was by invitation only, the gallery was full of
patrons who ought to know art and who were apt to buy. I tried
to cultivate the properly charming attitude, but openings always
made me surly, especially now, when my best inspiration came
from a claw hammer.

"Provocative," one severe-looking woman dressed in black
leather said to another severe-looking woman dressed in even
more black leather.

An aging patroness stroked the collar of her fur. "Adam

McCleet is in a rut," she proclaimed. "Why must there be nude women reclining on the backs of all his sea mammals?"

"Why must there be sea mammals beneath all his reclining nudes?" said her male companion.

"I believe he's going through his 'nude women riding on the backs of sea mammals' period," I interjected.

The lady sneered over the gold rims of her glasses, probably wondering how somebody who looked like me had rated an invite to this event. My clothes were acceptable—a navy blazer over khaki trousers and a chambray shirt—but there wasn't a damn thing I could do about my face, which looked roughly like it had been chiseled from a piece of stubborn mahogany. No matter how close I shaved, this face was more at home in a waterfront bar than at a fancy art opening.

She asked, "Are you familiar with this artist?"

"A. A. McCleet? I'm one of his biggest fans."

I strolled to a small room off the main exhibit area which contained a single piece—my favorite—a shimmering, slick, black ebonite killer whale, four feet long, thrusting skyward from its base. A slender nude woman straddled the whale's back, clinging to the dorsal fin with both hands, her spine gracefully arched, her head tossed back, her hair flowing in long wet tangles. I found myself craving a cigarette, and I hadn't smoked in ten years.

A woman's voice came in a breathy whisper from close behind me. "It's extremely sensual, isn't it?"

I turned to see who was speaking. Suddenly I felt like a small child on Christmas morning catching his first glimpse of the presents under the tree. She took my breath away.

With her eyes focused on the sculpture, she brushed past me so closely I could smell the clean in her hair. I could feel the heat radiating from her body.

She reached out a hand and lightly traced the soft curves of the statue with the tips of her slender fingers. "I like touching it," she said.

"It likes to be touched."

"Oh? And how do you know that?"

"Because I created it. I know how it thinks."

"What do you call it?" she asked.

"Orcinus Orgasmus."

"I see. And do you use live models?"

"Only the women," I said. "The last time I tried to get a live orca into my studio, the neighbors complained."

Her green eyes fixed on mine. "I could pose for you."

"I don't know. You see, I can't seem to do true justice to the beauty of my models unless I make love to them first."

She moved toward me and stood close enough for me to feel her warm breath on my face. "So, you like to be touched, too."

"Very much."

"That," she said, "can be arranged." Taking me by the hand, she led me out of the display room, through the crowd of people sipping wine and munching cheese in the main exhibit area, down a short hallway to an oak door with a brass placard exclaiming: PRIVATE.

She opened the door and pulled me into the tastefully decorated office. With one smooth motion, she closed the door and locked it. She had taken charge, and I decided to go along for the ride.

Slipping out of her burgundy velvet jacket, which she dropped to the floor, she walked to the center of the room, stopped in front of a large, antique desk and faced me.

Without speaking, she reached behind her head and removed the pin that held her hair in place. She tossed her head from side to side. Rich auburn locks fell gracefully to her shoulders, framing her delicate face in luxurious waves.

Her lips parted and she moistened them, seductively, with her tongue. "Could I model for you?" she asked softly. "What do you think?"

This is going to be a great day, I thought. "So far, so good," I said, trying to preserve what little objectivity I had left.

She leaned against the desk, causing her tight velvet skirt to rise to midthigh, exposing the dark portion of the tops of her hose. "Would you like to see more?"

"Yes," I said, feeling a little giddy. A result, no doubt, of all the blood in my brain rushing to my genitals.

Her enameled fingernails lightly played across the buttons of her pink silk blouse. She pulled the blouse back and allowed it to slip off her shoulders and fall to the floor.

Her stomach was firm and flat. Her narrow waist curved in, delightfully, from the hips. Her sumptuous breasts were only partly concealed by a provocative rose-colored bikini bra.

Her alluring green eyes spoke in a language all their own.

"More?" she asked.

I searched the recesses of my mind for precisely the right words. "Uh-huh."

She laughed. It sounded like angels singing. "You're a man of few words." She unfastened the clasp in the front of her lace bra and pulled it back, slowly, deliberately. Her breasts were a vision of symmetry, two perfectly proportioned mounds of firm, creamy flesh, crowned with hard pink nipples.

She finished removing her bra and tossed it toward me. I caught it with one hand as it sailed close to my face. The material felt soft and warm, and the scent of wild roses was intoxicating.

She touched an index finger to the tip of her tongue and lightly traced an exciting path down her throat, between her breasts, across her navel, stopping at the waist of her skirt. "More?" she teased.

I could barely keep from blowing saliva bubbles, but I managed to nod the affirmative.

She leaned forward from the waist and placed her hands around one ankle. An ankle made to look even more graceful by the presence of the burgundy-colored, three-inch, spike-heeled shoe adorning her foot.

As if smoothing her stocking, she slid her hands slowly up her leg, drawing attention to each tantalizing curve. At midthigh, her hands reached the hem of the skirt and continued up, revealing a creamy upper thigh that contrasted with a pink garter belt fastened to the top of her dark hose. She raised the skirt high enough for me to see the rose-colored, French-cut panties which matched the bra I held in my hand.

Rapidly approaching sensory overload, I could no longer be a spectator. Tossing the bra aside, I moved across the room and wrapped my arms around her slender waist. Pulling her body hard against mine, I kissed her delicate face, her luscious throat, her firm breasts.

She peeled the blazer off my shoulders and dropped it on the floor. Her hands slid across my chest and unbuttoned my shirt. She pressed her lips against mine and forced her hot tongue into my mouth. With mechanical precision, she unbuckled my belt and lowered the fly of my trousers. Her passion was overwhelming.

"Would you like to lie down?" she whispered.

Before I could answer, she pulled me toward the sofa.

"Wait," I said, "I have a better idea." And with one grand gesture, I swept the phone, papers, books, everything off the desk and onto the floor with a crash.

"Adam, what is it about this desk? Last time you did that, you broke a five-hundred-dollar statuette, a Lewiston original."

"Lewiston is a hack," I said, as I picked her up and laid her gently onto the cool surface. "What you need on your desk, Miss Brooks, is a McCleet original."

In fact, there was something about the sight of Alison's pale skin contrasted against the dark cherrywood of her antique desk. She brought out the beast in me, drove me to feats far beyond those of mortal man.

This seduction game, which Alison Brooks played so well, was one of our favorites.

A rapping at the door was followed by the sound of a slightly effeminate male voice on the other side. "Alison, are you all right? I heard a crash."

It was Monte, Alison's slightly effeminate assistant.

"I'm fine, Monte. I just dropped some, uh, books."

"Is Adam McCleet with you? Some of the guests would like to meet him."

"Philistines," I whispered, as I stroked her thighs. "Let them wait."

"Yes, he's here," Alison called back. "We're just finishing up some . . . business. We'll be out in a few minutes."

"A few minutes? You underestimate me," I said, as I pushed her skirt into a bunch above her hips.

"Well, please hurry," Monte whined. "There's a gentleman out here who's interested in purchasing one of Adam's sculptures. He wants to talk to the artist."

"Purchasing?" she questioned.

The temperature in her office went from hot and steamy to crisp. Though I insistently caressed the satin skin of Alison's buttocks, it was too late. She'd already changed gears, downshifted from *femme fatale* to astute businesswoman.

"Adam." She caught both of my hands in her own, held them together and raised them to her lips. After she brushed a kiss across my knuckles, she whispered, "We have to stop."

A groan started in the pit of my belly and crawled all the way up my throat. It was hard not to whine.

"Come on, Adam. This is your show, after all."

"Correct." I buttoned my shirt. "And live purchasers of giant sea mammals are not to be ignored."

While Alison gathered her clothing, I began picking up the mess on the floor. "Just leave it," she said. "It'll save you the trouble of knocking it all off again later."

"You give me hope." I placed a final kiss on the tip of her aquiline nose. "And inspiration."

I left Alison to rearrange herself and headed back out into the gallery to find Monte and the man with the money.

I didn't get far. When I spotted Trevor Ingersoll I came to an abrupt halt. Trevor was one of the most well-respected artists in the Northwest, and I held him responsible for causing me to take the leap from police officer to struggling sculptor. Seven years ago, he'd judged The New Oregonian Art Contest, which I had reluctantly entered. I didn't win, but afterwards, he sought me out. He had seen something in my work that the other judges had missed.

His encouragement was about as subtle as cutting a wedding cake with a chain saw. He'd bought me a beer and told me, like it or not, I was an artist.

I didn't like it. As far as I was concerned, art was a game, a hobby that I used to keep myself sane. But sculpting wasn't real life. I just couldn't believe that diddling around in a studio was a suitable occupation for a grown man.

Then, Trevor had informed me that the sex life of an artist was not to be believed. His offhand remark went a long way toward convincing me to quit the force, especially after I'd taken a good look at him. At that time Trevor was in his early sixties, but built like a lumberjack with a fierce glint in his eyes and confidence in his manner. He was a man's man.

Now I hardly recognized him. His skin had an ochre cast. His once-powerful shoulders slumped inward. I embraced him carefully. "Trevor," I said. "Thanks for coming, man."

"I knew you'd be famous." He gestured toward one of my smaller, more delicate pieces, a woman and a playful dolphin. "Now you are able to create like an artist. Can you talk like one? Explain this sculpture."

I shrugged. "It's a beautiful woman and a powerful animal. If it makes somebody smile, I've done my job. And if it makes them want to write a check, then I've done my job very well."

"Still pragmatic, I see. Still the cop mentality."

"Guess so."

"But now your art is not so fulfilling. You're in a slump."

I looked up sharply. How did he know? I made a point of never talking to anyone, not even Alison, about my aborted sculptures.

"Keep thinking like a cop," Trevor advised. "It will help you survive."

He almost laughed, but the effort seemed too much for him. Goddamn, I hated to see him this way. He waved me on. "Go, Adam, enjoy this while you can."

While not wanting to abandon him in the crowd, I respected him too much to hover. I was relieved when Alison appeared at his shoulder. There was a hint of the old glimmer in Trevor's eyes. I left him in her dainty but capable hands.

The search for Monte eventually led me back to the room where Alison and I began. There I found him, schmoozing a middle-aged man in a rumpled London Fog raincoat. Unfortunately, this man, who looked like he was assembled at the Kenworth truck factory, was no art collector.

"Oh, here he is," Monte squealed as I walked into the room. "Adam, this gentleman is interested in the *Lady and the Orca.*"

I doubted that very much. "Monte, this is Nick Gabreski of the Portland P.D."

Nick and I exchanged a bone-crushing handshake. Squeezing my fingers until tears ran down my cheeks was Nick's way of demonstrating affection. At six-feet-three-inches in height, he was only an inch taller than I was, but his two-hundred-sixty pounds gave him a seventy-pound advantage in weight. I tightened my grip. "This guy wouldn't buy a piece of art if it jumped up and bit him on his large, callused ass."

Nick winced and relaxed his hold. He hadn't counted on the strength that had developed in my hands from all the clay modeling. "Not true. There're no blisters on my large ass."

"Oh . . . I see," Monte said, unable to disguise his disappointment. "You're not interested in a purchase. You're only a friend of Adam's."

"Sorry," Nick said. "I figured the fastest way to get Adam front and center was to let him think there was money involved."

Nick's voice sounded like gravel sliding off a tin roof, the result of a gunshot wound to the throat his first year on the force.

His laugh made an infectious rattle, and I laughed along with him.

Monte glared at the both of us. "Go ahead and have your fun. It's just that these invitation-only openings are such a bother, what with crashers and the hired help guzzling the wine and gobbling up the hors d'oeuvres, and important guests to be attended to, and. . . ." His stream of consciousness bitching faded from earshot as he scurried from the room.

"Kind of an intense little fella," Nick rasped.

"So what brings you down here?" I asked.

"I got some information, and you're gonna buy me lunch."

"Nick, Nick, Nick, when we say, 'We'll do lunch,' it's just one of those things we insincere artsy types say. It didn't actually mean that I had any intention of feeding you."

"You don't get off that easy, McCleet. If you wanna know what I found out, we gotta do it over food."

"I'm a very busy man, you know. I'm scheduled to stand around here with my hands in my pockets for the next several hours. But . . . what the hell. Should we invite Alison?"

The orca-sized grin on Nick's face indicated an affirmative response. He was fond of Alison. The big guy might not know shit about art, but he could appreciate beauty.

After a brief search, we located Alison in the main display area. She was chatting with a male model type, but as soon as she spied me and Nick, shouldering through the crowd like a couple of misplaced thugs, she politely excused herself, and gave Nick a warm hug. "Good to see you."

"He's conned me into buying him lunch," I said. "We thought you might like to join us."

"Oh, that would be nice, but I should stick around." Her liquid green eyes misted slightly and there was a tiny furrow between her eyebrows. "I want to spend some time with Trevor."

There wasn't a damn thing I could say to make her, or me, feel better. Fortunately, Alison wasn't a woman who required a lot of hand holding. Beneath her satin exterior, she was tempered steel. She recovered in a blink and offered Nick a smile that would melt an iceberg. "Sorry."

"Whatever you say."

Nick was starry-eyed, under Alison's spell, and I hoped it would have an effect on his appetite when the two of us strolled across Second Avenue to Jerry's Trawler. Jerry's was a small, white-tablecloth restaurant with a casual nautical atmosphere and expensive food. I ordered clam chowder, and Nick ordered everything else on the menu.

"What's the matter, your wife not feeding you?"

"Ramona takes good care of me." Nick patted his gut and reminded, "And you owe me for helping out your sister. The woman's a loose cannon."

He had dated Margot once. I'd warned him that the tall, slender, expensive Margot McCleet package was a disguise for a she-werwolf who spent her life snaring dull-witted husbands. But Nick was the kind of guy who had to see for himself what happened in the full of the moon.

Nick elaborated, "Margot's a cold sore on the upper lip of womankind."

"But she's also my sister." That said it all. When your family calls for help, you've got to answer.

"So, you wanna know what I found out about Phil Stang?"

"Sure, let me have it."

"Nothin'."

"Nothing?" I snapped. "I buy you enough food to feed a small family of gypsies for a month, and you tell me, nothing?"

"I called an old bud at the Seattle P.D. by the name of Ed Forest. He ran a check on the hospitals and morgues, and none of them had anybody like your brother-in-law's description."

I was impressed. "Fast work. Is your friend in missing persons?"

"He's a lieutenant. Homicide."

Now, I was really impressed. "You got a homicide lieutenant to do your legwork for you?"

"Forest owes me."

He frowned suddenly, disturbed by something he had seen over my shoulder. I turned to see what had unnerved my old partner—this highly decorated hero of the Vietnam conflict—this hardened, twenty-year-veteran cop.

"Oh my God, it's Margot. Are you armed, Nick? Shoot her."

He shook his head dejectedly. "It wouldn't do any good. I don't have silver bullets."

"Then shoot me."

"And leave myself alone with her? I don't think so."

"Don't look at her. Maybe she'll go away."

But it was too late. I had stared into her cold dark eyes, which were outlined with precision. As always, her makeup was perfect and her Spandex outfit fitted like a second skin. Gargoyle though she was, Margot was tall enough, skinny enough and selfish enough to have been a model for three years. When she recognized me, her ruby lips contorted into an evil snarl.

"We're fucked," Nick said as we watched her push the maître d' aside and descend upon us like an avenging angel.

"You asshole," she hissed, poking a long silver-enameled fingernail in my face. "You were supposed to call me."

"How'd you know we were here?" I asked, trying not to show fear. I knew she could smell fear.

"That little pencil-neck across the street told me."

I assumed the pencil-neck to whom she referred was none other than Monte. Poor guy, I thought. If she made Nick nervous, she probably gave Monte a cardio infarction.

She transferred her Medusa glare to Nick, and he rose to his feet in a belated attempt to be charming. "Margot. What a surprise to see you."

"Shut up, Nick."

"Calm down, Margot," I said. "If you'll retract your claws and sit, Nick can tell us what he found out."

Nick attempted to pull a chair out for her but she jerked it out of his hands and dropped herself down. "Let's hear it."

Just then, the waiter appeared. "Would you like to hear our specials?" he asked, placing a menu in front of Margot.

She slapped the menu back at him. "Get away."

It was going to take a big tip, I thought, if I ever wanted decent service at Jerry's again.

"Well . . . what?" Margot shrieked at Nick.

Nick sat, cleared his throat and said, "A friend of mine who's a Seattle cop checked the hospitals and morgues. No John Does fitting your husband's description turned up."

"That's all? Couldn't your friend go to the hotel? Couldn't he make them tell him where Phillip is?"

"Not without a warrant," Nick said.

"You're pathetic."

"Margot," I said, hoping against the inevitable that I could keep her from ripping Nick or me or the waiter to shreds. "Nick is doing you a favor."

"And what are you doing? Nothing? As usual?"

"I called security at the Olympic Roosevelt and found out that Phil didn't sleep in his room last night. The mints were still on the pillow, and his luggage was still in the closet."

"Oh, my God. That proves something terrible has happened. Any moron—even one like Nick—can see there's enough reason to issue a warrant."

"Sorry," Nick replied, "there's no law against paying for a hotel room and not using it."

The waiter sidled toward us again. With a wary eye on Margot, he piled a small mountain of seafood in front of Nick.

Margot impatiently drummed her fingernails on the table. When the waiter left, she said, "There must be something you can do, Nick."

"Not without a warrant," he repeated.

"Don't patronize me, you big clod."

"He's talking about," I said, trying to take some of the heat off

Nick, "the Federal Privacy Act. It prevents the police from snooping into people's private lives, unless they have hard evidence that a crime has been committed. A hotel could get sued for distributing information about their clientele in the absence of a warrant."

"But my husband's missing," Margot said. "And anyone who knows him knows he wouldn't disappear without telling someone."

"Maybe. Maybe not." Nick snapped the leg off a king crab. "He's got a right to do whatever he wants, as long as he's not breaking any laws. Even if the cops found him, they couldn't tell anybody what he's doing if he doesn't want them to."

"So all you bozos can really do is gobble doughnuts and suck coffee. Is that it?"

I braced for a storm. Margot was baiting Nick, and he'd already taken more abuse than most reasonable men could stand. He gripped the massive crab leg with both fists and broke it in half with a resounding crack.

Margot flinched, but she did not relent. "What if I could prove that Phillip is a victim?"

That shouldn't be difficult, I thought. Anyone who knew Margot would testify that Phil had become a victim on the day they met.

Nick said, "You'd have a new ball game."

"Okay, what about the mints on the pillow? That's proof."

He set down the crab leg and poked a meaty index finger toward Margot's cleavage. "You still don't get it. We're not going to do a damned thing except put Phil's name on a list with a thousand other names. And the first people we look for are children, old people, mentally handicapped people and legitimate victims of crimes. We don't have time to track down every pussy-whipped dentist whose own wife provides all the reason any man, with one ounce of self-respect, would ever need for dropping out."

After a brief but extremely uncomfortable silence, Margot's

lower lip began to quiver, tears welled up in the corners of her eyes and her usual pale complexion turned crimson. She grabbed a water glass. Before Nick could react, the contents of the crystal tumbler were dripping off his chin.

Margot flung back her chair, grabbed her purse and, without speaking another word, raced for the ladies' room.

"Jesus Christ," Nick gasped, as he blotted his face with a napkin. "I should've shot her when she came through the door. Are you sure you're related?"

"Much as I hate to admit it," I said, "Margot has a point. Phil wouldn't have left his luggage behind if he planned on dropping out."

"I know." Nick paused for a moment. "There's something else, too. I couldn't talk about it in front of Margot. I shouldn't tell you, either. So you keep your mouth shut."

"What?"

His rasping voice lowered to a scratchy whisper. "Seattle has had three ripper-style murders in as many weeks. All males. All professionals. The cops think it's some cult ritual. They been keeping it out of the news."

"What do you mean by professionals?" I asked, not really sure if I wanted to know the answer.

"You know, yuppies. Like an attorney, a CPA and an architect. All tourists."

Like Phil, I thought, an orthodontist in Seattle for a convention. "What do you mean, ripper-style?"

"They've been cut up real bad. You know, mutilated."

Before I could find out more, Margot returned. Her eyes were red and swollen. Her lips were a little puffy. She poured on the guilt. "I'm sorry. I'm trying to be brave, but my husband, my dear, sweet Phillip, is in some kind of danger. I just don't know who else I can turn to for help."

Warily, Nick filled his mouth with shrimp.

"Could a private investigator do it?" she asked. "Get proof."

"I suppose so," Nick said. "A P.I. wouldn't be restricted by the Federal Privacy Act."

"Could Adam do it?"

"Oh, hell, yeah," Nick chuckled. "He'd be great. He already knows all that cop stuff."

I gave Nick the same look the waiter had given Margot when she nearly bit his head off.

"Oh, please, Adam. You have to help me."

Margot's helplessness was a transparent ruse. But she was making that whimpery noise in the back of her throat, the same evil whine she'd made when I was ten and she was eight and she'd pleaded with me to rescue her Barbie doll from the local twelve-year-old bullies. As I recall, that was the first time my nose was broken.

"Please," she sobbed.

What could I do? Margot the Manipulator was my sister.

Chapter
Three

Whatever shortcomings Phillip Stang may have had, his taste in lodging was not among them. The Olympic Roosevelt, built in the early 1900's and restored in 1985, was one of the finest hotels downtown Seattle had to offer. I didn't bother stopping at the front desk. Instead, I took the elevator directly to the fourth floor.

The Friday-morning traffic on Interstate 5 had been light. Though it rained all the way, my mood had brightened considerably. Due to this family emergency, I had escaped the dubious honor of standing around at my Brooks Gallery opening and discussing my new artistic directions—of which there were none—and I had managed to put miles between Margot and myself. Phil had not checked in with her for over twenty-four hours, and her panic had taken on the proportions of a great white shark, hungry to feed on my spleen. Of course, I was concerned, too, especially after what Nick had told me about the ripper murders, but I couldn't help feeling that this whole thing was some kind of simple misunderstanding.

I knocked at the door of room 427, hoping Phil would answer

and bring this impromptu manhunt to an end. My gentle tap echoed off the walls of the deserted hallway like a battery of howitzers firing in sequence.

After a moment's wait I was about to assault the door again but changed my mind in midknock. I had already decided that, if Phil didn't answer, I was going to break in. No sense making any more racket than necessary.

Fortunately for me, whoever restored the hotel was so concerned with preserving its old-world charm, they neglected to change the old-world locks. My credit card slid between the jamb and the latch like a knife through butter. The door swung open faster than if I had used a passkey.

The room was empty. Red-striped mints laid ominously on the pillows. Jackets, trousers and shirts hung in the closet. Socks and underwear were folded neatly in the dresser. I estimated that Phil had brought enough clothes for two complete changes a day, yet none were dirty. In the bathroom, the hotel soap was still in its wrapper, and the little strip of paper around the toilet seat was intact.

Then I saw the most disturbing thing of all. There, on the vanity, among the neatly arranged toilet articles, was Phil's dental floss. Even if he had been abducted, he would have taken a bullet in the chest before he'd leave his floss behind. For Phil, oral hygiene was not just a job, it was a way of life. This was not good.

In the bedroom nightstand I found a rent-a-car contract and Phil's convention name tag. I stashed them in the pocket of my leather bomber jacket.

The red message light on the phone was flashing. I was about to pick it up and call the desk for the messages when I heard the words, "Freeze, scumbag."

The voice was shaky, and I thought I'd try to bluff it out. "What seems to be the problem?" I said, turning to see a skinny little man with a big nose and no chin. The plastic name tag above the left breast pocket of his baggy hotel security uniform

spelled out Roy. This, obviously, was the patriotic and courageous Roy Fishman who had successfully quelled the assassination attempt on former Vice President Quayle.

I considered identifying myself as Special Agent Dullard, but
decided against it. The penalties for impersonating a federal
officer are fairly severe, and Roy was probably annoyed that he
hadn't received his medal yet. Besides, it would not be wise to
antagonize the little guy since he held a black .45 automatic in
his trembling hands.

I repeated, "Is there a problem?"

"Breaking and entering. That's the problem," he said. "Up
against the wall and spread 'em."

"You can't be serious, Roy. This is my room."

"Oh, sure. I suppose you always open your door with a credit
card. Now put your hands up."

The general rule is: People holding guns should be respected. Nervous people holding guns should be feared. I raised
my hands slowly. "I misplaced my key?"

He moved closer and demanded again that I put my hands
against the wall and spread my legs. I considered taking his gun
away and giving him a sound rap on his bald little noggin, but
decided that it would probably damage our relationship. "You're
making a big mistake," I said, as I assumed the position.

He quickly stepped in, jammed the gun against the base of
my skull and began patting me down.

"Jesus, Roy," I exclaimed as he stuffed his hand into the hip
pocket of my jeans and extracted my wallet. "You a security
guard or a proctologist?"

I felt the gun barrel press harder against my neck. "You'd
better just shut up."

"If you'll just give me a chance, I can explain—"

"Good job, Roy." A more authoritative voice interrupted.
"We'll take over."

I didn't have to look to know this was a real cop. He hand-
cuffed me in a most professional manner.

As I was escorted down the hall by matching blue bookends, I noticed several high-resolution video security cameras inconspicuously mounted in the chandeliers. These, no doubt, had been my undoing. If I'd known big brother was watching, I might have done things quite differently.

I wasn't exactly crazy about police stations when I was a cop. Now that I was a suspect, I liked them even less. The walls were government green. The floors were black and white speckled tile. And the rooms smelled like drunk people.

I knew the routine. The arresting officers weren't going to listen to anything I had to say until I was booked, which was exactly what I didn't want. If I allowed that to happen, it would take a court order, an act of God, and a tender-hearted bail bondsman to set me free. "Go Directly To Jail" was not the game card I needed. If I was locked up, I couldn't look for Phil, and I also had tickets for the Seahawks game on Sunday.

Fortunately, I remembered the name of Nick Gabreski's friend. When the baby-faced arresting officer seated me in an interrogation room and finally took off the cuffs, I said, "Call Ed Forest."

"Who?"

Wonderful, I thought. They'd never heard of him. "Detective Lieutenant Edward Forest, Homicide." I tried to sound as if Forest and I were old buds. "Ed can straighten this out."

"Ed?" The young officer's eyelids batted nervously.

"Bullshit," said his partner. "Forest don't have friends."

"Call him and find out," I advised. "Mention Nick Gabreski."

The two officers looked at one another as if each was expecting the other to make a decision. Finally, the older one nodded. "I'm doing it."

He stepped through the open door into another room, and I heard him making nervous "yes, sir" and "no, sir" noises on the phone. I decided Ed Forest might be a big shot, the Seattle P.D.'s version of Norman Schwartzkopf. The tense face of the cop in the room with me confirmed that suspicion. His partner returned in less than two minutes, looking at me with new respect. "You stay right here, McCleet. Forest says to wait."

Pretending that I had a choice, I checked my wristwatch. "Hey, guys. It's two-thirty and I'm missing my lunch date."

"Forest says you wait."

They left me and closed the door. After I had strolled the perimeter, done fifty push-ups and checked out my rear molars in the two-way mirror, only half an hour had passed. There was too much time to think, and I was painfully aware of what a sloppy job I had done of breaking into room 427. I needed to get a lot smarter. I needed a plan for locating Phil. Where would he go? What would he do? *How the hell could I think like a guy who saw Margot the Dreadful as a gentle and loving woman?*

At five-forty-five, the thought of escaping flickered through my mind, but I figured that the way my luck was running, I'd probably end up in front of a firing squad.

Twenty more minutes passed and I was about to doze off when, suddenly, I was jolted back to consciousness by an angry, booming voice that seemed to come from everywhere at once. "Who's this fuckin' guy?"

I opened my eyes and focused on a man who looked like a bowling ball in a wrinkled suit. His coarse gray hair pointed to all positions of the compass, as if he had combed it with a paint mixer. Filthy wire-rimmed bifocals balanced precariously at the tip of his bulbous, red-veined nose. A black and dripping stub of what might have been a cigar at one time was jammed into the corner of his snarl. If hell had a version of Santa, this was him.

"His name's Adam McCleet," the young cop said. "Says he knows you."

Forest looked like he'd run out of patience during the Truman administration. His explanation was terse. "I talked to Nick."

I nodded, pretending that I understood.

Forest rolled the mangled cigar butt from one side of his mouth to the other and motioned with one fat hand. "Let's go."

I grabbed my jacket and headed for the door.

Detective Forest politely informed his associates of his intentions. "I'm taking this fuckin' guy."

"Sure, Lieutenant," the older officer replied. "But what about the charges?"

"There ain't no fuckin' charges. Give him his shit back."

The booking sergeant handed me a manila envelope containing my wallet, car keys and assorted change and papers. "Thanks, man, it's been a genuine—"

Forest grabbed my arm and shoved me into the hallway, slamming the door behind us. "Listen, asshole," he hissed.

Asshole again. First Margot. Now Forest. I couldn't remember receiving as much negative input since boot camp.

"You're off the hook because of Gabreski," Forest snarled. "If you fuck up again, Jesus Christ himself won't be able to save your narrow ass."

"I've got no intention of fucking up." I shrugged free. It was hard to imagine Forest doing a favor for anyone. Nick must have pulled one hell of a thorn out of this guy's paw.

He poked the blunt tip of a stubby index finger hard against my sternum. "Now, you listen up, fuck wad. Nick says you were a good cop once. But you're not a cop anymore. You do what I say, then you get the hell out of my city."

"I get the point."

"Good," he grunted. "Now you're coming with me."

Outside, it was drizzling and dark. Forest indicated that I should get into the passenger side of his car, then he got down to the business of careening through the congested, post-rush-hour traffic of downtown Seattle with suicidal abandon. He steered with his left hand while his right alternated between coffee he'd poured from a thermos and the ever-present stump of a cigar butt.

As near as I could tell, nothing stood between us and certain death but a flashing red light plugged into the cigarette lighter of his trashed-out two-year-old Ford. I tightened the seat belt until the possibility of gangrene in the lower half of my body, from loss of circulation, became a legitimate concern. "Jesus, Lieutenant . . . you ever considered giving decaf a try?"

"I got no time to dick around," he said. "My watch was over twenty minutes ago and the little woman's got supper on the fire."

I imagined a bony crone in tattered hyena skins roasting road-kill over an open flame. "That's worth dying for."

"I guess you got no stomach for police work. No guts?" Forest taunted. "That why you quit the force?"

"The work didn't bother me."

Forest barked a flatulent note that might have been a laugh. "Oh, hell, yeah, everybody loves police work. It's so damned rewarding, isn't it? You didn't mind the fucked-up hours or the shitty pay. Or the maggot lawyers who thread child molesters through the eye of a legal needle. You were a champion of the people. The work didn't bother you? Bullshit."

"Not as much as the uptight assholes I had to work with."

"You mean, assholes like me," Forest said as he skidded sideways through a left turn, washing away a mustard stain on the fly of his trousers with scalding coffee.

"You're very perceptive," I said. "I guess that's why they made you a detective. The force needs men who know an insult when they hear it."

"Yeah? I also know a punk when I see one."

We could have continued exchanging insults indefinitely. But one of the more practical lessons I learned on the force was not to argue with idiots. It occurred to me, as I stared through the dirty windshield, that my last few minutes on earth would be put to better use trying to remember the words to the Twenty-Third Psalm.

I actually started to relax a little when Forest steered the car onto a south-bound ramp of the Alaskan Way Viaduct. At least we were away from the traffic lights and congested intersections of downtown. "You want to tell me where we're going?" I asked.

"To the beach." Forest stomped on the accelerator and laid on the horn. At eighty miles per hour, we weaved, dodged and lurched through forty-mile-per-hour traffic. "We're going to look at a body."

The dusk and heavy mist covered the city in a thick darkness. I felt cold inside. "You think the corpse might be my brother-in-law."

"What a fuckin' genius! How did the art world ever get along without you?" Forest jerked the wheel hard to the right, cut off a tractor-trailer and headed west on Spokane Street.

He didn't need to drive like a lunatic. He was trying to scare me. The very fact that he was succeeding, only served to strengthen my resolve not to show it. "You missed your calling, Lieutenant. You should have been a grief counselor."

"Fuckin' great," Forest said. "Then I could be just like you. Make a lot of money for blowing sunshine up people's asses."

I didn't correct his opinion of me and my work because somewhere between my ears or maybe in my heart, I had the feeling he was right. Real men didn't make a living creating delicate statuary. They built bridges and skyscrapers and railroads. The real manly men had grit and grease under their fingernails, not bits of clay.

Maybe I *was* blowing sunshine up the collective asshole of society. Forest's way, the cop way, was the most direct route to fixing the problems of the world. However, I had tried that approach to life in the Marine Corps and on the force. It didn't work. No matter how hard I beat my skull against other people's fists, the world continued to screw itself up.

"Kind of quiet, McCleet. You run out of bullshit?"

"Did you?"

"Shit, no," Forest said. "I could ride your sorry ass all the way to Walla Walla and back again."

I realized where I'd seen Forest before. Not him exactly, but his kind. "You were a drill instructor."

"Marine Corps Recruit Depot. San Diego. 1966 to '69."

"Been there," I said. "Third Marine Division, Northern I Corps."

"Well, *Semper* fuckin' *Fidelis.*"

"Hoorah," I replied. I usually identified with former Marines, but with Forest I felt no kinship.

A few more minutes of heart-stopping near misses and we were north-bound on Harbor Avenue, skirting Elliot Bay. Soon after we rounded Duwamish Head, Forest slammed on the brakes and skidded to a halt, needlessly closing off a portion of Alki Avenue, which the scores of police cars and emergency vehicles, already parked like jackstraws at the scene, had somehow carelessly overlooked.

The entire trip had only taken a little over twenty-five minutes but it seemed like hours. Forest burped and discarded his coffee mug on the floor among the assortment of fast-food sacks, wrappers and styrofoam cups. "We made good time," he said as he climbed out of the car and slammed the door.

A heavy fog settled on Alki Beach. I turned up the collar of my leather jacket, stuffed my hands into the pockets of my Levi's and followed Forest to the water's edge.

"Get out of the fuckin' way," he barked as we approached the crowd of cops at the scene. Like the honor guard at a military wedding, they parted reverently to allow his advance.

Voices were muffled by the dense air, the squawk of radio chatter and the far-away murmur of curiosity seekers. The dull background noise masked the lapping waves of the Puget Sound's receding tide, while red and blue flashing lights from emergency vehicles diffused into the fog like aborted fireworks. The thick, wet veil distorted space and time until everything seemed immediate yet just out of reach. Salvador Dali could not have created a more surreal image of organized chaos.

Everyone had come to the party. Firemen, paramedics, the county coroner, the Coast Guard. I couldn't see them, but I knew there would be reporters, held at bay by uniformed officers who shivered in the dark. Coldest of all was the guest of honor, who lay naked and motionless, face down in the wet sand.

The scene was familiar.

Most of what was unpleasant in my past seemed to fade, even disappear, with time. But the memories of every corpse I'd ever seen, many rendered extinct by my own hand, were more tenacious. They played and replayed in my dreams. Like the grotesque montage of a demented film maker, the images remained vivid, complete with sound and smell. Some had names, some only had faces and some had neither. Now, I was about to add yet another player to the ensemble, and I had to fight the urge to turn and run like hell. I didn't want the ghost of Phillip Stang parading through my dreams.

"Has it been moved yet?" I heard Forest ask.

"No, sir. You said not to touch him until you got here."

I avoided looking directly at the body. I wasn't ready yet. Instead I stared into the fog, wishing it was daytime, wishing it was warm, wishing I was somewhere else. To the southwest, a lighthouse beacon flashed at regular intervals. Nearby, the foghorn of a large, invisible ship sounded loudly.

"Who found it?" Forest said.

It, I thought, this was Forest's way of coping. Never acknowledging that *it* was once a living, breathing human being. Until very recently, the dead man had a life. He probably had a family, a wife sick with worry, children eagerly watching out the window for daddy's car to pull into the driveway. But Forest would avoid the use of other pronouns until he convinced himself that he was dealing with an inorganic object, just another clue at a crime scene. He was a hard man, well suited to the job. Homicide.

"A couple of kids found him," one of the officers said.

"Kids," Forest said disgustedly. "What the hell were they doing out here? They didn't know it was raining and colder than seven sides of dammit."

"Just getting out of the house. You know how it is, Lieutenant. A couple of boys, eleven and thirteen years old. They'd been playing around here most of the afternoon, and they said the tide must have left him behind and they found him."

"Jesus H. Christ," Forest said. "Why are half the corpses in the world found by fuckin' kids who wouldn't know a clue from a foreskin? Where are the little shits?"

"They were pretty shook up. A deputy took them home, but we've got their names and addresses if you want to talk to them."

In a rare show of sensitivity, Forest said, "Tomorrow's soon enough."

He nudged me on the shoulder. "Well, McCleet, does _it_ look familiar?"

"I don't know," I said. "He looks too heavy."

"It's bloated from the water. Take a closer look."

I didn't like being pushed. I remembered when I was five and my grandmother told me to kiss the cold dead face of my grandfather as he lay in a casket in the parlor of her house. Her voice was stern and her jaw tight, holding back her own tears as she ordered me to kiss Grandpa good-bye. I looked for Mom, but she wasn't in the room. Somebody in black had taken her out of there, weeping and hysterical. A stranger picked me up and held me over the coffin. I remembered the sickly sweet odor of flowers and the crazy look in my grandmother's eyes as she droned about how I was Grandpa's favorite and he would have wanted me to kiss him. I couldn't refuse, couldn't say I was scared. When I got close to his powdery white face, I thought his eyes were going to pop open and his arms would grab me and pull me into the coffin with him. The best memories of my grandfather vanished that day.

In a way, Grandpa's death prepared me for later. When my father died, I didn't go to the funeral. Some of my family had a hard time with that. But I knew that Dad would have understood. It's best to remember people's lives, not their deaths.

"Take a closer look," Forest repeated. He took a flashlight from one of the officers and handed it to me.

I shined the light toward the head. The face was not visible. The hair looked darker than Phil's, but it was soaked to the skull. Hair always looks darker when it's wet.

I checked the breadth of the shoulders and, in my mind, tried to compensate for the bloat. They could have been the right size and shape. But how could I tell? I never spent much time studying the rear view of Phil's physique. Then I remembered his wedding ring. It was one of a kind. I had introduced Margot to the artist who made it.

"Jesus," I said as I repositioned the light and saw that most of the skin had been torn away from the wrist and hand. Only a few ragged chunks of gray-white meat clung to the pale bones. The middle and ring fingers were absent.

"Fuckin' crabs eat everything," Forest said.

"I could have identified him by his ring. You think it's coincidence that the ring finger is missing?"

"The ring worth anything?"

"Twenty-four-carat gold. A couple of diamonds."

"Maybe stolen." Forest craned his neck, scanning the group that had gathered like official pall-bearers. "Where's the coroner? And why are all these fuckin' people stumbling around in the dark? Look like monkeys fuckin' a football. What am I running here, a homicide investigation or a shittin' circus?"

"An investigation, sir." A red-faced officer sounded confused about which question to answer first. "Uh . . . the coroner's sitting in his car. He already looked at this side of the body. He said to come get him when we're ready to turn it over. Everyone else is looking for clues."

"Clues!" Forest shouted. "If the corpse came in with the tide, what makes you think there's any fuckin' clues?"

"S.O.P., Lieutenant," the officer said.

"Oh, good. Monkeys two, football nothing."

The humor of Forest's response did not escape me. Under different circumstances I might have laughed out loud. But this was not a time for laughter. I heard him yelling, "Tell all these people to get back to work. All I want here is four officers and the crime lab team. Go tell the coroner to get his skinny ass down here. And nobody, but nobody, talks to the reporters."

I remained focused on the body, hoping to find something, anything, that could prove this wasn't Phil. The right hand and arm were in worse condition than the left. The thumb and first two fingers were gone, and all of the flesh had been torn from the forearm.

The crabs would have dined first, tearing away the spongy, water-logged flesh from the boniest parts of the body. Then the smaller, more timid scavengers would move in to nibble on the exposed meat. There are very few strict vegetarians living under the sea.

"Well . . . what do you think?" I heard Forest ask.

He sounded like he was running out of people to harangue.

"Hey . . . asshole."

I realized he was talking to me. "What?"

"Try to pay attention. Is it Stang or not?"

I looked at Forest, who was standing beside another man in civilian clothing who I guessed was the coroner, and I wondered how long I'd been staring down, motionless, mesmerized, unaware of anything around me except the profane sight of the grisly body. "I can't tell."

Forest shined a flashlight in my eyes. "You look like shit, McCleet. Not planning to yak on my shoes, are you?"

Looked like somebody already had. "I need to see his face."

"You ready? This isn't going to be artistic."

On Forest's command, two officers wearing rubber gloves knelt in the sand at the far side of the body. With a gentleness that would have been appreciated if the dead man could have known, they rolled him onto his back.

I felt another knot in my stomach as flashlight beams illuminated the chest cavity, laid open from the collarbone to below the sternum. The rib cage was spread wide apart. The gloved officers recoiled as two crabs darted from inside the gaping wound and skittered sideways across the sand.

"Just like the others," the coroner said. "This poor fellow was dead when he hit the water."

I looked past the chest to the face. What was left of a face. The nose and ears had been reduced to little more than shreds of cartilage. The lips were gnawed away, freezing the teeth in a permanent, hideous, sardonic grin.

"Something's weird about the eyes," Forest noted.

They were gone. The eyeballs were gone.

"Good observation," the coroner replied. He reminded me of a preschool teacher as he leaned over the body and pointed to the temples with his pen. "You see, right here. Take a look, Forest. Don't be nervous. You see, there's evidence of a clean incision. I'll know more later, but it appears the eyeballs were removed while he was still alive, surely before he was in the water."

"How long, doc?" Forest asked. "How long has it been dead?"

"He's been in the water two or three days. But I can't even guess at how long he's been dead until I've had a chance to conduct a thorough examination."

"McCleet," Forest said. I was beginning to hate the sound of his voice. "How long has your man been missing?"

"Long enough." Margot's last contact from Phil had been the night before yesterday. Almost exactly two days ago.

"Is it him or not?"

"Not."

I handed the flashlight to Forest and turned my back on him and his body and his band of merry men, who all seemed delighted to have something to do besides writing traffic tickets. It wasn't Phil, and they didn't need me anymore. I walked into the fog, parallel to the shoreline, not sure where I was going, unsure if I cared.

Forest lumbered up beside me. His flat feet made a pitterpat noise in the hard, wet sand. "How the hell do you know that's not your man?"

"I know."

"How? It's got no face. Body's all bloated, half-eaten and ripped to hell."

"It's not Phil."

Forest grabbed my arm to spin me around, but I'd been jerked around enough. I shrugged free of his grip. "Why'd you bring me down here? You knew what that guy was going to look like. You knew it would take dental records to make a positive I.D."

"Because people like you piss me off, McCleet. It's not your job to come to my town and play detective for the weekend. I drug your ragged ass down here to remind you what it's like in the real world. I wanted to make you puke up your toenails. Fuckin' artist." The cigar rolled across his face like an exclamation point. "So, you don't really know if that's your brother-in-law or not, do you?"

"It's not Phil." I lengthened my stride. I wanted to make it hard for his stubby cop-legs to keep up.

"How the fuck do you know?"

"The teeth," I said. "Phil's an orthodontist. He has the most perfect set of choppers you ever saw. You could throw a cat through the gap in that guy's two front teeth." I pointed toward the body site. "And he has silver fillings. Phil doesn't have fillings."

Forest grunted his acknowledgment. "Okay, McCleet. And I'll tell you one more thing."

"Great."

"You were a cop, so maybe you remember how bad the media can cock up a murder investigation. But just in case you forgot, if you breathe a single word of what you know to anyone, I'll jack you up so bad, you'll envy the next ripper victim. And that ain't no threat. It's a by-God promise."

I didn't respond. I didn't need to. We both knew I was going to do whatever it took to find Phil.

The wet sand felt like frozen concrete beneath my feet. I walked until I couldn't hear the radio squawk or see the flashing lights. The fog off the Puget Sound swallowed me whole.

Chapter Four

In the movies, disappearing into a dense fog in the dark is considered very dramatic. In reality, it is little more than an act of gross stupidity. I couldn't see past the end of my nose, which was still out of joint from having a corpse needlessly thrown in my face. Twice, I blindly wandered into the sound up to my ankles. Even in my leather jacket, the dank chill was so piercing that I briefly considered returning to the body site and begging Forest for a ride home. I decided against it. Slow death by hypothermia was preferable to another ride in Forest's slob-mobile. Besides, I wasn't sure if I could find the body site again. I wasn't sure of anything except that I was somewhere north of the equator.

Then I saw the vague outline of my salvation. Hallelujah. With my wet Levi's slapping at my ankles and my penny loafers making loud squishy noises, I dragged myself up from the beach toward that beacon of hope, the cheerful red and green sign of a twenty-four-hour convenience store. The gods had smiled on me. I had hot coffee and a greasy Polish dog in a stale bun while I waited for a cab.

The cab driver made me pay in advance, but I didn't care. I was glad to be around another human being who wasn't calling me an asshole, so I didn't mind being treated like one.

This time when I approached the Olympic Roosevelt Hotel, I had a couple of advantages: Number one, I knew about Fishman's surveillance cameras. And, secondly, I had Phil's convention badge and rental car agreement in my pocket. With any luck at all, I could manage to get his room without being arrested.

Before I left the cab, I sloughed off my jacket and pinned the badge above the pocket on my shirt. It read: "Pacific Northwest Regional Dental Association. Dr. Phillip Stang, Portland, Oregon." There were so many letters and words that the tag looked like an eye test.

The pale, long-nosed desk clerk regarded me with a bland but tactful expression. "May I help you?"

"I seem to have misplaced my key." After a pantomime of patting down all my pockets, I glanced toward the convention badge. "Dr. Phillip Stang. I'm in Room 427."

While looking down his long nose, the desk clerk punched buttons on his computer terminal. I chatted in a genial orthodontic manner, "And I know all about those messages from my wife. She doesn't understand that a man at a convention is a busy man."

The clerk presented me with a duplicate key for Phil's room and said, "You're right about those messages, Doctor. Over forty of them at last count."

"Persistent wench." I pivoted away from the front desk with Phil's room key in my fist. The simple ruse had worked smoothly . . . too smoothly. I found myself facing a small herd of dentists. Whether by happenstance or design, they were wearing nearly identical outfits, including dark slacks, cardigan sweaters and bolo ties. Their badges from the convention were prominently displayed, and their eyeballs swiveled in unison to check out the identification on my chest.

Odds were high that at least one of them knew I was too tall, too rough-edged and too wet to be Phil Stang. Before they could expose me as an imposter and summon Fishman of hotel security fame, I threw my jacket over my shoulder, covering the badge, and strode past the elevator, ignoring a gentle, dentist's voice that said, "Hello, there."

Another chimed, "Care to join us?"

"This won't hurt a bit."

I kept going past the lounge, past the men's room. In the hallway with rooms on either side, I sidestepped a burly chambermaid and casually discarded Phil's identification in her cart. "Nice evening," I said.

"For a duck," she responded sullenly.

When I circled back, the dentists were gone, and I took the elevator to the fourth floor.

Alone in Phil's room with only a relentlessly blinking phone-message light for company, I concentrated on the mission that had brought me to Seattle in the first place. A more thorough search of Phil's room did not reveal any new clues. The mints still lay on the pillow, and the floss had not been moved from the bathroom counter.

I sat on the edge of the bed and took stock. The dead guy on the beach wasn't Phil, and that was good. But I wasn't any closer to finding Phil, and that was bad. Maybe Forest was right, and I should give up on my weekend detecting and call on a real private investigator, somebody better suited to talking to contemptuous cops and looking at dead people.

Just like the others, the coroner had said. He didn't elaborate but I knew what he meant. The chest had been cracked open and the insides scooped out like a Halloween pumpkin. That was no coincidence. The coroner and Forest had both seen it before. Now, I was a member of the elite club who shared the sick honor of viewing the handiwork of the Yuppie Ripper.

Much to my credit, I had not retched. To my dismay, I experienced a familiar burning deep in my gut, a sensation that had nothing to do with logic or the rational pursuit of information.

As I stared at Phil's suits and shirts that hung in a neat row in the closet, a savage rage spread heat through my veins. Although I never considered myself a violent person, I knew I was capable of violence. And at that moment I would have given anything for a few minutes alone with the Ripper.

Obviously, I needed some balance, a strong dose of sanity. I picked up the telephone receiver and placed a long-distance call.

Alison answered on the third ring. "Hello?"

I lowered my voice to an obscene growl. "Hello, baby. What are you wearing? Is it silk?"

"Black lace teddy."

"What else?"

"Nothing."

I imagined Alison's soft, warm, live skin contrasted against the red satin sheets I'd given her last Valentine's Day.

"Are you in bed," I asked.

"Who is this?" she asked.

"Who is this? It's Adam. Who'd you think it was?"

"Some other pervert."

"Just for the record, I'm the only pervert you're allowed to have this kind of conversation with."

"Adam, is something wrong?"

"Tell me about your teddy. Is it that one with the little rose-bud right between—"

"You sound strange. More strange than usual. Did you find Phil? Please tell me what's going on?"

I had fallen into a mess that wasn't my problem. I shouldn't have been involved, but I felt somehow responsible. "I don't know what's going on. I don't even know why I'm here."

"Because you're one of the good guys."

Not according to Forest. He believed I was a weenie artist.

"And you care about Phil," she continued. "Whether or not you're willing to admit it, you care about your sister, too."

"Are you referring to Margot the Malignant?"

"Joke about it all you want, Adam. I know you. And I know you care. You might even love her."

"Nail my toes to a ceiling fan, I'll never admit it."

"So, tell me what you did today."

I gave her the short report. "I haven't found Phil. He's not in his room. Looks like he wasn't there last night. He's not at the convention. He's not on the beach."

"The beach?"

I didn't explain. Suddenly, having her with me seemed like the most important thing. "Come up here tomorrow instead of waiting till the game on Sunday."

"Oh, yes," she said, without enthusiasm. "The football game. I'd almost forgotten. Aren't you going to be busy? Detecting?"

"I'll hire a good P.I. to find Phil. You and me can take a ferry to Victoria." I wouldn't beg, but I wasn't above bribery. "We'll spend the night at the Empress. We can skip the football game and sleep in. Have breakfast in bed."

I could hear her flipping pages in her Day-Timer. "I'll be there before noon."

"Good." Her promise didn't make everything all better, but it went a long way toward brightening the end of an otherwise bleak day. "I'm staying in Phil's room, so ask for Phil Stang."

"I don't believe for a minute that you're going to give up on this so easily."

"Believe it."

"We'll see. Good night, pervert."

As I hung up, I realized how much of a stabilizing factor she had become in my life. Even though it had only been a little over twenty-four hours since I'd last seen her, I missed her. It occurred to me that somehow, quietly and effortlessly, our relationship had developed into what, for lack of a better word, I could only describe as a relationship.

I called down to the desk and informed them that Dr. Phillip Stang would be joined by another party tomorrow at noon.

There were a good fifteen hours to kill before then, and so, like all good Americans, I reached for the television remote control. Between the canned laughter of a tired sitcom rerun and a ridiculous commercial for a fast-food taco store, I stared blankly at a news update. The anchorwoman, a cool brunette with a huge mouth and a detached look in her eyes, salivated over what she obviously perceived as a scoop.

"This just in," she announced, licking her lips. "Earlier this evening, the body of an unidentified male was discovered on Alki Beach. According to official sources, this is the fourth victim in a series of ritualistic cult slayings. More at ten."

So much for Forest's order against talking to the media.

I clicked off the television and lay back on the pillows. After ten minutes, I lost interest in the ceiling. Although I fully intended to call a real P.I. in the morning and turn this whole mess over to him, there was one more bit of detecting I could do tonight.

From Phil's rental car contract, I had the make, model and license number of the car. If the white Pontiac Grand Am was still parked at the Roosevelt garage, it was a sure bet that Phil hadn't taken it anywhere. That conclusion would, at least, rule out the possibility that he'd driven off into the sunset of his own accord. I could look for the Grand Am and get my own luggage at the same time.

The Roosevelt on a Friday night was a hot gathering spot for swinging senior citizens and starry-eyed dentists. The management had wheeled a white baby grand into the downstairs lobby, and a piano man with slicked-back hair and a powder-blue tux tickled the ivories. A full-figured woman bounced the dentists' name tag on her ample bosom as she belted out a smoky version of "I Am Woman."

Outside, the cold drizzle made me glad that I'd decided to wear a rag-wool sweater under my jacket. I turned up the collar and followed the awning-covered walkway to the nearby underground parking. I had checked out the first row of parked cars before I realized I wasn't alone.

Another person stayed in the shadows, moving only when I looked away. I continued the search for Phil's car, trying not to let on that I was aware of his presence. I monitored the movements of the shadowy figure through the periphery of my vision until I was certain that he was following me.

Christ, I thought, it's probably Roy Fishman, come to blow me away with that big hogleg of a .45. Even if hotel rules didn't specifically state anything against lurking in the garage, Roy probably had a vendetta against coveting other people's cars.

Whoever it was, he was making me nervous. I decided that a confrontation was in order. Since there was no other exit from the garage, I figured I'd deprive him of the element of surprise. If I was going to be mugged, now was as good a time as any.

I turned and walked back up the ramp toward the exit. When I came abeam of the pillar where the spectator was lurking, I turned and walked directly toward him. This tactic, the alternative to run-and-hide, was employed by the Marines in case of ambush.

When I was within spitting distance of his hiding place, the stalker stepped out of the shadows. He was massive, with the physique of a body builder. At first, I thought he was unarmed, except for his pecs and abs. Then I saw the knife in his hand. Calling this weapon a knife was like comparing a squirt gun to an AK-47. The blade was eight inches long, serrated on one side and shimmering razor sharp on the other. The bone handle balanced lightly in his hand, and his cool gaze indicated that he was accustomed to using it. His voice was a low whisper. "Where's Sterling?"

Sterling? I didn't know who or what a Sterling was, but I figured it wasn't a wise idea to antagonize this behemoth. "In a safe place."

I took a slow, deliberate step backwards, toward the exit. This guy was a heavyweight, probably not built for speed. I might be able to outrun him, of course he'd probably stab me in the back before I sprinted across the finish line.

"Don't move," he said.

"You're a man of few words. I like that."

"Where's Sterling?"

"Your boss," I said, figuring that guys like this are never masterminds and always have bosses. "How much would your boss pay to know about Sterling?"

For his size, the big guy moved with amazing, light-footed agility. But I didn't have time to express my admiration for his style because as soon as he was within striking distance, he drew back his left hand to deliver a backhanded blow to the right side of my face. I saw it coming, but there wasn't much I could do but block the open-handed slap. Even so, the force was enough to stagger me. I felt my rage starting to build from within but kept it check.

My meager resistance seemed to please him. I saw a flicker of life in those dark eyes, like the reflection of rain on asphalt. Apparently, he liked a challenge.

"I want Sterling," he said. "Now."

Talk about a one-track mind. "Okay, man, but we have to drive. My car's right over here."

He kept just the right amount of distance between us as I led the way to my car. He was too far for me to make a grab for the knife, but close enough for him to keep me from dodging behind a car and escaping. The guy was a professional—a bodyguard, a hit man, an enforcer—and he seemed to love his work.

At the car, I reached into the pocket of my jeans for my keys and immediately felt a shiver of pain in my ribcage. His commando knife had sliced through my leather jacket like it was butter.

"Car keys," I explained. "I need to get something from the trunk."

My tire iron, I thought. It was back there, nestled amongst my luggage. Though a gun would have been better, it was a weapon, and I was going to need everything in my arsenal to take this guy on.

"The trunk." He sounded doubtful.

"Yeah, I've got a map in there that I have to use to locate Sterling."

He took a step back and gestured with the knife for me to open it. I popped the lid and reached inside. I unzipped my suitcase and fumbled around inside. My fingers closed around the tire iron.

There must have been something suspicious about my movements because he demanded, "Tell me about Sterling."

"He's quite a guy."

"His name. Tell me his first name."

"You know, it's the craziest thing, but I forgot. I know it like I know the back of my—"

"You don't know shit."

When I looked over my shoulder, I saw him grinning. We both knew that I'd been bluffing, and this guy who made Arnold Schwartzenegger look like a ninety-eight-pound weakling was going to enjoy punishing me for not telling the truth.

Without warning, I lashed out with the tire iron and struck the blade of the big knife. The ringing sound of metal against metal reminded me of one of those old sword-fight, swashbuckler movies. The knife flew out of his hand. I swung again. The tire iron bounced off his solid gut as if I'd clubbed an over-inflated tractor tire.

He lunged and I sidestepped, rapping the side of his cranium with a blow that would have rendered a normal man unconscious.

Godzilla merely grunted.

A shout echoed in the underground garage. "Hey!"

I turned and saw a small man at the far end of the row of cars. The big guy saw him, too. Apparently, he decided I wasn't worth killing in front of a witness. With blood dripping from his noggin, he scooped up his knife and ran up the ramp and out of the garage.

When I faced the small man, intending to offer my thanks, I

saw a cardigan and a bolo tie. His name tag said, "Pacific North-west Regional Dental Association. Dr. Stuart Hall." He had as-sumed an attack position. What was this little guy going to do, floss me against my will?

"You're not Phil Stang," he proclaimed assertively.

"You got me there, Doc. I'm his—"

The wiry, fiftyish-looking man interrupted my explanation with a lightning-fast kick to my ribcage which knocked me into the side of a nearby BMW and hurt like hell.

"Goddamn it," I exclaimed, "why'd you do that?"

"What have you done with Phil?"

"I didn't do anything with Phil. He's my—"

A leg whip to my ankles took me off my feet, and I dropped to the concrete floor like a sack of lead.

"You'd better tell me," he said. "Where's Phil?"

I was on one elbow when he moved in to deliver another blow. This time, I was ready. I caught his foot with my right hand and punched him in the groin with my left. Now we were both on the ground, but the karate dentist was holding his crotch with both hands.

I quickly pounced on top of him, cinched his bolo tie tight around his neck and delivered two rabbit punches to his fore-head. If it hurt his head as much as it hurt my fist, I had the advantage. "Now . . . why are you so goddamned concerned about Phil?" I demanded, threatening his nose with my fist.

"I'm his friend," he moaned.

"Yeah?" I dragged him to his feet by his string tie. My ribs hurt and I was considering another rap on Hall's forehead. "And I'm Adam McCleet. Phil's brother-in-law."

"Margot's brother?"

"The jury's still out on that."

"Excuse me?"

"Okay, Stuart. I'm in Seattle, looking for Phil. Have you got any information that might help me find him?"

His eyeballs swam into focus. "Please accept my apology.

But when I saw you wearing his name tag, I thought you must know what happened to him."

I released Stuart and he pulled himself together. "Can I buy you a drink, Adam? To make up for what happened here."

"When you tried to kick the shit out of me?"

"Well, um, yes."

"A drink sounds good. Let me drop off my suitcase and I'll meet you in the lounge."

In less than five minutes, I went to my room, changed shirts and headed back to the elevator. The lounge at the Roosevelt was named, appropriately, the San Juan Hill. Bully.

Stuart Hall looked harmless enough, perched on a stool at the bar with a drink that contained at least five maraschino cherries and enough miniature umbrellas for the entire Munchkin cast of *The Wizard of Oz.*

I kept my distance, not wanting to startle the miniature Jean Claude Van Damme. "Hello, Stuart."

He bounded off the stool and faced me. At least, he faced my armpit which was eye level for him. "What are you drinking? I recommend the Roosevelt Rough Rider. That's what I'm having."

I ordered a double Wild Turkey, neat.

"I'm concerned about Phil," Stuart said. "It's not like him to be irresponsible. I haven't seen him since Wednesday evening. And I heard that today he missed giving his ultrasound plaque removal workshop."

"Did he?"

"Indeed, he did. I most certainly do not blame his charming wife Margot for being worried about him. When I spoke with her on the telephone, she seemed quite distraught."

First, Alison had accused me of actually liking the shrew. Now, Stuart was charmed. I bit my lip, sipped the Wild Turkey and savored the burn. "What did the charming Margot have to say?"

"That you were looking for Phil, but could possibly use some assistance. She implied that you might be in over your head."

"A vote of confidence." I ducked my head to look the little dentist in the face. "Tell me about you and Phil."

"Oh, dear me. We go way back. Almost all the way to dental school. We did our first root canal together. The patient was an older man, and his gums were in terrible—"

"More recently," I interrupted. I wasn't up for a detailed description of the inside of an old man's mouth. "At the convention. When was the last time you saw Phil?"

"I believe it was the night before last. Yes. It was definitely Wednesday, right here in this very lounge. We were sitting in the corner over there." He gestured toward the Pac-Man game. "It was quite amazing, really."

"What was?" I had the feeling that I'd better get any information I wanted from Stuart before he had another Rough Rider. He was almost misty-eyed with the memory of two nights ago. "What was amazing, Stuart?"

"The ladies," he whispered. "They were magnificent. Two of them. They were blondes and they had the biggest, most beautiful, whitest smiles I've ever seen. And, believe me, I've seen a lot of smiles."

I believed him. "What about these ladies?"

"They walked right up to Phil. He was coming out of the men's room and they walked right up to him. One on either side. And, dear me, they were smiling to beat the band."

So, good old Phil got himself propositioned two nights ago. Though that was not an unusual occurrence in a downtown convention hotel, I suspected that two grinning blondes would be a red-letter day in the life of Phil Stang. Or a lead, I reminded myself. Hopefully, I asked, "Did Phil go with the ladies?"

"Rest assured that he did not. Phil is not the sort of man who betrays his charming wife."

"Too bad," I murmured.

"And the ladies were most insistent. They flashed smile after smile. They must have talked to Phil for a good five minutes."

I wondered if these two desperate women had legs or

breasts. Reality was starting to distort itself. I felt like Gulliver being attacked by Lilliputian dentists, tying me down with floss and filling my head with ridiculous tales of big beautiful teeth.

"It's my guess," Stuart said, "that these ladies were dental technicians."

"They couldn't have been hookers, I suppose."

"I never thought of that. I've never seen a hooker. But these women were ladies, and they seemed to enjoy Phil's attention very much, and he said that before they started talking to him, they read his convention badge." He shot me a squinty, resentful look. "The badge you were wearing earlier."

Stuart made a slurping noise with his straw as he polished off the remnants of his Rough Rider. He ordered another with extra cherries.

"So, Phil didn't go with the girls. What happened next?"

"He had a phone call. 'Probably Margot,' Phillip said, and went off to answer."

"Good boy, that Phil."

"But it wasn't Margot. It was another dentist, a local chap, who asked if Phil could assist him with a procedure. Quite a compliment, really."

Finally, we were getting somewhere. "Did Phil mention this guy's name."

"Oh, you know him?"

"Know who?"

"Guy."

"Guy who?"

"Fellowes."

"What?" Who's on first? I resisted a strong urge to lift Stuart Hall off his tiny feet and throw him head-first through the cheesy stained-glass window depicting Teddy's charge up San Juan Hill.

"Guy Fellowes," said Stuart. "Dr. Guy Fellowes."

"So the person who called was Dr. Guy Fellowes. Right?"

"Correct."

"And have you ever met this g—, this person?"

"Never heard of him. However," Stuart said, "Phil recited his degrees, and I was very impressed. Then, at about ten o'clock, Phil went to meet with him."

"On Wednesday night?" I questioned. "Let me get this straight, Stuart. Are you telling me that Phil went to do a dental procedure at ten o'clock Wednesday night?"

He bobbed his chin contentedly.

"Is that usual?" I asked. "Do dentists make house calls?"

"We have emergency circumstances," he said huffily. "What do you think people do when they have a toothache in the middle of the night?"

"I thought they took two aspirin and suffered till morning."

He chuckled condescendingly at my abject ignorance. "Laymen," he said. "Non-medical people never understand."

There was one thing I did comprehend. Phil had been called away on a supposed dental emergency. Then, he'd disappeared. I wanted to know more about this Guy Fellowes.

"Stuart, did you happen to see Dr. Fellowes when Phil went to meet him?"

"Just the limo. A long white one. Like enamel."

"And you didn't see Phil after that?" I clarified.

"I guess not."

Poor Phil. Abducted by his sense of duty. He should have gone with the hookers.

Chapter
Five

After I left Stuart crying into his frilly but potent Rough Riders and returned to my room, which was really Phil's room, I flopped onto the bed and stared up at the familiar ceiling. A thought bubble had begun to form over my head when I heard a loud banging at the door. I assumed it was not Ed McMahon, arriving to inform me that I had won ten million bucks.

Without moving, I yelled, "Who is it?"

"Open up, asshole."

I opened the door. "Lieutenant Forest. How nice to see a friendly face. I was beginning to think I wasn't welcome in Seattle."

He blustered into my room and shook himself like a wet, smelly dog. Unplugging the cigar from his face, he said, "You talked to those fag reporters, didn't you?"

"Moi?"

"Not funny, McCleet. I've got bodies popping up all over Seattle like fuckin' Whack-A-Moles, and you're playing games. I told you not to talk to anybody."

"You got it wrong," I said.

"It had to be you." Darkly, he added, "I hope you're not saying that one of my people leaked to the press."

Was it possible that Forest was that naive? "Come on, Lieutenant, the police force is like Congress. If it's a secret, you only tell one reporter . . . at a time. And if it's top secret, you ask them not to use your name. An official source? Isn't that what they said on the news?"

"Not this time, McCleet. This is *my* homicide. You got that? Mine. *Everybody* around here knows that. And *nobody* wants to piss me off. Nobody except you."

Though I liked the distinction, I couldn't accept the honor of being the only person in Seattle—possibly in the free world—who was willing to piss off Ed Forest. "That wasn't exactly a private party you threw this evening. There were Sheriffs and Coast Guard. Everybody in a uniform but the French fry man at McDonald's. It wasn't me who talked to the press."

He paced across the room, leaving wet tracks on the carpet. "I thought you'd take this more seriously after seeing that pile of meat on the beach."

"Thanks for reminding me." I watched him fume and wished to high heaven that a sane homicide detective, if there was such an animal, had been assigned to this case. "How did you find me here, anyway?"

"An asshole always returns to the scene of the crime. Breaking and entering, right?"

"I prefer to think of it as visiting my brother-in-law." And I preferred not to dwell on my own trespassing. "Actually, Forest, I'm glad you decided to drop by."

"This ain't a fuckin' social call."

"I've got a couple of leads on *your* homicide. First, I need information on a dentist named Guy Fellowes."

"I know you're not exactly a criminologist, McCleet, but what do you think? Is that an alias?" He sat, spreading out his wet raincoat on my bedspread. "Guy Fellowes? Maybe I should check out Harry Butz and Master Bates, too."

"This could be tied in to your Ripper." I hoped not, but I had to face the possibility that Phil was the fifth victim.

"Explain."

"I'd rather not."

"Fine. If you want a favor, call the Make-A-Wish Foundation. I don't owe you squat."

"A lead is a lead, Forest. Are you telling me you've already got so much data on these mutilations that you don't need anything else?"

"Guy Fellowes," he said. "I'll check on it."

"And I've got another name for you. Sterling."

"First or last name?"

"Don't know." And I definitely did not want to tell him about the knife-wielding Godzilla in the parking garage. The guy was too suspicious, and I didn't want to spend the night and most of tomorrow at the cop house looking at mug files.

"If you're jerking me around, McCleet, I'll—"

"All I know is that Sterling is missing and somebody wants him back pretty bad."

Muttering, he slopped toward the door. "Fucking yuppie-killing son of a bitch. I ought to be helping the guy."

"Oh, Lieutenant . . ."

"What?"

"Thanks for bringing a little ray of sunshine into my day."

The door slammed shut.

I should have asked him to refer me to a good P.I., but I didn't. Maybe Alison had been right when she said I wouldn't give up so easily. And that was before the bodybuilder had come after me. I tend to take physical assaults personally, and I generally want revenge. Maybe, tomorrow, I'd let Alison talk me out of it.

That night, I dreamed about Phil Stang. He was standing between two blondes with Cheshire Cat smiles, and he was grinning from ear to ear, and when he opened his mouth to laugh, two crabs skittered out. His face decomposed in slow motion. Eyeballs yellowed and fell from their sockets. But he was still laughing. Or was he screaming?

And the phone rang. I hadn't left a wake-up call, but when I groped across the bedside table for my wristwatch, I saw that it was after nine o'clock. It had to be Margot.

Never disembowel yourself with a claw hammer or talk to Margot before . . . I considered letting it ring, but I wasn't that anxious to get back to my dreams.

I pulled the phone to my ear, and muttered, "Hello, Margot."

"Dr. Stang?"

"No. What? I mean. . . . Yes. This is Dr. Stang."

"This is the front desk. The party you were expecting has arrived."

Alison? Maybe there was a God in the universe. "Send her up. Now."

I stuck the receiver back on the hook, untangled myself from the sheets that I had kicked into a twisted knot, and unlocked the door. Then I hit the shower. Cleanliness wasn't the first thought on my mind, but I hoped that Alison would come into the room, hear the water running and join me. A warm shower with a goddess would take my mind off the events of the day before.

She'd gotten to Seattle quickly. Must have taken the first shuttle in the morning. I hoped she was as anxious as I was.

I heard the door open and close. There was no sound of conversation with a bellman carrying luggage. That didn't surprise me. She was good at spontaneity and she could travel very light when she wanted to. Maybe Alison hadn't even brought a suitcase. Just herself and a toothbrush.

"I hear you out there," I called out. "Come in here."

Through the translucent shower curtain, I saw the bathroom door open. The blood was pounding in my head and in my groin. "In here," I coaxed. "Come on. Take off those travel clothes and join me."

She wasn't saying anything, playing another one of her teasing games. "Do I have to beg?"

"No, Adam. Just tell me you mean it."

A man's voice. My burgeoning erection vanished instantly. I stuck my head through the shower curtains. "Monte?"

He was leaning against the vanity with his arms crossed. "Aren't you the pixie?"

"Get the fuck out of my bathroom."

"But, Adam, I thought you wanted me to slip out of my traveling clothes and hop into the shower with you."

"Tell you what, Monte. How about if I help you undress? I'll start by pulling your underwear off over your head."

Monte giggled. Perhaps that wasn't a threat to him.

I stuck my face into the shower. I couldn't believe my luck. "Where's Alison?"

"She had to change her plans at the last minute, but she's worried about you and didn't want you to be alone."

Alison, a normally intelligent and perceptive woman, had sent Monte as a nursemaid. The image boggled the mind. What had she been thinking?

Monte said, "I hope you're not too disappointed."

"Disappointed? Me? Not at all, Monte. Would you do me a favor?"

"Your wish is my command," he chirped.

"Good. Would you please wheel the TV in here, plug it in and hand it to me?"

"In the shower?" he gasped. "Dear God, you'll be electrocuted."

"What's your point?"

"Adam, this is a rather severe mood-swing. Do we need to adjust your medication?"

"What was so important that Alison couldn't come?"

"Well, you know what an angel of mercy she is."

I knew very well. "Just tell me."

"Not on your cute little life, Adam. I want you to beg."

I braced my hands on the steamed tiles of the shower wall

and let the water beat on my head. This couldn't be happening. I wanted Alison in Seattle. "I'm not in the mood for this shit."

"All right," Monte said. "But all this steam is wilting my ensemble. You finish your shower and I'll order breakfast. The airline food was, as always, unpalatable, and I'm famished. We can talk when you get out."

"No croissants," I said. "Don't order me croissants. I want ham and pancakes and eggs over easy and orange juice and black coffee with caffeine in it."

It occurred to me that the last thing I'd eaten was a greasy convenience-store Polish dog. I heard the door close behind Monte, and I was back at the beach, but this time I refused to wallow in it. Since Alison wasn't coming, I might as well get back to the business of finding Phil. Before I turned the case over to a private investigator, there were a couple of things I could check on myself. Nothing dangerous. Nothing weird. I had to call Forest to see if he'd found any information on the redundantly named Guy Fellowes. I might as well stop by the dentists' convention. And, as much as I wanted to, I knew I couldn't permanently avoid touching bases with Margot.

I shaved, wrapped myself in the terrycloth robe provided by the Roosevelt and stormed into the bedroom where Monte was unpacking a suitcase on wheels that was roughly the size of a U-Haul van. He was humming "I Feel Pretty" as he dragged a mind-boggling array of bright-colored clothing from the huge bag. I was reminded of a magician who pulls a scarf from his sleeve, then another and another until he has enough scarves to stuff a mattress. "What are you doing, Monte?"

"Settling in. I'll take the bed by the window." He pulled a silver-framed photograph of a scrawny Siamese cat from his suitcase and propped it on the windowsill. "There. I never go anywhere without my picture of Madonna."

"What is going on in your head, Monte? You're not staying here. This is my room. Mine."

"I did ask for a room of my own at the desk. But they're full."
He fluttered a happily colored shirt.

"I don't care. Go to another hotel. Better yet, go to another town."

"Oh, don't be silly. You can't sleep on both beds, can you? Besides, Adam, we're going to the football game together tomorrow."

That was the first I'd heard about going anywhere with Monte. Why, in God's name, Alison had thought he was a suitable surrogate, was beyond me.

"I just love football," Monte extolled. "Seahawks and the Broncos with those orange shirts and—"

"Stop. I don't want to talk about the Broncos. I hate talking about the Broncos. I want to talk about why Alison isn't here."

"She's at the hospital."

I could feel all the light going out of the day. "Why?"

"Your friend, Trevor Ingersoll. He's taken a turn for the worse, Adam, and Alison just couldn't leave him there alone. He has no family, you know."

I knew. I should have been there, too. If I could have chosen a replacement for my own father, it would have been Trevor. He was everything I found admirable in a man. He was creative and vital and generous enough to care about an artistically challenged cop who aspired to be a sculptor. The image of Trevor in a hospital bed stank, and I didn't begrudge him a minute of Alison's time.

"Adam?" Monte called. "Are you upset?"

"I'll live." But maybe Trevor wouldn't, and that was the hell of it.

Before I could sink any deeper into the morass of depression that seemed to be the trend of the day, there was a rap at the door and the announcement in an accent that might have been French, "Reum Ser-veese."

"That must be our croissants," Monte trilled.

It was his idea of a joke. He had managed to order me a

decent breakfast and I braced myself to inhale enough saturated fat to refloat the *Titanic*.

I politely waited for the room-service guy to leave before I attacked the meal with a vengeance.

"My God," Monte said. "If I'd known it was going to be like this, I would have worn my safety goggles. I just can't stand to look at you."

He was a fine one to talk. I'd seen Monte eat before. It was not a pleasant sight. He was one of those people who cut up everything into dainty pieces, played with it, arranged it in varying mosaic patterns, then nibbled, dabbing his mouth with a napkin after each bite. It might take him an hour to put away that croissant. What the hell kind of breakfast was a croissant?

In fact, I had eaten every morsel, gotten dressed and had my hand on the telephone when Monte called out, "Finished. Now, what are we going to do today?"

"*We* are doing nothing. *I* am going to look for my brother-in-law."

"I can help, Adam. Really. I'm very good at making contacts."

"Fine." I gave him Margot's number. "Ask if she's heard anything. Tell her I don't know anything. And hang up before she slithers through the phone and eats your liver."

"And where are you going to be?"

"The main convention center for the dentists' convention is the Puget Madrona," I said. I could call Forest from there, probably I didn't need to call him. If I spit on the sidewalk, a squad car will undoubtedly appear.

"But, Adam, how will I find you?"

"I'll be the only guy not wearing a bolo tie."

I left him to deal with Margot and went to the parking garage adjacent to the hotel. Daylight made a world of difference. Last night, there had been drizzle and lurking shadows. Today, the garage was nothing but innocent concrete and the aroma of oil leaks.

Though Stuart said Phil had taken off in a limousine, he might have returned, picked up his rental car and driven off into bachelor heaven. If anything made sense, that did. Nasty as it would have been for me and the others who were left behind to deal with Margot, it was preferable to the Yuppie Ripper scenario. At least Phil would be alive . . . until Margot caught up with him.

But I found the rental car, looking as shiny and new as if it had just come off the showroom floor, with the engine cold and the windshield clean. This baby had been driven from the airport, parked and not used again.

I left the hotel. The chill of autumn was in the air, but the sun was shining, so I walked the few blocks to the Puget Madrona. I didn't have any trouble figuring out that this was the right hotel. Even without the huge sign welcoming the Pacific Northwest Dentists' Association, there was a vehicle parked outside the hotel entrance that I could only describe as a toothmobile. The white enameled van was fashioned after a giant bicuspid and said "Mobile Clinic" on the side.

A single morose dentist leaned against the van door, offering free examinations to passersby. I assumed there were no takers, and I wasn't about to be the first.

"Come on," he urged, "it's free."

This was, apparently, the Dentists' Association idea of a carnival pony ride. "You'd have to pay me," I said.

He started digging in his pocket for change, but I kept walking. I'd been arrested, threatened, physically attacked and verbally abused. The last thing I wanted was someone stabbing into my rear molars with a sharp instrument.

In the convention hall, I approached the attractive young woman who was sitting at the conference registration desk, looking bored. I asked for Dr. Guy Fellowes.

She rifled through a stack of computer printout pages, then searched a card file, then consulted a booklet. She was a woman with a mission. Her wide blue eyes looked like they had tears in them when she gazed up at me and shook her head.

Guy Fellowes was not registered anywhere.

"I don't suppose you've seen Dr. Stang this morning."

She shook her head dejectedly. "Sorry."

I went to the hotel desk and had Fellowes paged.

Nothing. Nobody. So, the twenty-thousand-dollar-question was: Who was Guy Fellowes, and what did he want with Phil? I couldn't think of any good reason that Guy Fellowes would target Phil in a convention hall full of men with approximately the same credentials.

On the off chance that I might get some useful information, I called Forest. He wasn't there, but I talked to another homicide detective who laughed at my vague reference to somebody named Sterling. With first name and last name, there were dozens of them in the Seattle metropolitan area alone. At the opposite extreme was Guy Fellowes. There wasn't one. Nobody by that name in the medical profession. Or in any other.

The last lead, and the most pathetically hopeless, was the convention hall itself. There were dozens, possibly hundreds, of dentists inside. And one of them might also have been approached by Fellowes. Or, at least heard of him.

I left the hotel lobby and sauntered inside. It was apparently a break period, because dentists were all milling around in the central area like bacteria in a petri dish. Several displays on skirted tables lined the walls and formed a bulwark in the center of the room. Floss displays, appliances and instruments of every description. The drills were whining, and the spit sinks were gurgling. I was intrigued by an anesthesia display where the salesman was offering free blasts of nitrous oxide.

Almost the entire center section was devoted to The Chair. There were extra large seats with reinforced steel arms for the more ample patient. I overheard one of the dentists referring to this chair as the "Big Momma." A special comfort model with the name "Easy Rider" was prominently displayed. It included a heavily padded seat, vibrator and stereo speakers in the headrest. As if it were possible to achieve Nirvana while losing your wisdom teeth.

Stuart Hall stood beside a particularly sporty model with black leather, tuck-and-roll upholstery and chrome trim. The only thing missing was fuzzy dice. But Stuart apparently liked it. He was holding forth in the midst of his colleagues, on the virtues of this chair, which was the model he had chosen for his own office.

He left his pals and greeted me importantly. "Well, Adam, have we located Phil yet?"

"Do you really use that chair?"

"Absolutely."

I eyeballed the black leather chair. "What do you call it? La Bamba?"

His grin was high wattage. "I enjoy a fine piece of machinery. I am the proud owner of a fully restored 1967 GTO."

A muscle car. I was impressed; Stuart Hall was a complex character.

He continued, "I got the car as a trade with a gentleman who needed a full set of uppers. Then my interest was piqued. I started fixing up junkers and driving them in the demolition derby once a month on the first Sundays."

Amazing. I wondered if Phil had any similar hobbies. Secret passions he didn't share with Margot or me, habits that could have gotten him into trouble. "About Phil," I said.

"Yes?"

Stuart was so expectant that I hated to dash his hopes. "The only lead I have is Guy Fellowes. The police say there's no such person. And he's not registered at this convention."

"But I'm sure I heard the name correctly. It's rather unusual, and I asked Phil to spell it for me."

He looked past my shoulder, and a frown pinched his little forehead. I turned and saw Monte, fondling the leather on La Bamba.

"Hi, Adam," he said. "Don't you just love this piece. It's almost art, you know. Wouldn't it be great in my bedroom?"

"I don't know," I said. "I've never seen your bedroom."

Stuart was beaming. "I've often thought the very same thing. The chair is rather costly. I believe five-year financing is available. With unlimited warranty for parts and labor."

It was almost unnecessary to introduce these two kindred spirits, and I was amazed to discover that Monte also was an auto nut. I'd always thought of him as a wing nut. "Does Alison know about this car thing?"

"My dear Adam, Alison has come with me to car shows."

I never knew. In spite of her passion for ballet and gourmet cuisine, I did know that she liked the Three Stooges and smothered burritos and Twinkies and really bad jazz. Though her home was filled with incredible artwork, she had occasional lapses in taste which only served to make her even more adorable. As I thought about Alison, I could feel a smile starting to form. I brought myself back to earth by remembering the unpleasant task I'd left for Monte. "Did you talk to Margot?"

"Yes, I did. We had a lovely chat. What a charming woman."

Stuart bobbed his little head in agreement. "Charming."

Monte pouted and said, "She hasn't heard a thing from Phil, and she's very concerned. The poor, dear woman."

Feeling pity for Margot was like worrying if it hurts Godzilla's feet when he steps on skyscrapers.

"Well, Adam," Monte said. Both he and Stuart looked expectantly at me. "What shall we do next?"

For some unknown reason, the gods had chosen me to lead this merry band. I might have been flattered if I'd had a clue how to do it. "Stuart, can you introduce us around here at the convention? Maybe somebody else has heard of Fellowes?"

Stuart whisked us around the hall. We met short dentists, tall dentists and dentists with big noses. Some of them were rude. Others were sweet. Others were stupid. They all looked at my teeth.

Nobody had heard of Fellowes. And nobody knew anything about Phil.

We were sitting in the hotel lobby, tired of smiling and still without a lead, when Stuart bolted upright in his chair. "Those are the girls."

"What girls?" I asked.

"The ones I told you about. In the bar. The two nice dental technicians who wanted to chat with Phil."

I translated. The hookers. I headed after them like a bloodhound who's finally got a scent. Two incredible, statuesque blondes sauntered toward the exit. The doorman practically genuflected as he escorted them out onto the red carpet. These were no ordinary hookers. These were two-thousand-dollar-a-night call girls, and they didn't look like they needed to waste time approaching Phil.

On the curb, I caught up with them. "Ladies," I said. Then what? Haven't we met before? What's your sign? I opted for the semi-direct approach. "I'm looking for a friend."

"I'm so sorry, you darlin' thing." Her voice was deep South, sweet as honeysuckle on the vine. "But we're busy."

Her partner was displaying a long, tantalizing stretch of thigh as she slid into the back of a white stretch limo. The same sort of limo that had abducted Phil. I muscled forward, determined that they wouldn't get away from me.

The doorman had leapt to her aid and, as doormen often do, was holding the door for her and blocking my way.

"Wait!"

She cast a glance over her shoulder at me. "Not today, darlin'. Maybe I can be your friend some other time."

One of the women was already in the car and the other was about to follow.

"You misunderstood," I said. "I'm looking for a specific person. I believe you and your friend spoke with him a few nights ago in the lounge at the Olympic Roosevelt. His name is Phil Stang."

There was a flicker of recognition in her eyes. Maybe something else. Maybe alarm.

"You know him," I said.

"Sweetheart, I know a whole lot of men."

I took her arm, gently, but she made a squeaky annoyed noise and slapped at my hand.

The doorman came to her rescue. He tapped my chest. "The lady isn't interested, sir."

My hold on her was obviously too gentle, because she pulled away from me and joined her friend in the limo. From behind me, I could hear Stuart and Monte joining in the chase.

I yanked the limo door ajar and stuck my head inside, planning to follow with the rest of my body. There was a man with the two blondes. Dark glasses, suit and a hard-edged sneer on his lips that said he could afford these women, both of them, and the limo. That was all I noticed before the Southern belle blasted me in the face with Mace.

It was a glancing shot, but it was enough. I fell back on the curb. The pain went right through my eyeballs to my central nervous system. I felt paralyzed. I might have screamed.

The limo was pulling away and I could do nothing to stop it. Stuart and Monte were next to me. I heard their excited voices and I might have mumbled something about following the limo. I couldn't be sure because I was preoccupied with writhing on the ground in agony.

Stuart and Monte made the next logical decision. Our only lead was getting away.

I supposed that getting in a cab and telling the driver to follow that limo would have been too cliché. My two squires half-carried, half-dragged me across the drive-through and tossed me into the back of something. I heard a woman shriek.

Chapter
Six

Stuart and Monte had hijacked the toothmobile.

And the traveling dentistry unit was occupied. The shriek had come from an apparently elderly lady. Not being able to see, I assumed her age from the antiquated ravings, which included such phrases as "Jumping Jehosaphat" and "Hoo, Lordy."

The dentist who had been working on her tried to step over me on his way to the front, but he missed. His Reebok landed in the center of my chest.

"Hey, Stuart," he shouted. "What the hell are you doing? I almost took out this lady's tonsils."

"Fasten your seat belt," Stuart returned. His voice was annoyingly gleeful. "This is an emergency."

I had a fairly clear mental image of Stu, hunched over the steering wheel with his little dentist foot stomping on the accelerator. I felt the van flying over a curb, like a stubborn molar yanked too hard from its mooring.

Monte cautioned, "Jesus, Stu. Slow down. They mustn't know we're following. Try not to be conspicuous."

Good thinking. We'd want everyone to think we were just another giant tooth, out for a leisurely Saturday afternoon drive. This crew was in need of leadership . . . and a group rate on lobotomies.

The lady in the back wailed a plea to "Great Caesar's Ghost," then fell silent. A heart attack, no doubt. I was probably riding in a tooth with a dead woman.

My eyelids blinked a couple of times. The pain had gone from paralyzing to merely devastating. And my vision was beginning to clear. I could see the traveling dentist hovering over me. "I don't want a check-up," I said.

"How about some nitrous oxide?"

The old lady had apparently taken her dose of laughing gas. Between giggles, she crooned the words to "Moon River."

I pushed the druggy dentist away. "Get out of my face."

"Oh, Adam," Monte called, "are you okay now?"

I was a mess. But with the karate dentist at the wheel and Monte riding shotgun, I was sure everything would be just fine. I lurched to my feet. Stu came to a stop and the traveling dentist and I crashed together into a wall.

"Don't worry," he said. "That's only my x-ray equipment."

Radiation poisoning seemed to be the next logical step in the chain of events. "My eyes," I said. "I need to wash out my eyes."

He helped me to the spit sink, right beside a lady whose frizzed hair was a noxious shade of blue. She gazed at me with unfocused eyes and said, "Hiram, is that you? I think it's milking time again."

She passed out. I envied her.

By the time I had regained vision and the skin on my face only stung like a thousand paper cuts, Stuart and Monte had worked out a plan. They told me so.

"Oh, Adam," Monte squealed. "We have a plan."

I wondered if anyone in the Seventh Cavalry experienced the same kind of apprehension when they heard Custer's plan to turn the valley of the Little Big Horn into a war memorial.

_____

While we were stopped at a light, I shot forward. The cab of the van had two bucket seats. One for Stuart. One for Monte. Monte patted the leatherette beside his skinny butt. "You can sit here, Adam."

I kneeled and braced myself between the seats as I stared through the windshield into downtown Seattle traffic. The sunlight glared painfully bright.

"We've just gotten on Aurora Avenue," Stuart announced. "The limo is still up ahead. I don't think he's spotted us."

The rest of the free world had. Virtually every vehicle we passed held at least one person looking up at the white enameled van with awe-struck eyes.

"What's this plan?" I muttered.

"The plan," Stuart said, "is to follow the limo at a safe distance. If they stop, we stop. If they go, we go. If somebody gets out, one of us will follow that person on foot."

Some detailed plan. Must have taken pretty high-level brainstorming to come up with it.

"Stuart's very good at this," Monte said.

I tried a smile. The skin around my eyes and across my cheekbones felt raw and flayed. I checked my reflection in the rear-view mirror. My face resembled the back end of a baboon. "Who's going to follow?" I asked.

"I'm driving," Stuart said. "And Monte isn't—pardon the expression—inconspicuous. So, I guess that leaves you, Adam."

Somehow, I could have predicted this roll of the dice. I was going to follow, inconspicuously. I made a silent vow to back off if one of the blondes got aggressive again. There was only so much humiliation I could handle in one day; rolling around again on the ground, blind and in pain, was stretching the envelope.

When we merged onto the George Washington Memorial Bridge, heading north across the ship canal, Stuart made a small gurgling noise in the back of his throat. His toe eased off the gas pedal, and his fingers clenched on the steering wheel. He looked like he was having a seizure.

"Stuart?" I touched his shoulder, and his arms clenched against his chest. His knees pulled into a fetal position. Then, in the midst of multiple lanes of moving traffic, he squinted his eyes shut.

"Monte, take the wheel," I instructed. "Stuart, what the hell are you doing?"

He gasped on the edge of hyperventilation, "I don't . . . like . . . heights."

Now was a fine time to announce this phobia.

Monte stretched his leg across the front of the van and floored the accelerator. The problem with this position was that he couldn't reach the brake and had to compensate with erratic lane changes while steering one-handed from the passenger's seat. As if this juggling act wasn't enough, Monte saw fit to dispense self-help advice. "The best thing, Stuart, is to force yourself to look down. Really! It's an embrace-your-fear kind of thing."

"No," Stuart said.

"We're almost to the end of the bridge," I informed him.

He nodded gratefully, but didn't open his eyes.

"We're there."

Stuart snapped back to normal, grabbed the wheel and drove. His breathing was ragged, but otherwise he seemed fine.

Monte clucked his tongue against his teeth. "Listen, Stuart, you have to control your fear. Or it will control you."

"I do control it," he explained. "I never go to high places."

The limo was still in sight, but changing lanes. Stuart gunned it and we roared forward, increasing our speed by a bone-jarring, brain-crushing three miles per hour. He wedged the tooth-mobile between a semi-truck with a likeness of Mother Teresa painted on the back and a double-wide mobile home on a low-boy trailer.

"Now we're getting nowhere," I noted.

"You've got to change back," Monte said. "We can't see anything from here."

Stuart Hall, the demon of the Sunday demolition derby, bounced back into the original lane, crept forward and edged around the truck. The driver of the Living Saint Moving And Storage truck was not amused. Just in case nobody had noticed a giant molar rolling across the bridge, a blast on the airhorn and the middle finger salute from the saintly driver alerted the rest of the state to our progress.

Amazingly, the limo didn't speed up or try any diversionary tactic. Either they'd seen the tooth and had a good chuckle, not knowing that we were on their tail, or the limo driver was heavily medicated.

"He's turning," Monte shouted. "Right lane."

"Make up your mind," Stuart yelled. But he managed the turn, cutting off only two cars in the process.

We followed a modified cloverleaf which took us off and under Aurora to the west. At this point, it seemed likely that we were heading toward the waterfront district, and I wasn't pleased with that destination. The waterfront wasn't known for hospitality. As the designated follower on foot, I would have felt a lot more cozy in practically any other part of town.

The streets down here were less crowded than Aurora Avenue. It was only a matter of time before the limo driver realized he was being pursued by a tooth. "Fall back, Stuart. Give them a couple of blocks lead."

Stuart slammed on the brakes. I jolted forward, catching myself on the dashboard. There was a low moan from the rear of the van. I glanced over my shoulder and saw that the blue-haired lady had regained consciousness. It was only a temporary state, because the traveling dentist was turning the crank on another bottle of gas.

"You're going to be in big trouble for this," he yelled. "Do you hear me, Stuart?"

Stuart didn't flinch. His beady little eyes focused straight ahead. Now that we were past the bridge, he was enjoying the chase. As I watched his jaw tighten, I could almost hear the James Bond theme music in the background. In future, Stuart would probably order his Rough Riders shaken, not stirred. Double-oh-seven dentist, licensed to drill.

"Oh, my God," Monte said. "They're stopping."

Stuart whipped around a corner and parked, blocking traffic. The honeysuckle blonde climbed from the car and sashayed into a bar called the Turk's Head.

Stuart nodded toward the door. "Your turn, Adam."

I had been considering staying with the limo, since the last time Phil was seen, he was getting into one. By the time I got around to sharing my concerns Stuart had made the decision for me. The limo pulled away and Stu didn't.

I was on the street. It smelled like salt water and diesel oil. An assortment of Harleys parked outside the Turk's Head indicated a biker bar. With blisters forming on my face and the collar of my leather jacket turned up, I looked bad enough to be there.

Though it was only one-thirty, the place was packed. There was standing room only at the bar, but I elbowed my way to an open spot. Bob Seeger music blasted from the juke box. The pool tables were full. It was like a scene from an old Peter Fonda movie.

In this bar, the expensively packaged blonde was easily as conspicuous as the toothmobile on the bridge.

The bartender growled at me. "What're you having?"

A brain tumor, I thought. "Long neck . . . light."

The blonde sat at a table in the corner. When she crossed her legs, there was a pause while every male in the bar thought about dropping to the floor for a better view.

Her companion at the table was a heavy-set woman who looked vaguely familiar. She had a low forehead and thick lips. When she raised her cigarette to her lips, I saw a tattoo on her forearm. A heart pierced with a dagger and dripping blood. She reached into her bag and picked up a large, thick, padded envelope.

The blonde surreptitiously slid a letter-sized envelope across the table. Her stealth was wasted, however, because her companion peeled it open and thumbed through a stack of cash before handing over her own envelope.

I drew the obvious conclusion. Drugs. That was why the classy stretch vehicle had ventured into this part of town. The blonde was making a significant buy, either for herself or for the man in the back of the limo.

But how was Phil tied into this? He wasn't a user, and even if he was, dentists could write their own prescriptions. The idea of Phil as a dealer wasn't even worth considering. I needed to talk to the blonde.

She rose from the table and straightened her skin-tight miniskirt. The temperature in the bar rose by ten degrees. I heard several gutteral moans. But nobody moved in on this intimidating Southern beauty. I was the only one. I tapped her arm and stepped out of Mace range.

"Why, look who's here?" she said. "You mind getting out of my way, hon? I'm in a hurry."

"You'll save yourself grief if you talk to me right now."

"Why? Are you a cop?"

I glanced at the padded envelope she'd tucked under her arm. "What if I was?"

"How much?" She sighed. "How much to leave me alone?"

"The answer to one question: Where's Phil Stang?"

"I don't know anyone by that name."

"You and your friend talked to him night before last, in the lounge at the Roosevelt. Then, he disappeared in a white limo, just like the one you're riding in."

Her sultry, heavy-lidded eyes did not change expression. But her pink tongue crept out to moisten her lips. "Sorry, sugar. I don't remember a thing."

"Do you remember Guy Fellowes?"

She rolled her eyes. "Oh, please. That can't be a real person."

I threw out another lure and hoped she'd rise to the bait. "What about Sterling?"

"What about him?"

Bingo! She'd taken the hook. "Let's talk. I'll tell you about Sterling. You tell me about Phil."

A loud chorus of obscenities interrupted our conversation. I turned to see, much to my chagrin, that Stuart and Monte had entered the bar. Stuart was still in his James Bond mode. Monte beamed like a prom queen.

A biker with a red beard and arms the size of Virginia hams hitched up his Levi's and stepped in front of Monte. "You're in the wrong bar," he said.

Monte said, "My, you're a big one, aren't you?"

"Get the fuck out of here, and take your girlfriend with you."

One insult was all Stuart needed. He assumed the karate stance, and everybody in the bar went, "Ooooooh."

"That's right," Stuart said. "I'm a brown belt."

In the instant that I had turned away from the blonde, she made her way out the rear exit. I should have pursued her. If memory served me, that was my part in Stuart's plan. Follow and be inconspicuous.

I heard Monte say, "Let's all settle down now."

The red-bearded giant heaved an evil chuckle. He'd been joined by three more guys, equally large. They could have been the front four for Satan's football team.

"I know," Monte chimed out. "I could buy you boys a drink. Okay?"

"You got money?" said the giant.

"Well, of course, I do. Don't be silly."

I couldn't allow Stuart and Monte to be eviscerated, even if it meant I was going to be chained to the back of a Harley and dragged up and down the waterfront. Not that I planned to let that happen. This was not a stand-and-fight situation. I moved fast, crossing the bar in a few strides. I lifted Stuart off his tiny feet and slung him over my shoulder in a fireman's carry. Then I continued swiftly toward the door. Monte followed, blowing kisses.

On the street, I ran for the toothmobile. Stuart was protesting his less-than-macho retreat, but now was not the time for a sensitivity encounter group. I pitched him into the back of the van.

Monte jumped behind the wheel.

Behind us, I heard the ominous sound of a Harley Panhead revving up, and I recalled a cartoon commercial I'd seen as a kid where a pristine set of teeth were being attacked by nasty characters called the Mr. Tooth Decay gang.

"We can outrun them," Monte said.

The traveling dentist in the back seat yelled, "What have you done now?"

His blue-haired companion was singing a medley of Andy Williams's greatest hits.

Stuart sat up on the van's floor and straightened his bolo tie. "We can't outrun shit in this thing."

"Good point," I said.

Nonetheless, after riding half a mile or so, there were only two men who bothered to continue their chase after us—Redbeard and a tall lean man with a stringy Fu Manchu mustache. It was safe to assume that they intended to put some major dents in our behemoth bicuspid. Which was far preferable to letting them put major dents in our bodies.

At a stoplight, the choppers pulled up beside us, flanking the cab. The big red-bearded guy swung a heavy chain. The metal crashed against my window on the passenger side, and the glass shattered in a cobweb pattern.

"Let's go, Monte."

"But the light's still red." He bounced nervously in the seat, but did as I said. "Jesus, Adam. We're almost out of gas."

I checked the gauge. We were running on empty.

"We should find a phone booth," Stuart said reasonably. "Call 911."

I imagined Forest's delight at hearing that I was riding in a hijacked mobile dentist office on the waterfront, being menaced by a couple of fuckin' Harleys. I felt like an asshole for getting into this mess, but I preferred embarrassment over serious bodily injury. The problem was that I doubted these two guys would sit casually by and wait while we called the cops.

I charged into the back of the van, dodging around the babbling blue-haired lady who made a lunging grab at my butt before her arm fell loosely to her side and a blissful smile stretched the skin on her wrinkled face.

"Is there anything back here we can use as a weapon?" I asked the traveling dentist.

"I don't think so."

There were all kinds of things for in-fighting. Scalpel-type tools and picks. Of course, the dentist's drill was fairly intimidating, but I doubted these guys would hold still for an examination.

The van made a sputtering noise, harmonizing with the crash of the chain against the side of the white enamel.

"I do have a flare gun," the traveling dentist said. "I just bought it for my boat. In case I get stranded somewhere."

Interesting, I thought. Under less stressful circumstances we might have had a nice chat about boats. "That's good," I encouraged. "Anything else?"

"A pistol."

"That's a weapon," I said.

He dug into the back of a drawer by his radiation equipment and pulled out a gun. "But I'm not sure where I put the bullets. I don't keep it loaded. You know, safety measure."

"I understand."

I told Monte to pull into a gas station. "First, call the cops. Then, if you can, fill the tank. But don't get in the way."

"Adam, I didn't know you cared."

"I don't, but Alison will kill me if you get mangled."

Four blocks later, he pulled into a full-service bay.

"Full serve?" the traveling dentist protested. "You know how much it costs to fill this thing?"

I waited, hoping the two pursuers wouldn't be stupid enough to attack us here in front of witnesses. I stopped hoping when the gas-station attendants refused to leave their glass-and-concrete building. I heard the hammering of a hard fist against the van door. The red-bearded giant smashed the front windshield with his chain.

Stuart and I were both armed. He had the flare. I had the dirty .38 snub-nose special without bullets. "Whatever you do," I advised. "Don't hurt their bikes."

He nodded. "I'll take the fellow with the beard."

"Yeah, Stuart. Swell."

We slid the van door open and emerged. Both bikers focused on the gun in my hand.

"That's right," I said. "This is a gun, and I will shoot you."

They looked at each other and nodded before moving wide apart. They'd done this sort of thing before. I heard the car door opening on the opposite side of the van. Monte should be scampering toward the gas-station telephone.

Instead, I heard him call out, "Regular unleaded? Or premium?"

"I don't think you'll shoot," said the Fu Manchu mustache. "If you miss me and hit one of the pumps, we're all dead."

"I won't miss."

The bearded one charged at Stuart, provoking him enough to fire the flare, which soared overhead like the beginning of Fourth of July. Now the flare gun would have to be reloaded. I groaned. Red-beard grinned. He took a wide stride toward Stuart and was rewarded with a swift karate kick in his gut. His grin turned to puzzlement, then to pain.

His partner moved in on me. He grabbed for the gun, and I let him have it. Pulling him toward me, I used his forward momentum to sink a punch into his hard belly. I followed with something resembling an uppercut, but not so pretty.

He thought he had something with the gun. Backing away, he aimed at my face. I charged, knocking him backwards into a gas pump with a thud. I grabbed his shirtfront and slammed him against the pump again.

He held the gun to my head. "Die, asshole," he hissed.

The hammer clicked against an empty chamber. While he stared in disbelief at the gun, I popped off a series of quick blows to his head. His eyes were still disbelieving as he sank to his knees and fell face-forward on the concrete.

I turned around in time to see Stuart deliver the *coup de grace* to Red-beard—a graceful flying side kick to the head.

Both men were sufficiently disabled.

"Back in the van," I ordered. But Stuart had pounced on the chest of the big man, nearly twice his size, and was preparing to deliver a death blow to the throat.

"Stuart," I shouted.

His head turned. His features reflected the calm of a mild-mannered dentist.

"It's not worth it, Stu."

"You're quite right. I don't know what came over me."

We climbed back inside the van as Monte hopped into the driver's seat, and we were out of there. Monte squinted through the cracked windshield, and drove us safely back toward the Olympic Roosevelt.

I've been in enough fights to know that after the adrenaline wears off, the aches and pains start. It was now time to retreat quietly to a dark corner and lick my wounds. Stuart, on the other hand, hadn't had that much experience, and he was absolutely exhilarated. By the time we reached the hotel, he was singing victory tunes with the blue-haired lady in the back.

Since I didn't think there was much to be gained by another sojourn into the halls of dentistry, I left Stuart and the traveling dentist and staggered back toward the Roosevelt. Monte marched along beside me.

"Jesus, Adam, that was really exciting."

"A good time was had by all," I muttered. "Unfortunately, I learned almost nothing. I was making headway with the blonde before you two showed up."

"Sorry, but we were worried about you."

"I'm touched."

"The way you handled that thug was just magnificent."

"Do me a favor, Monte. Don't talk."

"What's the matter? Can't take a compliment?"

"All I can take right now is a nap." I glared at him. "By myself."

"Well, sure. If that's what you want."

"Then," I said, "I'll figure out what comes next."

"I have a couple of ideas."

"Shut up, Monte."

We walked in silence and split up in the lobby. Monte went toward the lounge. I hit the elevators.

The message light was flashing on the phone in my room, and I figured I might as well get all the unpleasantness over with at once. I called Margot.

It wasn't her voice that answered the phone.

"Who's this?" I asked.

"I clean for Ms. Stang on Fridays. Is this Adam?"

Margot would insist that the hired help address her as Ms. Stang. I nodded before I realized she couldn't see me. My eyes were still burning from the Mace. My skin felt like raw meat. My knuckles were swollen. "This is what's left of Adam."

"Margot said to tell you that Mr. Stang has been found."

I waited for her to continue, dreading the news that Phil had been found chopped to pieces.

"He's in the hospital," she said. "Let me find the note from Ms. Stang, okay?"

She read, "His condition is, um, crucial."

"Critical," I translated.

"That's right. Critical. But he's expected to recover."

I exhaled slowly. Tension I didn't even realize I was carrying slipped away. Though I hadn't been the least bit useful in finding my brother-in-law, he was all right. Mission accomplished. I could go back to my regular plans, my regular life.

"There's something else," she said.

"What's that?"

"He's been operated on, I guess. Gosh, I didn't know Mr. Stang had health problems."

"What kind of operation?"

"He had a kidney removed."

Chapter
Seven

Phil Stang had come to Seattle for a dentists' convention, but he'd never had a chance to present his paper on ultrasound removal of plaque. Instead, he'd been propositioned by two amazingly beautiful blond hookers, one of whom was probably into drug dealing. He'd met with a doctor who didn't exist, Dr. Guy Fellowes. And he'd lost a kidney.

There had to be some logic to all this, but it escaped me. I lay back on the bed with my head propped up on the pillows and telephoned the hospital in Portland where I was informed that Phil was in ICU and had no telephone. I asked them to page Margot Stang and waited, listening to a watered-down Muzak version of "Louie, Louie." It sounded more like "Louis, Louis."

Margot cut in, "Nice job, moron."

"Is Phil okay?"

"He almost died. No thanks to you."

"Could we forego the insults for once, Margot? Tell me what happened, I'll say fine and hang up. And this whole ridiculous chapter in our lives will be over."

"Except for Phil." Was that a catch in her voice? "He'll never be a whole man again."

"Just tell me."

"Phil really can't talk yet, so he hasn't explained anything. All I know is that he was dumped on the hospital steps this morning. His right kidney had been removed. The doctors here say it was a very neat, professional job." She paused. "He looks so tired and weak. My poor darling Phil. But he's going to make it." Her voice took on a ferocious determination. "He's got to make it."

In a straight-on clash with the Angel of Death, Margot had an even chance. She was at least as tough and twice as mean. Reassuringly, I said, "He'll make it, Margot. He's a strong man."

"Shut up, Adam."

"What?"

"This is all your fault. If you'd gotten up to Seattle when I wanted you to, you could have found my husband. But no, you wouldn't listen to me. You thought I was being a pain in your artistic ass."

I still thought she was a pain, but I knew better than to say so. "I'll be back tomorrow. Maybe even tonight."

"What about your precious Seahawks game?"

"How did you know about the game?"

"I have my ways. I know you used my husband's disappearance as a reason for going to Seattle to see a football game."

Maybe. Before I realized that Phil's disappearance was serious. Now the idea of attending a football game with Monte doing the color commentary didn't work for me. "I'll skip the game. I want to see Phil."

"Good. Because I can't wait to get my hands on you."

To sink her claws into me. I sighed. My sister's overwhelming gratitude gave me a gurgling sensation in my lower intestine. "Take good care of Phil. I'll see you at the hospital."

I decided to suck it up and cover as many unpleasant bases as possible in a brief period of time. First, Margot. Then, Forest. I hit a home run. He was in his office.

"My brother-in-law turned up in Portland," I informed him.

"I know," he said. "Gabreski called me."

Not that it was any of my business, I asked, "Did you ever find out who the dead guy at the beach was?"

"We think we know who he is but we can't get anybody in his family to come to Seattle and I.D. the poor fucker. Not his ex-wife or his kids. Some clown from the engineering company where he worked is flying out to have a look. But only because he was coming on business anyway."

"Sounds like a fun guy. An engineer?"

"That's right. Another yuppie."

He seemed pensive, perhaps considering what would happen if it had been his own unpopular carcass that had washed up on the beach. I took advantage of his momentary lack of raging hostility to ask, "So, what's the deal here, Lieutenant? Can you make some kind of connection between Phil's kidney and your Yuppie Ripper?"

"How the fuck would I know?"

"How, indeed." I no longer had to put up with Forest's abuse. "See you around, Lieutenant. It's been swell making your acquaintance."

"Hold on, asshole. Your brother-in-law's a witness. Has he said anything yet?"

"Nothing yet."

He muttered, "By the way, you can blab to the fuckin' media all you want. They already know as much as we do about the dead engineer."

So Forest had a leak in his department. I wasn't shocked. "When I saw the first mention on the news, they said there was a cult involved."

"What do you think, asshole? The Loyal Order of Kidney Snatchers?" He tried to chuckle but it turned into a raspy cough.

With any luck, I wouldn't need to talk to him again. Phil was safe, and that was all that concerned me. That was the nice thing about being an *ex*-cop. I wasn't getting paid to stick on the case.

The only problem was . . . I still thought like a cop. I wanted answers. It wasn't enough to know Phil was going to be okay. I wanted to know who did it. And I wanted revenge. I'd been Maced, chased and threatened. I didn't want the bad guys to get away. That cop instinct was enough to keep me on the phone. "I'm thinking voodoo. Blood sacrifice, you know?"

"Not your problem," Forest said. "Real cops take it from here."

I didn't protest.

"Get out of town," he continued. "Oh yeah, and be sure you give my regards to the art world."

It gave me great pleasure to respond, "Fuck you, Lieutenant."

Gently, I placed the phone back on the hook. I didn't want to disturb Forest as he cursed my family tree, branch by branch.

No sooner had I hung up when the phone rang again.

This time, I ignored it. I was stiff. I was sore. And I was going to take a bath. After that, since I'd already blown the check-out time, I'd get a massage at the hotel spa. I checked my watch. It was just after three. If I left Seattle by four-thirty, I'd make it to Portland around eight, early enough to visit Phil at the hospital.

I started the water running. Hot. Extra hot.

My half-hearted attempt at playing detective was over, finished and done with . . . except I hadn't been playing. For a few minutes, my adrenaline ran hot, and it felt good. I shook my head. Now I needed to rearrange my thinking toward sculpting, claw hammers and shapeless lumps of clay.

There was a timid rapping at the door, and I was sure it was Monte. Hopefully, he had found another room elsewhere, far away from me.

I yanked the handle. "What, Monte?"

Instead of Monte standing in the doorway, I saw a creature from another planet, one of Margot's alien forebearers. He was about my height, wearing little round sunglasses, a Z. Z. Top beard and a gas mask.

There were only a few occasions in my life when I'd been completely, totally surprised. My seventh birthday, my mother hid all the presents where I couldn't find them and arranged for my little buddies to pop up after baseball practice. Then there was the first time I got laid. I'd been hoping, but not expecting. And there was now.

The guy in the mask didn't speak. He raised his hand and he sprayed me, directly, right in the same face that had been Maced only hours ago. My last conscious thought was: Don't inhale.

Apparently, my brain wasn't listening.

When I emerged from what felt like a heavy sleep, I was lying on my back in bed. The drapes had been drawn. I couldn't tell if I'd been out for a day or for a few minutes, and I tried to focus on the ceiling, looking for some kind of answer in the light fixture.

I said the first thing that crossed my mind, "Guy Fellowes." But the words didn't sound like that. It sounded like "Ggguhd-aows."

"Good. You're awake."

I was in trouble. I should have been scared. But my body didn't respond, wouldn't move. My brain sent a message to my arms to move. I could feel the bicep attempting to flex, but my arm was limp. Relaxed in absolute lassitude. There seemed to be soft pleasant music playing between my ears.

"Adam," said a disembodied voice.

I gurgled.

"Are you comfortable?"

"Obladee," I threatened.

"Try to concentrate on talking, Adam. I can't understand you."

I wasn't going to tell him anything. I tried to clamp my lips shut, but I knew they were hanging open. A sliver of drool ran down my cheek into my ear. It felt good.

"Tell me about Phil, Adam. Is he all right?"

"Phil Stang," I said. It sounded almost right. I tried a couple more coherent words: "Who're you?"

"I'm Sterling."

Sterling? Why couldn't I move? I needed to grab him, to warn him. The Terminator was after him. But that didn't make sense. Was he a good guy or a bad guy? "Why?"

"I never meant to hurt anybody. You believe me, don't you? It was an experiment that went wrong."

I was the one who was drugged, but he was whacked out. "Hurt anybody?"

"I hope and pray my discoveries won't be lost. That the benefits to mankind will be accepted when I turn myself in to the police." Above the beard, his eyes filled with tears. "I hope someday that I can talk to Phil, that he can forgive me."

"Phil Stang."

"That's very good, Adam. Tell me about Phil Stang."

"Nice guy. Don't know how he can stand Murglah."

"Murglah, Adam?"

"Margot," I said. "Margotmargotmargot."

This was fun. I needed to be thinking clearly, but I regressed to childhood, to infancy. I wanted to suck my thumb, but I couldn't get my arm to move. There was only one organ in my body that seemed to be functioning with any sort of precision. I was aware of the hardest hard-on in the history of hard-ons. "Alison," I murmured.

Just like Pavlov's dogs. Hard-on. Alison. Hard-on. Alison. Conditioned response.

"Who is Alison?"

Why should I tell him? Let him find his own girlfriend. "Beautiful," I said.

"You answer some questions for me, Adam, and you can see Alison."

"Alison?" Was she here?

"First, you've got to tell me about Phil. He's at a hospital in Portland."

"That's right," I said with some surprise. "Gonna be okay? Phil's gonna be okay?"

"Have you spoken with his doctors?"

I tried to see the guy who was talking, but my eyes wouldn't move. I was just staring up at the ceiling. "You gonna take my kidney?"

"No, Adam. I do not intend to hurt you."

"That's good. Only got two kidneys to give for my country. Ask not what your kidney can do for me, but . . ."

"This is very important, Adam. Listen to me."

". . . but what I can do for my bladder."

"Adam." His voice was sharp. "Pay attention."

If I could have nodded, I would have. But I was hopelessly immobile. And I really didn't care.

"Tell Phil I'm sorry. When you see him, tell him that I'm very, very sorry."

"How come?"

"He's one of us. I didn't know."

Phil was an alien? I didn't know, either. But there were big, bunchy pink clouds rolling over me like huge breasts.

"You can go back to sleep now, Adam."

"Thanks," I said. "Thanks for the mammaries."

I heard the door to my room crash open. There were lots of people. The bodybuilder with the knife. Sterling looked like he was going to cry. I had to keep watching. Witness. I was a witness. But my eyelids closed and I drifted.

When I woke again, the breasts were gone. My hotel room was still dark, and there was somebody knocking persistently at the door. My brain sent a message to my arm, and it shot up over my head. All systems seemed to be functioning, and I felt great. This was like the morning after fantastic sex, but without the soreness.

That had been one hell of a dream.

I sprang to the door, vaguely recalling an alien in a gas mask. The door opened to Monte.

"Jesus, Adam. I've been out here knocking for five minutes."

His whining didn't bother me. A truck could have run over my left foot and it wouldn't have bothered me. "What's up, Monte?"

"Well, I was wondering if you were going to use your bed tonight."

I told him that Phil had been found and was resting safely at a hospital in Portland. "And I'm heading back tonight."

"So you won't need this room?"

"Guess not. Why?"

"I made a friend in the lounge, and I thought maybe we could—"

"Say no more." There were limits to my good mood. "The room is yours, my twisted friend."

"You're in a perky mood, Adam."

"I had a nap. And a bath."

Monte wrinkled his nose. "You haven't bathed."

I looked down at my clothes, still grungy from the encounter with the biker. Blood still crusted on my knuckles. Monte was right. I hadn't gotten to the tub.

I went into the bathroom. I remembered turning the water on, and after that, I wasn't sure what had happened. Somebody had turned off the tap. The tub was full of cold water.

When I last checked my watch it was four-thirty. Now it was eight-fifteen. That was some nap. I remembered a pair of granny glasses and a gentle voice. And spray. *Don't inhale.* Either I'd been fantasizing about Bill Clinton's college days or something very strange had happened.

"Tell Phil I'm sorry," I said.

"Whatever," Monte piped up. "Can my friend come in now?"

"Sure." I paced across the room, trying to remember. There had been a guy at the door in the hallway. He was wearing a gas mask and he'd blasted me. Which meant there must be some record on the hotel security system.

I turned and faced the most savage brunette I'd ever seen. Her red and lavender striped dress hiked up over perfectly formed legs. She smelled like expensive perfume, and she was gazing lustfully at Monte.

"Adam, I'd like for you to meet Rachel."

"Nice to meet you, Adam." Her voice was a husky alto, but she didn't sound like a cross-dresser. And her breasts, displayed discreetly in a V-cut neckline, were one-hundred percent real.

"Pleased to meet you, Rachel."

Monte's hand clasped gently around her waist. "We were going to call room service. Adam, do you want anything? Or were you in a hurry to leave?"

"Could I have a word with you, Monte." I separated him from Rachel and pulled him toward the door. In a hushed voice, I exclaimed, "Monte, I'm surprised."

"Why?"

"I thought you were gay."

"Jesus, Adam. Whatever would make you think such a thing?"

I dug out the tickets to the Seahawks game out of my wallet and presented them to Monte. It only took me a minute to pack. "Have a wonderful time," I said as I left.

There was one more stop I needed to make at the Olympic Roosevelt before I left Seattle. I bypassed the front desk and went directly to the security offices where Roy Fishman was sitting with his feet up on a console table in front of several television monitors. He wasn't happy to see me.

"You," he said. His feet came down with a crash. His right hand rested on the butt of his gun. "What do you want? How come the police let you go?"

I could have pretended to be Agent Dullard, but I decided to try the truth. "I'm an ex-cop."

"Connections, huh?" He sneered. "I hate it when dirtbags like you get off with a slap on the wrist because you happen to know—"

"Spare me the canned speech, Roy. I was up here looking for my brother-in-law who disappeared from your hotel."

"Are you a licensed private investigator?"

His eyes were wide and gullible. The temptation to lie was overwhelming, but I stuck to the straight story. "I don't have any kind of badge. I'm just a guy who's trying to do the right thing. Will you help me?"

He thought for a minute, sized me up. And Roy Fishman must have seen something that escaped Forest, Margot and all the other people who looked in my eyes and called me an asshole.

"Okay," he said.

"At about four-thirty this afternoon, did you happen to notice anything unusual?" Like a weird bearded man wearing a gas mask and spraying hapless hotel patrons. Sterling, I remembered. "In the fourth floor hall?"

"There was a blackout," he said nervously. "At exactly 1627 hours, the monitors on floors four through nine blanked out for exactly thirty-three minutes and fourteen seconds."

"Did you find the cause?"

"I called in the technician, but by the time he got around to responding, the system was back up."

"Thanks, Roy."

That covered it for me. Thirty-three minutes and fourteen seconds must have given the guy time to zap me, talk to me and get the hell out of Roy Fishman's hotel. And all I could remember with clarity was that I should apologize to Phil.

There was another memory—mammary?—my total lack of muscular control and my bionic erection, which returned when I climbed behind the steering wheel of my car and aimed due south to where Portland and Alison were waiting.

Along the route, I recalled bits and fragments of my babblings with Sterling. He'd mentioned the police, turning himself in. And somebody grabbed him. The big guy with the big knife. But that couldn't be possible because I was still alive, and professional killers don't leave witnesses.

At midnight I crossed the interstate bridge between Vancouver and Portland. Since hospital visiting hours were surely over, I wouldn't bother to check in with Phil and definitely not with Margot.

I headed toward Council Bluffs. Though I'd put in a long and gruesome day, I wasn't tired. After my gas-induced nap, I felt like I could go on for hours in a state of semi-euphoria.

Momentum was with me as I parked in front of Alison's house and used my key to enter. Dodging the furniture, I went through the house to her bedroom where the light was still on. She lay across the red satin sheets. Her auburn hair was spread in disarray across the pillows. Her eyes opened groggily. "Adam?"

"How's Trevor?" I whispered.

"Holding his own." She opened her arms, welcoming me.

Chapter
Eight

Until that night, I had never believed it was possible for a man to have multiple orgasms. Perhaps my inspiration came from the contrast between Alison's serene beauty and the gross violence I had recently been subjected to. It could have been the Mace in the face delivered by the thousand-dollar hooker, but I suspected my persistent erection was related to the happy gas administered by Sterling. Whatever the cause, I didn't mind the effect.

My first climax happened almost immediately. I pulled her off the bed and into my arms, reveling in the softness of her creamy skin and the silken texture of her long auburn hair. As always, I made every effort to prolong foreplay, but her encouragement matched my urgent passion. Our lovemaking was fast and furious. Too fast. She made a soft, disappointed moan and heaved a ragged sigh.

Any other time I would have felt completely inadequate, but this was different. The profound feeling of exhaustion was conspicuously absent, and my superhuman erection remained outstanding. Alison was delighted. I couldn't attribute my prowess to sexual abstinence, because I had certainly gone without sex for longer periods than three days without turning into a lusting stallion, which was what she called me when I rolled against her again.

My senses had never been more alive. Alison had never looked more provocative, smelled more delicious or felt more tantalizing. I reveled in the pure eroticism, tasting every hot, wet inch of her body. We made love into the early hours, experimenting with positions that would have blown the collective mind of Masters and Johnson.

I had never had sex like this before and I didn't think that I ever would again, without ingesting massive quantities of mind-altering drugs. I didn't want to stop, and I wouldn't have, if Alison hadn't insisted that she'd run out of orgasms.

Alison rested her head on my chest and lightly caressed my shoulder. "My God," she sighed. "That was inspired."

"Thank you," I said modestly. "I couldn't have done it without you."

"Are you saying I bring out the best in you?"

"You bring out the beast in me."

"We must do this again sometime." She pressed a gentle kiss on my neck. "Sometime soon."

It occurred to me that I might have created a monster. I had delivered a performance which exceeded the abilities of mortal man. I might have spoiled her for all other men. It would be a tremendous responsibility.

"Maybe tomorrow," she murmured. "Your sculptures are selling so well that I can probably sneak away early. Actually, if this keeps up, we can both retire early."

I thought I was retiring when I left the police force.

"I'm not sure if I can stand to retire again." I felt myself wilting. "How well am I selling?"

"Only four pieces left, including the big one of the orca. Everything is going for full asking price." She snuggled closer. "You're a genius."

Much as I would have liked to believe her, the title of genius was something I could not claim when my sculpting productivity had dwindled to a few smashed lumps of clay and a total dearth of new ideas. I felt like a phony. I hadn't paid enough dues as an artist. And I had just walked away from a fight. Maybe there was some truth to all those insults Forest had hurled at me.

"Adam, when can I schedule your next showing?"

"Soon as I have some more stuff, I guess."

"Adam?" Her voice was husky and concerned. "What's wrong?"

A change of subject was in order. "Speaking of things that are wrong. Why did you send Monte to Seattle?"

"Didn't he tell you? Trevor had to be rushed to the hospital."

"Yes. I understand why you didn't come. I'm glad you stayed with Trevor. But why did you send Monte?"

"He insisted. You know, Adam. Monte really admires you."

That knowledge might have concerned me if I hadn't seen Monte's choice of sex partners with my own eyes. "The feeling is mutual."

"Besides," Alison added. "When we spoke on the phone last night, you sounded like you needed a friend."

She was right on target. "I was just tired. And I missed you."

"Adam, is there something you're not telling me?" She turned on her bedside lamp, brightening the flow of moonlight through the French windows in her bedroom. Her intelligent green eyes studied my face and she lightly stroked my cheek. "What happened to your face? It's all red."

"Allergies." I definitely wasn't going to tell her that I was zapped by a hooker.

She traced a line down my arm with her fingernail. "And how did you get this bruise?"

"Fell in the shower."

Her tone of voice sharpened when she spotted a large yellow discolored area that stretched from my armpit to my hipbone. "What's this? What happened here?"

"I don't know." I really didn't. It could have come from the knife-wielding thug in the parking garage or from Stuart Hall, karate dentist, or when I fell to the curb after being Maced. Or even from my latest encounter with the bikers. It had been an eventful couple of days in Seattle.

"You might as well tell me." The palm of her hand made a smacking noise against my chest. "If you don't say anything, Monte will. He can't keep a secret from me."

"Good old Monte."

"I don't like this, Adam. You've gotten yourself into something dangerous. I don't want you to get hurt."

"I appreciate your concern, but it's not necessary. Phil's back, he's going to be okay, so there's no more need for me to be playing private eye."

Alison yawned. "Good. Otherwise I'd have to shorten your leash."

"Did you know Monte isn't gay?"

"Whatever made you think he was gay?"

"Never mind," I yawned. With Alison's soft, warm body nestled snugly against mine, my erection and I drifted into a deep blissful sleep.

The next morning, my dreams of Alison riding bareback on a dolphin were interrupted by Alison—the real thing—scampering into the bedroom wearing her hot pink with black stripes Spandex jogging suit that looked like it had been applied with a glue gun. The Oregon Ducks half T-shirt and matching headband gave her the look of a serious athlete.

She whipped open the drapes, chirped something and sprinted out of the bedroom. When she returned, the aroma of the two mugs of fresh-ground Sumatra coffee preceded her. She set one down on the bedside table beside me, snuggled in on the other side and patted my morning erection.

"I'm shocked," she murmured. "After last night, I wouldn't have thought you'd be . . . up."

"Don't get any ideas. This is just a routine drill. Doesn't mean a thing." I wondered if this was the same woody I had when I left Seattle, or had it taken a break during the night. It concerned me. If this was going to be a permanent condition, I would need to have all of my trousers specially tailored. I might even have to have a custom harness constructed.

She sipped her coffee, sighed and stared up at the small blue chandelier on the ceiling. "Last night was . . . well, Adam, words fail me. What got into you, anyway?"

I decided not to tell her about the Z. Z. Top beard and the gas mask and the happy gas. Better to let her draw her own conclusions. And I knew she would.

Men are content to have sex, enjoy it and move on. Women have to analyze. Was it the way you touched me right here? Was it the phase of the moon? Was it the new bedroom drapes?

"Maybe it was because you missed me," she said. "Do you think I'm too available? Should I play hard to get?"

Encouraging Alison to play more sex games was like offering Cher a tattoo-parlor franchise. "You are perfect," I said. I meant it.

"Drink your coffee, Adam. It's after eight o'clock."

She didn't need to remind me that today would be hectic. I needed to visit Phil at the hospital. And Trevor. And there was something else I'd decided sometime during the night when my unconscious brain reminded me that I'd spent fourteen years as a cop. I needed to fill Forest in about knife-wielder in the garage, the hookers, the Turk's Head and, of course, about Sterling. In that morass of events, he might be able to cull out a useful clue that would lead to the arrest of the Yuppie Ripper.

After sucking down the whole mug of coffee and holding it out to Alison for seconds, I decided to talk the whole thing over with Nick Gabreski first. We'd been partners, and he'd understand what was useful to Forest. I called his number and learned that he'd be happy to meet me for donuts at the Muffin House downtown.

Alison returned with more coffee and sat on the edge of the bed. "I'd appreciate it if you would stop by the gallery today."

"Not a chance. I'd jinx sales."

"Possibly," she agreed. "But people love to meet the artist, even when he looks like he's been riding on the inside of a cement mixer. Adam, how did you get all these bruises?"

"Doesn't matter. It's over now, and I'm back to being a tame sculptor."

"Hardly tame." She stroked my forehead. "But I'm glad it's over. If anything happened to you . . ."

"Nothing did." Except for several attacks of gross ineptitude that should have gotten me killed. "Do you know which hospital Phil's in?"

She told me that Phil had been dumped outside the emergency entrance to the City Hospital where all the derelicts, gunshot victims and poverty cases were taken. "Margot was not amused."

"Of course not." It wasn't enough for Phil to have survived; he should have known better than to be discarded on the steps of a measly general hospital.

"Last night he was still in intensive care, but they were almost ready to upgrade his condition to serious. Then we can visit."

I dragged myself from Alison's bed. "I'm going to head over there. Wanna come?"

"Actually, I wanted to stop by and see Trevor."

So far, we hadn't talked about Trevor. I hadn't planned to avoid this discussion, but we hadn't talked much at all. "How is he?"

"Holding up. Just barely holding up." Alison lowered her eyes. "He's already had two bypass operations, Adam. The doctors say his heart can't stand another."

"So what comes next?"

"They don't know. Keep him quiet. Put him on oxygen. Trevor has been talking about some kind of experimental procedure. I don't like the idea, Adam."

"What kind of procedure?"

"He won't explain." She sighed. "He's been through so much already. Two bypass operations. I saw the scar, Adam. It went from his neck all the way down to the waistband of his pajama bottoms."

I sat beside her on the bed. The only things I could think of were so clichéd that I didn't speak.

"He hates being in the hospital."

"Who's doing this procedure?" I asked.

"The man I talked to is a Dr. Moorcroft, but he's not the one who will operate. Trevor said the work would be done by a renowned surgeon. Moorcroft as much as admitted that the A.M.A. would not approve of what he's doing. He needs to keep this quiet."

"I don't like the smell of it, Alison."

"Neither do I. But Trevor wants it. He thinks it's his only chance, and he swore me to secrecy before he let me contact Moorcroft."

"Damn." I didn't like it at all, but the decision was up to Trevor. He'd always lived life on his own terms, and I figured he'd done a fairly good job of it. "You think I can talk him out of it?"

She cleared her throat and looked away from me. "He doesn't want to see you, Adam. Not in the hospital with tubes and wires coming out of him. But he asked me to tell you that after this procedure you two could go sailing on a three-masted schooner to Micronesia. Maybe around the world."

Trevor and I shared a love of the open sea, and I much preferred to think of him standing at the helm of a schooner than lying helpless in a hospital bed.

"I'm sorry, Adam."

"I understand."

Just in case he changed his mind, Alison gave me the name of his hospital—a swanky resort type of place, exactly the sort of health care facility that Margot would select for Phil.

Alison and I separated, dressed and went our separate ways, making a tentative plan to see each other at Phil's bedside. I sidestepped any mention of visiting the gallery.

In downtown Portland at the Muffin House, I ordered more coffee and a healthy selection of bran, banana and blueberry. At least they weren't croissants.

Nick looked more rumpled than usual when he sat down opposite me and waved to the waitress who began loading a plate with what I assumed was Nick's usual assortment.

Without prologue, he said, "I talked to Forest."

"And did he say kind things about me?"

He pulled his head back, like a turtle going into a shell. "He hates your guts. Your fuckin' guts is what he said." Nick barked a gravely laugh. "That means he likes you."

"Well, you can tell him that I hate his fuckin' guts, too." I swallowed a gulp of coffee. "You know, Nick, the more I think about this, the more I know I'm going to have to go back to Seattle and see Forest again."

"Whoa, Adam. This is gonna come as a surprise to you, but you already quit the force."

"I keep telling myself that, but it doesn't ring true. I turned up pieces to his Yuppie Ripper puzzle. Maybe Forest can put them all together and make an arrest."

Nick settled back with a mountain of muffins and two large coffees. He knew exactly what I wanted. "Tell me what happened."

I ran through the events, sparing none of the embarrassing details. Nick and I had been partners, and he'd seen me screw up, heard me cry and scream in pain. He'd been there when I'd lost control at a domestic violence scene and came within a heartbeat of killing a man who had pummeled his wife into unconsciousness. He had physically restrained my rage. Next to Trevor, I trusted Nick more than anyone else in the world.

When I finished, I asked for his opinion. "You think any of this stuff is useful? Should I go back up there?"

"You wanna go, don't you?"

"I don't know. It's a part of my life that I've buried."

"But it's not gonna rest in peace, Adam. You can't turn off your sense of duty. Know what I mean? When life goes wrong, you can't look the other way."

"So?"

"But you're not a cop, anymore. You don't have backup."

There was something he wasn't telling me. "Why did Forest call you, Nick?"

"There was an accident. He wanted you to know."

"An accident?"

"Stuart Hall is dead."

I blinked once. I wanted to tell Nick that he was wrong, that the karate dentist was a tough little guy. "How?"

"Forest said he'd had a lot to drink. He was up on the rooftop of the Puget Madrona counting stars and wasn't watching where he was going. He fell thirty stories."

"Anybody with him?"

"No."

"Stuart Hall was murdered." He hadn't wanted to embrace his fear, and the last place in the world Stuart would have gone was to a rooftop. I was going back to Seattle, and I was going to find the son of a bitch who killed that brave little man who wanted nothing more than to drive in demolition derbies and work on other people's mouths.

I stood and clapped Nick on the shoulder. "It's your turn to pay for the muffins."

"What are you gonna do?"

"Go fishing." I thought about the body on the beach. And about Stuart. "I'm going back."

My old buddy knew better than to try to talk me out of it, but he offered a word of warning. "Forest doesn't want you messing in this. If you go back to Seattle, he's gonna get you off the streets and into protective custody."

"A man's got to do what a man's got to do. Whatever the hell that means."

We stood and walked through the double doors of the Muffin House, shoulder to shoulder. I wished I could take Nick with me. We'd been a good team.

"What's next?" he asked.

"The hospital," I said. "I need to visit Phil and his charming wife."

Nick shuddered. "Give my regards to Margot."

The drive through town took forever. Though it was Sunday, the traffic downtown was loud and annoying. Both parking lots outside City Hospital were full, and I was almost sideswiped by an ambulance before I found a space.

After I found the ICU, it wasn't difficult to locate Margot. I just followed the screeching.

"A private room," she snarled at a doctor-type wearing aqua scrubs. "My husband must be transferred to a private room."

"Mrs. Stang, there are no private rooms available. Besides, your husband is going to be just fine. He'll be out of here in a day or two."

When I heard that, my spirits rose. Phil was going to be fine.

"I want a private room," Margot repeated, more loudly and more shrilly.

"The hospital is full."

"Move the other people. They're sick. They won't notice."

It was nice to see that my sister was coping with her husband's hospitalization in her usual calm and rational manner. Hoping to avoid this particular screaming match, I kept my distance, lurking just beyond Margot's peripheral vision. This would be a good test for the doctor's Hippocratic oath. Practically anybody who was around Margot for any length of time wanted to kill her.

And it seemed that my intervention was unnecessary. Margot had clearly met her match. A nurse who was roughly the same body type as Dick Butkis in his prime, muscled up beside my sister. "The doctor is busy," she snapped. "What's your problem?"

"He's not a doctor," Margot snapped back. "He's only an intern. I want a real doctor. I want the head of administration."

"You got _me_, Mrs. Stang. And I will not put up with your whining. Your husband is being moved to the seventh floor."

"Where there had better be a private room. With a bath."

"This isn't the Hilton."

"You can say that again." Margot actually looked distressed. Her makeup was less than perfect and her designer slacks were so badly creased that she must have slept in them. "I'm telling you right now, Nurse Rachet, if there's anybody else in that room, I'm pushing them out in the hall."

"We'll do what we can," the intern said.

Further shrieking was halted when a hospital person in scrubs wheeled Phil into view. The guy was probably an orderly and he was taking the whole bed with IV attached toward a freight elevator. Margot reacted. She leapt up beside him. "Don't worry, Phil. I'm going to get you the very best of care. You won't be put in some sleazy room with sick people."

Weakly, Phil looked up at her. His lips moved, but I couldn't hear what he was saying.

Then Margot whipped around. She spotted me. "Adam, get over here. Tell them that they have to give Phil a good room. With a view."

Phil whispered again, and Margot leaned over him. "What is it, my dearest? What are you trying to tell me?"

Very clearly, he said, "Shut up, Margot."

When she looked up, Margot was grinning. "He's getting better."

I would have trailed along at the end of the procession, but the aqua-suited intern pulled me aside. "Adam McCleet? Mr. Stang wanted to talk to you."

"What did he say?"

"It was all pretty much jumbled up. But there was something about Stuart and you and all the other fellows."

"Guy Fellowes?" I asked.

"That's right. Guys. Fellows." The intern shook his head. "This is the strangest case I've ever seen. You know about his kidney?"

I waited for him to fill me in.

"It was surgically removed. An exceptionally neat job. Sutures like a seamstress, you know what I mean?"

I didn't. Comparing cross-stitches on surgical wounds was outside my realm of expertise, and conventional wisdom told me that I didn't want to know any more than absolutely necessary. "Were there any other injuries? Lacerations? Bruises?"

The intern shrugged. "A few bumps. But he hadn't been beaten, if that's what you mean."

"Just the kidney."

"Isn't that enough?"

My mind went back to the hollowed-out corpse on the beach. He'd been minus fingers and toes. Sans innards. It made me think of cult rituals. Had Phil been victimized by a kidney cult, some modern-day weirdos who believed the tide wouldn't come in unless they offered up a kidney? But why stitch Phil back up and deliver him home? I knew Sterling was involved enough to want to apologize. But I didn't know why.

I trailed after Margot into the room which was, thankfully, unoccupied except for Phil. In the absence of this source for conflict, she made sure to direct every step of Phil's transfer into the bed. She set her small Gucci suitcase on the vacant bed beside Phil and unzipped it. In her claws, she flourished a pair of baby blue silk jammies. "He needs to wear these."

"Doctor's orders?" one of the orderlies questioned.

"Witch doctor," I muttered.

"Very funny, Adam. I just want Phil to be comfortable."

"Margot, he's lucky to be breathing. I'm sure Phil can live with the cotton hospital-issue gown for a while."

"You're damn right he's lucky. No thanks to you."

Now was not the time to educate her about the corpse on the beach and all the fun times I had in Seattle. I moved up beside Phil and watched him inhale and exhale. His chest moved with reassuring regularity. His color was pasty and through the pale skin on his forearm I could see the blue veins. He looked fragile, but he also appeared to be recovering. His eyeballs waved around in his head and focused on my face. He made a croaking noise.

"What is it?" I asked softly. "Do you want to rest?"

His hand caught hold of mine and he tugged weakly.

"He wants to talk to you," Margot said, brilliantly pointing out the obvious. She'd be a lot of fun at a mime show. "Lean closer to him."

I put my head close enough to smell the antiseptic that had been used to treat Phil's wounds. And he whispered, "You've got to do this for me, Adam."

It was a long sentence for somebody who could barely gasp, so I didn't ask for more explanation.

"Got to do what?" Margot demanded. Her face was right down next to mine. She moistened Phil's lips with a damp cloth. I don't know where she got it, but the Stang family crest, a possum holding a shovel, marked one corner. "Phil, honey, what is it that you want Adam to do?"

Very clearly, Phil pronounced, "Adam, I want you to avenge my kidney."

But there was a hard determined look in his eyes that made me think this was one serious orthodontist, and I was glad that I'd already decided to go back. I didn't want to argue with him. "Whatever you need, Phil. Just concentrate on getting better."

His eyes closed and he appeared to relax. I straightened up and moved away from the bed. Phil needed rest, and I needed to get away from the hospital without being dragged into another confrontation with Margot.

She circled the bed and snatched my arm, pushing me up

against the hospital-green wall for a low-volume conversation. Her voice sounded like the hiss of a cobra. "You're going back to Seattle, Adam. And this time you'll do it right for a change."

"Okay, Margot. If that's what you want."

"You just promised Phil that you would avenge his kidney. You're not backing out—because I won't let you." She paused. Her brow furrowed. "Did you say okay?"

I nodded. "But you've got to tell me, Margot. How the hell do I avenge a kidney? Is this some kind of jousting thing? Do I need armor? Do I wave a banner with that possum family crest?"

"It's a griffin, Adam. You know that. A griffin holding a fleur-de-lis. The Stang family goes all the way back to the Crusades."

"No doubt Phil's ancestors took the Moors captive and threatened to straighten their teeth."

"If I want smart-aleck comments, I can afford to hire a stand-up comic."

"That's good, Margot, because then you can afford to hire me as a private investigator."

"Hire you?"

For once, I had the upper hand. I'd already decided to go back to Seattle, and the fact that I could annoy Margot by doing it was gravy. "And I've got to tell you that my charge for kidney avenging is fairly high."

"How much?"

"You've got to go to Brooks Gallery and buy one of my sculptures."

"You are the most pathetic, ridiculous—"

A groan from the bed drew our attention back to Phil, and Margot flew to his side. Even after he'd lost a kidney, the guy was rescuing me from the wrath of Margot. I owed Phil. There was no way around it. The whole McCleet family owed Phil big-time for taking care of Margot. But the whole clan wasn't here. Just me.

Margot looked over her shoulder at me. "You're hired."

Mentally, I hoisted the McCleet family crest—a cherub with a lily up his butt. "Okay, Phil, if a kidney can be avenged, I'll do it."

I'd do it for Phil, for Stuart Hall, and for that unpopular dead yuppie on the beach. And for myself. Because I couldn't walk away and leave it alone.

I was going back to Seattle. I wondered if Monte was done with the room.

Chapter
Nine

My excuse for not calling Alison before I left Portland was that I had to rush to catch the next flight up to Seattle. The actual reason was decidedly more complicated. I knew she wouldn't approve of my plans. But I couldn't base my decisions on her lack of approval. She'd said, many times, that we got along well because we were independent, gave each other enough space and, of course, because we had great sex. She was a womanly woman, and I was a manly man. I shouldn't have to check with her every time I decided to risk life and limb to avenge a kidney.

So, I took the non-confronting, coward's way out. I left a message on her answering machine, saying that I had unfinished business with Lieutenant Forest in Seattle and I'd be back as soon as possible.

Like a homing pigeon, I returned to the Olympic Roosevelt, my hotel away from home.

As the strange and wonderful effects of Sterling's gas wore off, bits of memory recurred to me with startling clarity, like fragments of shimmering glass. When I recalled the incident at the Turk's Head, I vividly remembered the delicious blond hooker receiving an envelope from a tattooed and surly woman. She'd looked familiar, and it occurred to me that I might have seen her at the Roosevelt, working as a chambermaid.

The more I thought about that exchange, the more it bothered me. Drugs were the most likely substance, but why bother with a complicated drug exchange when cocaine was readily available at the nearest schoolyard? Most upscale dealers were happy to deliver. Unless the drug in question was Sterling's happy gas. But how did Sterling connect with the Yuppie Ripper and Phil's missing kidney?

At the Roosevelt, I dodged behind the desk and slipped into Fishman's video command central, the heart of the Roosevelt security system.

He squinted up, recognized me and his chinless face scowled. To Roy Fishman, I was as appealing as a bad case of psoriasis. "Now what?"

"I need your help again, Roy."

"Get out," he said.

"Your choice." I shrugged and turned toward the door. "But it doesn't look good for the Roosevelt security to have one guest assaulted and another murdered."

"What?" he squeaked.

"Stuart Hall," I said.

"But that happened at the Puget Madrona. You think it was murder?"

I nodded.

"And who was assaulted?"

"My brother-in-law, Dr. Phillip Stang, was staying at your hotel last week. As a matter of fact, he was still registered through check-out time today." I paused to get my bearings. Today was Sunday, before noon. If things had gone according to my original plan, I should have been in my room, getting ready to leave with Alison for the Seahawks versus Broncos game.

"So what?" Fishman demanded, impatiently.

"Phil's registration should have been up today, but I'm pretty sure he's not going to be here for check-out."

"If this is a registration problem, take it up with the front desk."

"Phil was abducted. Somebody cut out his kidney and dumped him on the steps of a hospital in Portland."

"His kidney?" Fishman pursed his lips like a carp, an expression of disbelief. He sputtered, then said, "I suggest you take this up with the police. I believe you know the way to the station."

"The police are working their own angle. This is my own private investigation."

"Are you a private detective?"

"No." While I was being honest, I decided to add, "I'm a sculptor."

"A sculptor?" Fishman's sneer deepened, and he actually snickered. To studs like Barney Fife and Roy Fishman, artists were one step away from eunuchs. "I don't have to tell you anything, do I? As far as I'm concerned, you're just a troublemaker, and I want you out of here."

"Okay, Fishman. You're too smart for me. I didn't want to break my cover, but you've caught me." So much for direct, honest communication. Fishman deserved to be led down the garden path. "I'm Agent Dullard of the Secret Service."

Fishman was skeptical. "Got some I.D.?"

"I just told you, man. I'm undercover."

"And the investigation?"

I lowered my voice. "The Quayle assassination attempt. Code name: White Bread."

"Right. Got it. Undercover." He stood, nearly saluted. "What can I do to help, Dullard?"

There are some people who just can't take the truth. Fishman was one of those. "We need to do surveillance on one of the chambermaids. She's a husky woman. Dark. And she had a tattoo of a rose dripping blood on her forearm."

"She's Indian. Sylvia Erthpouch."

"Sylvia Earth Pouch?"

"That's right. She's been working here for almost two years. Come to think of it, I've always been a little suspicious of her. What's she done? Is she an assassin?"

"Can't tell you that, Fishman. Classified. Can I get a look at her personnel file?"

"Done," he said. "I'll make a copy."

"What shift does she work?"

"Days. She's working right now." He gestured to the bank of monitors. "We can start the surveillance immediately. She's on four."

That was the floor where Phil had been staying. Then me. Now Monte. It occurred to me that Sylvia Erthpouch would have been easily able to direct Sterling to my doorstep, and she might have been the one who had taken Fishman's cameras off line.

I pulled up a metal folding chair beside Fishman and watched. The reception on the high resolution cameras was excellent, and Fishman played them with the skill of a cinematic director, a veritable Steven Spielberg of security.

"There are five cameras on each floor," he explained. "So there are no blind spots. I set this system up myself. Each monitor has five channels, one for each camera. The system automatically switches to each different camera every five seconds. But I have an over-ride that allows me to focus on what I want."

I was impressed. Despite a set of door locks that could be picked by a two-year-old, the Olympic Roosevelt had spared no expense in programming their security, but the program on all these channels was still people coming into and going out of their hotel rooms, just slightly more interesting than watching golf on TV.

Then, I saw Monte, matching luggage in hand, leaving my former room. "Hold it."

"That's your friend," Fishman said, knowledgeably. "Is he an agent too?"

"Right. Under deep cover."

Monte looked dashing in a silky orange and blue outfit he'd undoubtedly worn to honor the Broncos. He escorted Rachel into the hallway, plastered her against the wall, and performed a major examination of her oral cavity with his tongue.

"Your friend fooled me," Fishman said. "I never would have thought he was, you know, interested in women."

"He's good."

Monte and Rachel swiveled toward the elevators, and Fishman changed cameras. Sylvia plodded into the hallway. In her tangerine-colored maid's uniform, she looked like a bear in a Barbie doll dress. Sullen would be an accurate description of her attitude as she dumped trash into her cart, then disappeared back into the room. Fascinating as her routine was, I wouldn't learn much by watching her on the monitor. Especially since she, and all the other housekeepers, were well aware of the hallway security. "Can we get up into one of those rooms?" I asked. "For close surveillance."

"Sure. I do that all the time. To keep a check on the housekeepers. Sometimes they find things the guests left behind, and they don't turn them in."

"No?"

"Oh, yes. Even the most trustworthy."

"Then it might not be a good idea to have you come with me. Might put her on her guard."

"I'll get you a key to the room your friend just left."

Now that I was Dullard, Fishman was bending over backwards, contorting himself to fulfill my every whim. In seconds, he was back and I had the key to what was once my room. I pushed my luck with another request. "Tell you what, Fishman, I'll need a reservation for tonight and this room has already been swept for bugs."

His eyes popped out. "Bugs? Did you find anything?"

"It was clean."

"Thank God. I'd hate to think that our guests were being bugged."

"Can you arrange for me to use the same room? The name I'm using as a cover is McCleet, Adam McCleet."

"I'll take care of it," Fishman said. He gave me a broad wink and added, "Mr. McCleet."

My arrival at Room 427 was perfectly timed. Sylvia stood just outside and watched me as I unlocked the door.

"Past check-out time," she said.

"Yeah, I think I might have forgotten my lucky underwear. You go ahead and do what you need to do. I'll be out of your way in a minute."

She mumbled something and followed me inside. I didn't have the impression that Sylvia was too bright. There wasn't even a glimmer of recognition in her eyes when she looked at me, and she must have seen me in the biker bar.

While I pretended to search, I kept an eye on her. When she went into the bathroom, she half closed the door. Slamming a drawer, I moved to an angle where I could peer through the small opening. She hovered over the bathroom counter, but she had her back to me and I couldn't see what she was doing. When she turned, she had an envelope in her hand which she filed in a stack of towels. Emerging from the bathroom, she flung a disinterested glance in my direction. "Find your stuff?"

"Not yet." I went down on all fours to supposedly search under the bed. I hoped she'd leave the towels there and I could grab the envelope, but I wasn't so lucky. Sylvia lumbered into the hall to her cart, taking the towels with her.

After watching her dump the towels into a laundry bag, I dodged into the bathroom for a quick check. What could she have taken from this room? Since it was Monte's former bathroom, I knew this wasn't the site for a drug drop-off. The only nefarious item in this bathroom was the lingering scent of Monte's cologne, Eau de Stud and the wasted end of an eyebrow pencil. Monte had, of course, taken all the complimentary goodies like soap, lotion, shampoo, toothbrush and comb. At least he had enough class to leave the towels.

I stepped into the hallway as Sylvia was entering the room again, armed with bathroom cleaning equipment. She aimed the toilet brush at me. "You done?"

"Me done." I went into the hall, nonchalantly grabbed the laundry bag and strolled down the hall. Since I knew Fishman was watching, I waved to the camera before rifling the contents of the laundry bag. There was nothing but dirty towels. Apparently, Sylvia had hidden the envelope in the trash bag.

When I returned to Fishman's command central, I asked him if he'd seen the envelope. He gaped like a large-mouth bass. "Envelope? I didn't see an envelope?"

After watching her clean another two rooms and seeing no sign of envelope or anything more interesting than a nifty trash dumping technique, I used Roy's phone to place my call to Forest. He was out of the office, of course, and I left the message that I could be reached at Fishman's number.

I told Roy I'd be checking in with him and to expect a call from Forest.

"Okay." Eagerly, he added, "Sylvia is off her shift now. Are we going to follow her?"

We? His enthusiasm touched me. At the same time, it hurt. After what had happened to Stuart, there was no way I would team up with anybody. No more jolly rides in a toothmobile that ended with the finality of death.

"Thanks, Fishman," I said. "I'll take over the surveillance from here. In the meantime, don't breathe a word to anyone about my cover. You're the only one who knows. Not even Lieutenant Forest knows."

He looked pleased and proud. The first time I'd talked to Fishman, I'd promised him an engraved commendation from the Secret Service. It would be fun to design such a thank-you with lots of eagles and banners. "You're a good man, Roy Fishman."

"Thank you, Agent Dullard."

I swaggered away from security, got my rental car and found a parking spot in the employees' lot. My plan was to follow

Sylvia Erthpouch, which I figured would be a piece of cake. Even if I lost her, Fishman had given me her address.

Within fifteen minutes, Sylvia marched soddenly through the exit, glared angrily at the sky to assure herself it wasn't raining and proceeded toward a beat-up, rusty green pick-up truck. No vanity plates on that vehicle. In fact, Sylvia showed no evidence of vanity at all. What you saw was what you got. I couldn't imagine Sylvia being flirty or cute or giggling. Instead, she was solid and predictable, and her stoic calm was somehow reassuring. When she reached her car, the key was already in her hand so she didn't have to fumble in her purse, which happened to be the size of a mailman's bag, easily large enough to carry several envelopes.

I merged into traffic behind her, staying two cars back and out of sight. I'd done this drill before on the force, and Sylvia made it easy by staying on main roads until she pulled off on a side street and swung into the parking lot of an apartment building with a rusted metal sign planted by the door. "Natalie's Arms," it said, and there were vacancies for one and two bdrms. The address corresponded with the one Fishman had given me.

Driving further down the street, in case Sylvia had a sudden burst of paranoia and noticed that she was being followed, I parallel parked and watched over my shoulder. Like Sylvia, "Natalie" was solid but run-down. The building was five stories, red brick with curlicue wrought-iron trim that had been painted shocking pink, but the enamel was chipped like old toenail polish.

Sylvia climbed out of her truck, still carrying the huge purse. Using a key on the glassed front door, she went inside.

As I settled back to wait, it occurred to me that I was woefully unprepared for any sort of organized investigation. At the very least, I should have been carrying a notebook. Since I'd flown to Seattle on this trip and hired a rental car at the airport, I didn't even have scrap paper in the car.

Hoping that Sylvia would stay put for fifteen minutes, I drove to a convenience store where I bought a pocket-sized spiral notebook, a large sketch pad and a giant coffee. The additional purchase of a jelly donut was a nostalgic reminder of my days as a detective on the Portland force.

When I returned to Sylvia's street and found a parking place that allowed me a clear view of the front door and her truck, I felt like I'd traveled back in time, like I was ten years younger, with defined muscles, a washboard gut and a nickel-plated attitude. Back then, I had reeked with toughness and cynicism. Dirty Harry had nothing on me. I was Adam McCleet, former Marine, Vietnam veteran, cop, detective. Maybe I'd been an asshole, but I remember being damn proud to be one. And there was also the rush, the adrenal pump of danger that was second only to the glandular activity of making love. There was nothing else quite the same.

Sculpting came close. The physical act of creation, when I could see the form emerge from clay or stone, gave me a thrill, turned me on so I could work for hours that seemed like minutes, days that seemed like hours. That excitement was why I worked with big hard things instead of paints or watercolors. I liked the fight with raw material, the sense that I could conquer the element and force the shape that was in my head to come into being. There had been times, especially in the early days of my sculpting, that the materials had won the battle. A stone would crack. I'd miscalculate a balance point and the whole damn thing would lean like the Tower of Pisa. But when I succeeded, the final result felt so good. I could touch it and savor it and know that it was mine. To tell the truth, it really didn't matter to me if my work was shown or bought. If I hadn't developed a need for significant cash flow, I would have been content to sculpt just for myself—an attitude that Alison found almost as bizarre as my lack of concern for critical opinion.

Even thinking about the critics, with their smooth fingers curved around disposable wine glasses at gallery showings, made me sneer. Alison called it a throwback to my earlier careers. In my opinion, nobody got macho points for a rave review, and too many of the so-called geniuses were nothing but dilettantes. Assholes, as Forest would say.

I took a bite of donut, washed it down with coffee and stared at Sylvia Erthpouch's door. Stake-outs had to be the most boring part of police work, but it felt good to be here, trying to make a difference.

I took out my little notebook and jotted down Sylvia's address, her license-plate number and the phone number listed on the vacancy sign.

Then I settled back with the sketch pad. Now, I was really going back in time. On my fourth or fifth stake-out, I started sketching, a habit that a series of three different partners had told me was distracting, a waste of time and unmasculine. Real cops, they told me, didn't draw. Based on my conversations with these former partners, they didn't read or write either.

Nick Gabreski was different. We were a good match.

Using a number-two pencil, I sketched the thick square outline of Sylvia's face. Her high cheekbones and low forehead gave some indication of her heritage. Her thick raven hair might have been attractive if she'd occasionally used a comb.

I glanced up at her pick-up. It hadn't moved.

After I finished the sketch of Sylvia, I tried to recall the features of the blond hooker who'd sprayed me with Mace. Like many beautiful women, she'd been artfully made-up, but I remembered an extremely upturned nose, possibly the result of an aggressive rhinoplasty, and unusually long earlobes. From my police days, I remembered that ears were almost as good for identification as fingerprints. From sculpting, I had grown fascinated with ears, molding their delicate structure from clay, shaping the details in stone. Alison had perfect ears.

Without thinking, I turned the page and began to draw my favorite model. No memory problems here. I was intimately acquainted with every delectable inch of Alison's body.

Before I turned another page, I recalled my purpose in being here and took another quick gander at the entryway to the "Natalie." Nothing had changed. The shadows from a thick oak had grown longer, indicating that the overcast day was fading gently into dusk. A couple of lights had gone on in the apartments, but Sylvia hadn't left.

I shifted positions behind the wheel, acutely aware of my own kidneys and a pressing need to purge my bladder. This might be a good plan before nightfall, but it would be just my luck to time my break with the moment Sylvia chose to depart. Of course, there was always the emptied coffee cup, but I wasn't quite that desperate.

It was dark when Sylvia Erthpouch finally emerged from "Natalie." She had pulled her thick hair into a sort of braid. Her clothing was a study in black leather. Her jacket with silver studs, huge purse and heavy boots must have set her back a pretty penny, lots more than her take-home pay from the Roosevelt. Biker attire might not be to everyone's taste, and it might not be attractive, but it sure isn't cheap.

When her truck rumbled out of the parking lot, I waited until she was at the corner, heading west, to follow. I almost lost her once when she made a sudden left turn in traffic, but I circled around and caught up with her as she cruised the streets outside the Turk's Head, looking for a parking spot.

Now that I was sure of her destination, I parked first. A disguise might have been handy, but I was fresh out of trenchcoats and fedoras. The last time I'd been in this bar, I was wearing a leather jacket. This time, I was wearing a lightweight wool plaid. My disguise would have to be attitude. In this setting, a guy like me with a busted-up nose and a face aged like an old tree wouldn't stand out unless I wanted to.

I ordered a longneck beer and settled on a bar stool. When Sylvia stalked inside, she scanned the patrons, then motioned to the bartender. He was a giant bald Cro-Magnon-looking creature. They met at the far end of the bar. With no subtlety or pretense whatsoever, she dug into her huge leather purse and pulled out a large padded envelope.

The bartender took the parcel, stuck it behind the bar and went back to work.

The exchange had been too simple, I thought. But maybe I'd been away from police work too long. The lack of prudence among perpetrators never failed to amaze me. Nick and I once arrested a thief who was actually watching a tape of himself describing how he'd stolen the VCR, television and camcorder. His exact words, if I remembered correctly, were, "You got nothing on me, coppers." In vice, they were constantly arresting drug dealers who kept their stash on the kitchen table beside a weighing scale and an ashtray full of roaches. Nonetheless, I kept my attention focused on the envelope, expecting some kind of switch or shell game.

After about half an hour, the bartender took the envelope and went down a hallway at the far end of the bar. I took that opportunity to find the men's room. I saw the bartender go into a door marked "Private."

The bathroom was empty. I relieved myself, then took up sentry position at the door, peeking out a crack until I saw the gleam off the bartender's bald head as he lumbered back to his position behind the bar.

If I'd still been a cop, this was the time I would have called for backup. But I doubted that Lieutenant Forest would respond to an emergency summons from me.

I took a deep breath, went into the hall and took the twelve big steps toward the "Private" room. I didn't know if there was anybody else in the room or not. If I knocked, I'd find out. But I'd also be caught. I decided to barge right in and claim that I was selling Amway products.

For a change, luck was on my side. The door was unlocked, and the room was vacant. I closed the door behind me.

The office looked like a bag lady had exploded inside. Stacks of correspondence spilled across every surface. Defunct liquor signs and pieces of motorcycle and crushed beer cans littered the floor. The place looked like it had already been ransacked. Not that searching was necessary. Sylvia's padded envelope was tossed casually in the center of a forest of mildewing glasses on what I assumed was a desktop.

I opened it. Inside was a computer-generated list of hotel patrons and several smaller envelopes, similar to the one I'd seen her take from Room 427 at the Roosevelt. Each envelope was marked with a room number and a date. The first one I looked inside contained the Roosevelt-issued toothbrush and a plastic comb with a few loose hairs.

A second envelope contained the same items and used tissue.

The envelope for room 427 had only a comb with a few hairs from Monte.

Okay, this was weird. But I didn't think it was illegal. Before I had a chance to ponder the meaning of Sylvia's gatherings, the door swung inward. The bald giant stepped inside. In one practiced move, he slammed the door and picked up the Louisville Slugger from behind an overflowing trash basket.

Chapter
Ten

Beneath his wide shining forehead, the bartender's dull eyes seemed unreceptive to snappy repartee. "So," I bluffed, as I casually tossed Sylvia's envelope back onto the landfill of his desktop, "this isn't the men's room."

"You came in the bar right before Sylvia."

Before he could draw any further conclusion, I offered, "That's right. We came together. She's quite a gal, that Sylvia. We're engaged, you know."

"Sylvia's a dyke."

"I'm her brother."

"Sylvia's an orphan."

"Orphans' got brothers," I said. "There were dozens of us Erthpouch kids back at the orphanage."

The behemoth appeared to be confused. Clearly, he had a dilemma. I might actually be an insane relative of Sylvia's and she probably wasn't any too mentally stable herself. Or I might be in his office, pawing through the trash for an acceptable reason. In which case, we should shake hands, smile and go our separate ways. That's what I told him. "See you around."

"You're going nowhere," he said, blocking the only door with his considerable bulk.

"Why don't we go talk to Sylvia?" I figured that was safer. If there were other people around, even the patrons of the Turk's Head bar, one of them might feel compelled to report a bludgeoning to the police.

"No more talking."

"Come on, man. What else are we going to do?"

"I'm going to teach you a lesson."

"You can't kill me here. Not in your own office." It had, however, occurred to me that a body could have disappeared for weeks in this clutter without a chance of being discovered. In fact, the room smelled kind of like dead people. I pointed out the obvious. "You'd get caught."

His frown went all the way to his chin, and his sloping brow wrinkled. He was dazzled by my logic, and so I pushed to the next inevitable step. "I might even be a cop, you know."

"You're not a cop."

Was it that obvious? "How do you know?"

"No gun."

His expression showed that he'd made some kind of decision. I desperately wanted to believe that his current line of thinking involved my continued good health.

He gripped the Louisville Slugger with both hands, as if he were stepping up to the plate. The tip of the bat made a little circle in the air, and he flexed his fingers the way Ernie Banks had done in his prime.

My brain flashed back to Little League days, then fast forwarded to the Police Athletic League games I used to coach. In high school, I'd been a fair pitcher with an amazing sinking fastball.

I picked up an empty beer bottle and went into my stance. Just my luck, the bartender batted left-handed.

I flipped the brown glass at his head.

He grinned and smacked it out of the air.

"Center field single," I said enthusiastically, hoping he'd run the bases and leave me a clear escape route.

He took a step toward me, and I loaded both hands. One with another bottle, and the other with a desk lamp. This time, I didn't bother with the wind-up. I threw and ducked, thinking he might be distracted enough for me to make it to the door.

But I was facing the Babe Ruth of the All-Seattle Thug Team. When I peeked up from behind the desk, I felt the disturbed air as the bat passed over the top of my head. And the bartender laughed evilly. I could easily imagine him pointing to the far wall of a stadium, promising the bleacher bums that he would knock my head into the cheap seats.

I crouched and faked to the left. The bat made a splintering crash on the desktop.

I went right, aiming for the door. I saw the label of the Slugger coming at me in slow motion, growing steadily larger until it was the size of a billboard. My head bobbed in reflex, and the blow glanced off my shoulder, whirling me around. I felt myself falling, trying to stop my backwards spin, trying to slide safely into third. But I was too late to catch myself. The back of my melon smashed against the desktop. The black-suited umpire jerked back his thumb. "You're outa there!"

Blackness sucked me down to that lonely, unconscious place where sometimes it's so quiet you never want to leave. Here, there were no answers. But no questions, either. I couldn't feel a thing. The bartender could have been beating my body to a pulp, but I didn't care. The next stop might have been the blinding white light that people who had near-death experiences said they saw. I didn't give a shit. Maybe that's how it had to be. Since I had already achieved more longevity than my father and grandfather, I was living on borrowed time.

"Adam McCleet."

That might have been St. Peter, waiting to read off my list of sins before I gained admission through the pearly gates. Or I might have been transforming to my next karmic reincarnation.

My vision of my own demise had an ecumenical bent. Any religion or philosophy was fine with me, as long as I didn't have to lie on the sea bottom and watch as the crabs dined on my flesh.

"Wake up, McCleet."

My eyelids snapped open, and I saw a pair of dark glasses. Behind the shades was a face I'd seen before. A rich man's face, so closely shaven that his cheeks glistened. He was the man in the back of the limo, the man who could afford to be flanked by two of the classiest hookers I'd ever seen.

"Guy Fellowes," I said.

"I'm delighted your brain is still functional. It wouldn't have been much fun to have you killed if you weren't aware of what was happening."

I was at a distinct disadvantage in this meeting. Not only was I swimming half-consciously out of a probable concussion, but my hands were tied together at the wrist in front of me. It took me three tries to sit up, and I realized that my ankles were similarly bound. I wasn't surprised. From the moment the bartender discovered me—going through that envelope—I hadn't really expected to get off with a severe tongue-lashing and a slap on the wrist. The only puzzle at this point was why they hadn't already finished me and dumped my worthless carcass into Puget Sound.

I looked beyond the shoulder of Guy Fellowes, noting the sharp tailored cut of his sharkskin suit and saw the broad face of Sylvia Erthpouch. Her black eyes regarded me with a hatred that burned, and I couldn't really blame her. Obviously, I'd gotten her in trouble with her boss because the bald bartender clenched his meathooks on her upper arms.

"One question, Adam McCleet." It was Fellowes talking. "Have you ever seen this woman before?"

"What's your name?" I demanded. "We can't carry on a sparkling conversation when I don't know your name."

He laughed. From my position on the floor, I saw a brilliant set of upper incisors—a perfect disguise to entice Phil into the back of his limo. "You called me Guy Fellowes," he said. "That will do."

"Why'd you take Phil's kidney?"

"That, Mr. McCleet, is none of your concern."

"And what's with all the dead yuppies? I thought you rich people stuck together."

From the corner of my eye, I saw the sharp toe of his oxford wingtip coming toward me. The center of my chest absorbed the full force of his kick. I gave the pain an eight-point-five on the sphincter scale.

I fell back on the floor behind the desk. However, like one of those round-bottom punching-bag dolls, I popped right back up.

"Are you familiar with the ancient Aztecs?" Fellowes's question was rhetorical. He assumed that a dope like me who'd get himself caught in the Turk's Head bar wasn't familiar with shit, much less an ancient culture.

I decided to surprise him. "They wore a lot of feathers didn't they?"

"The Aztecs," he said, "required a daily sacrifice. Their priest would cut open the chest of the victim and offer the still-beating heart to the sun gods. In this way, they were assured of the sunrise."

"No wonder they're extinct."

"But the principle is sound. The sacrifice of one so that many might enjoy the benefits of the rising sun."

"Are you the high priest?" I asked.

He paused for a moment, considering. His hand raised to his mouth and he tugged at his lower lip. I noticed the dull gleam of a solid gold ring on his pinkie. "Perhaps, I am." He swung back around and faced me. "You should never have returned to Seattle."

I'd come to avenge a kidney, but that was clearly a stupid cause to die for. Stuart Hall was a better reason. I hardly knew him, yet he'd risked his own hide to help me and wound up paying the ultimate price.

"Something to prove," he mused.

There was that. The unexplainable urge to set right what was wrong, the same inane motivation that caused me to become a cop so long ago. In another lifetime. "A lapse in good judgment," I said.

"Correct." He gestured again toward Sylvia. "This woman. Do you know her?"

"We've never met."

"Was she clumsy enough to allow you to follow her from the hotel?"

"What hotel?" I had a feeling that if Sylvia had screwed up enough to let me catch her in whatever she was doing for Fellowes, she would be the next victim on the Aztec altar. I didn't want her blood on my hands. "I came here because this is where I saw your whore."

The toe was coming at me again, and I raised my arms, taking the blow on the bicep.

"I don't believe you," Fellowes said.

"Ask your bimbo," I advised.

This time, he didn't aim at my head. His foot connected painfully with my ribs. Once, twice. I doubled over on my side, curling up like an armadillo.

The blows stopped.

"Kill him," Fellowes said.

"Yes, sir," the bartender responded eagerly. "How should I do it, doc?"

"Do I have to tell you everything?" Fellowes made an impatient sound. "Do it so the police won't bother with an investigation. Pour alcohol down his throat until he's unconscious and throw him in the sound. He'll drown, and his death will be chalked up to another drunk who fell off the wharves."

I felt fingers twisting in my hair and Fellowes pulled my face up to his. "It's really a shame, you know. I own one of your sculptures."

I tried to work up enough saliva to spit in his face, but he threw me back on the floor.

Fellowes went to the office door. "You will come with me, Sylvia."

Apparently, she plodded after him. I couldn't see her leave because I was flat on my ass on the floor behind the desk, but I heard the door open and the merry rumble of the Turk's Head patrons. I considered screaming for help, but the way my luck was running, the first people through the door would probably be the two motorcycle guys, Redbeard and his skinny friend. I heard the door close before the bartender yanked me to a sitting posture. He pushed me. The back of my head, sore and bleeding, collided painfully with the unpadded seat of his desk chair.

"Shit," I yelped.

"Don't make this hard," he warned.

"Or what? You'll kill me?"

"There's some things worse than dying."

To make his point, he rested one foot on my left kneecap. To make his point even more clearly, he moved his giant foot to my groin and gave enough of a nudge that I got the picture. "What do you want me to do?" I asked.

"Open wide."

He wasn't about to waste the good stuff on somebody who was about to become flotsam. His vodka tasted like gasoline and burned like acid going down.

I tried to close my throat so I wouldn't be too drunk to swim when the behemoth flung me into the water. But after a few slugs, I realized that it didn't matter. He was going to render me unconscious anyway. Rendering? I wondered what that meant. Wasn't meat rendered? Weren't we all advised to render unto Caesar that which was Caesar's?

My eyes were crossing. My bodily aches and pains blended into one general sensation of pain, losing reference to the specific places where Guy Fellowes used me like a soccer ball. Guy Fellowes? The doc? The bartender called him doc.

He pulled the bottle away from me, and I sucked after it like a piglet looking for its mother's teat. When I looked up, I saw him holding the Louisville Slugger again.

"Whoa," I said. "Didn't the good doctor tell you not to make it look like I was beat up?"

"Yeah, kind of. No investigation."

"Give me a couple more drinks, and I'm gone. Unconscious. Whacked out. Totally blitzed. Hammered. Knee walkin', commode huggin', falling down shit-faced."

I could see him nodding his head. Both images of his huge face were bobbing up and down in a blur. I squinted. Now there were four of him. "And give your friends a drink, too."

He snickered. "You can't hold it."

"Hell, no. I'm just an artist, man. A weenie. I shouldn't even be mixed up in this shit. Guess this'll teach me, huh?"

Almost gently, he tilted back my head and sloshed more vodka down my gullet. The stuff was beginning to taste good to me. I lapped at the trickle that rolled down my chin.

My eyelids fell to half-mast. "Sailboat," I muttered to the bartender. "Always thought. 'Fore I died. Big schooner. Sail 'round the world."

"I got a boat," he said, sanely.

The big man wasn't tracking on my stream of semi-consciousness, but I didn't bother to explain that this was my dream. "What kinda boat?"

"Twenty-six-foot Sea Bird yawl. Cedar on oak, bronze fastened with a Yan Mar diesel."

"You're a sailor? I'm a sailor. Us sailors gotta stick together. You go round the world?"

"Up to Alaska. Down to Mexico."

The guy was experienced in offering a sympathetic ear to drunks. His few words created a picture in my head of a sailboat. God, I loved sailing. I closed my eyes so I could clearly visualize the clean blue skies and trade winds and rolling seas and me, standing at the helm. In the distance I saw great, gray thunderhead clouds, and I braced myself for a rough passage. The storm was coming in fast. Beneath my feet, the deck buckled and rolled, making it hard to keep my footing as I hauled in the sails and battened down. Blue skies vanished in a frigid, angry, wet mist as I was overcome.

In my head, I worked furiously against the cyclone forces of nature. But I knew this was a dream. My physical body was being hoisted to an upright position, my arm flung loosely over a broad shoulder and somebody was telling me to walk. I couldn't make my feet move, so I drifted back to the dream.

Straight as the masthead that pierced blackening skies, I stood against the gathering storm. Winds howled and shrieked like the raucous voices of men, raised in challenge.

Somebody grabbed my other arm, and the two men held me between them, dragged me while my feet tangled helplessly on the rough wood floor. We were outside the Turk's Head.

For a moment, the storm in my mind went still as I entered the eye of the dark, furious winds. Though the air was heavy with moisture and the deck surged beneath me, I was miraculously dry.

"Jesus, this fucker's heavier than he looks."

"Dead weight." I recognized the voice of the bartender.

The other guy laughed. "That's a good one. Dead weight."

Maybe I could outrun the storm with its towering waves that threatened to break over the transom. I hoisted sail and clung to the helm with both hands.

I could hear the waves splashing inside my head. My feet stumbled on the planks of a dock.

"Let's just dump him here."

"No, we'll take him to the end. Even if he comes to, he won't be able to swim back."

They didn't know me very well. I wasn't a graceful swimmer

and I had never won a race in my life, but I made up for my awkward style with stamina. I could swim for days.

A tidal wave rose up in my mind. I could see it coming from far away, an impenetrable dark wall of water cresting white at the top and draining the action of the small waves that preceded it. Ten feet tall, then twenty. The wave came closer and closer. I waited, knowing I had to dive through the center and swim like hell until I came to the surface on the other side. The wall of water towered over me and hung there for an instant.

"There he goes."

"Sleep with the fishes, asshole."

I was immersed. The cold paralyzed my limbs, and I took a mouthful of oily salt water. I couldn't breathe. My lungs were about to burst. I was sinking. Down, down into a dark peaceful world.

The hell with that.

I stroked with my arms, kicked with numb legs, I think I even tried flapping my ears. By the time I finally broke the surface, air had never tasted so good.

Though the pier area was not well-lit, there was enough light to see the shape of the two men standing at the railing, looking down.

One of them pointed. "Hey! Is that him?"

If I'd been even semi-alert I would have known to paddle a distance away from where I'd been dumped before I surged from the water like a drunk dolphin. I filled my lungs with air and dove under.

When I came up, I heard the bartender's voice. "There."

A pistol crack echoed across the dark waves. I guessed they'd given up on the accidental drowning scheme.

I went back under. Rather than fighting the tide and swimming toward shore, I swam further out. Maybe it wasn't a brilliant plan, but my survival instincts told me to put some distance between me and bullets. The way I figured, I had ten minutes, maybe less with the alcohol, before hypothermia sapped what little strength I had left and I would sink to the bottom, sucking sea water as I went.

The next time I breathed, I was a good forty yards away from the pier. The bartender and his buddy were staring down at the water below them, assuming that any sane person would try to find a ladder and climb back on the pier.

I swam cautiously on the surface, looking for escape from the icy water. There were other piers, but they were behind me now. I needed to find a boat or a ship or a garbage scow, anything to ferry me to shore.

And that's what I got. A small working tug putted through the torpid waters, slowly enough so I could snatch a dangling line and be towed to a wharf.

My fingers were frozen claws by the time I was near enough to a dock to flail my way to a ladder. I climbed, forcing my stiff legs to move. On the wharf, I staggered.

The bartender and his buddy might still be out here, looking for me. I had to get to my rental car, which was somewhere on the street outside the Turk's Head, but my final destination was far less important than keeping myself in motion. The breeze on my wet body was worse than being in the water. At least while I was in the drink, I had a kind of floating, liquid illusion that I was going to be all right. Out here, I was cold and miserable. My legs felt like they were going to snap off at the knees.

As soon as I hit the end of the pier and stood on solid land, I heard a deep, rumbling voice that cut through the coldest night of my life. The resonance was familiar, and I knew what I had to do: Hide.

This was easier thought than done. I lurched forward. Painfully, my head whipped back and forth on my neck, scanning. Just a few more steps and I'd reached a low building that looked like a fishing shack. I flattened myself against the rough wooden wall just as two figures rounded the corner. One of them was big and burly. The other was skinnier, bouncing along beside his larger companion like a flea on a bull. Or a remora on a shark.

A Fishman, I thought. Taking a closer look at the chinless profile of the angular man, I recognized Roy Fishman, the security man for the Olympic Roosevelt. How the hell did he figure into this picture? Was Sylvia working for him? If so, why the secrecy in smuggling out toothbrushes and combs?

Roy and his big buddy ambled on down the pier, not saying another word, just walking and listening to the lap of water against wood pilings.

If I'd been smarter, I'd have been home free by slipping away from the fishing shack and hightailing it back to my rental car. But wisdom wasn't the course I had laid for myself. When I set out from Portland to avenge a kidney, I was gliding through the starless night at the helm of the SS *Stubborn,* sailing a rhumb line to disaster.

Jolting my stiffening body away from the shack, I yelled, "Hey, Fishman. I'm over here."

Fishman spun around. He turned and pointed at me, and I think he even did a little victory jig. "I knew we'd find him. Good thing I called you, huh? Good thing I followed him after he left Sylvia's place, huh?"

If Fishman had been tailing me, he'd done an amazing job. I hadn't for one minute suspected that I was being followed.

His companion turned and glared through the darkness while the stub of his cigar rotated in his mouth. "This fuckin' guy can't stay out of trouble."

"Lieutenant Forest," I said, "lovely evening, isn't it."

"Didn't I tell you to stay out of my fuckin' town?"

He certainly had done that, and I probably should have listened to him, but I wasn't in the mood for regrets or apologies. The fact of the matter was that I'd made a little bit of headway in Forest's case. He should have been kissing my battered, cold wet ass. I took one step forward, then another, bringing my feet together. When I looked down at my squishy, sopping shoes, I could feel the walkway rising up to meet me. When I toppled, neither Forest or Fishman attempted to break my fall.

Chapter
Eleven

When I opened my eyes, Fishman was hovering over me like the ugliest nurse I'd ever seen. He patted my hand and murmured something that sounded like, "There, there, you'll be all right." Encouraged by his wharfside manner, I had an urge to curl up in the fetal position and whine.

Fishman blinked into the darkness and said, "I believe he's coming around, Lieutenant."

"About time. Get up, asshole."

Just like that? The man didn't understand that I'd just been whacked with a Louisville Slugger, kicked in the head, bathed in vodka and flung into the sound. I deserved some sympathy and some credit. I addressed the glowing tip of his cigar. "I met Guy Fellowes."

"He's delirious," Fishman diagnosed.

"Fellowes practically admitted that he cut out Phil's kidney, and that he's the one behind the Yuppie Ripper murders."

Forest leaned down. His big face loomed over me, like the Bullwinkle balloon at the Macy's Thanksgiving parade. "Shut up, Adam."

I closed my eyes again. With all the alcohol circulating though my veins, my blood must have been in the neighborhood of fifty proof, which moved passing out near the top of my list of things to do. In my younger, more resilient days, I had learned that there are several misconceptions about how to sober up a drunk. Drinking gallons of coffee or splashing cold water in the face of an inebriated person does not make them any less drunk, it just makes them alert enough to be cranky.

From far away, I heard Forest growl an order, "Stand up, asshole. I'm not carrying you."

He was an echo from my past, a drill sergeant echo. From the depths of my memory, I responded like a good little Marine. "Sir, stand up. Aye, aye, sir." It hurt to move, but some reflexes are more compelling than pain.

Then I was standing, weaving like a piece of seaweed on the tide, but standing.

"Follow me," Forest barked.

I fell into single-file formation. Left, right. I followed Forest and Fishman to the slobmobile. Before ducking inside, I hesitated. "You're not going to drive, are you?"

"No, I thought we'd hold hands, click our heels together three times and wish ourselves back to fuckin' Kansas."

Fishman giggled, and Forest turned on him. "That wasn't funny, Troutman."

"It's Fishman, sir."

"Whatever."

I gritted my teeth and crawled into the back seat amid stacks of unfiled police reports and discarded coffee cups and fast-food wrappers. Something made a loud crunch as I sat down, and I didn't look to see what it was—probably a piece of vital material evidence. Or a petrified hamburger bun.

Forest came around from the trunk of his car with a rough Army blanket in his hands and threw it to me. "Here, wrap this around you. And don't puke in my car. I just cleaned it."

Fishman had taken a position in the passenger seat and he

hung over the back to keep an eye on me. "You're in pretty bad shape."

"You are absolutely correct, Roy. Jay, tell our contestant what he's won."

Roy chuckled. "This guy is funny."

"This guy is a fuck-up," Forest said.

If I'd been a pugnacious drunk, I would have taken issue with Forest's unfair assessment of my achievements. In one night, I'd managed to make more progress on his case than all the cops and sheriffs and Coast Guard and Boy Scouts and Daughters of the American Revolution combined. I should be a candidate for a medal. "About Guy Fellowes—"

Before I could continue, Forest interrupted, "I don't want to hear it. I can't take a statement from a fuckin' drunk."

I sat as straight as I could with a blanket wrapped around my shoulders and the rest of the world slanting precariously to the left, no, to the right. "I only had a couple of beers."

"Right. Jesus, McCleet. Why don't you go back to Portland and drive Gabreski crazy?"

"Because Phil lost his kidney here, and Stuart Hall got tossed off a building here, and I want the guy who's responsible. Guy Fellowes."

Forest stared straight ahead, through the filthy windshield. He turned on the ignition, and I groped around for a seat belt.

"Relax," he ordered. "I'm just turning on the heat."

"Thanks."

"Not for you, asshole." He placed a cellophane-wrapped package on the dashboard. "I want to melt the cheese on my submarine sandwich."

Fishman started to snicker again, but thought better of his impulse and coughed instead.

"Okay, Bassman," Forest said. "Why don't you ask this sorry son of a bitch what happened?"

"Hold it," I said. "I thought you didn't want a statement from a drunk?"

"I don't, but Carpman does. Right, Carpman?"

"Fishman, sir."

"Whatever."

Roy dangled the upper half of his body over the seat and tried to look authoritative. "Well?"

My teeth were chattering too hard for my words to be coherent. "You first, Roy. How come you're here?"

"It's like this," he said eagerly. "After I got off my shift, I thought I might be able to help you out, so I went to Sylvia's address. I saw you sitting there on stake-out, making notes or something, and I didn't want you to think that I was horning in on your investigation."

Forest gave a disparaging, snorting noise and flipped his sandwich on the dashboard.

"Anyway," Fishman continued, "I watched you while you were watching Sylvia. Then I followed you when you followed her to this bar."

Fishman was a master at finding the most complicated way of explaining anything. I made a foggy mental note to never ask him for directions.

"You were in the bar a long time," he said. "Finally, I saw a gentleman—Caucasian, approximately six-feet-two-and-a-half-inches, weight of about one-hundred-and-eighty-four pounds, tanned complexion, brown hair wearing an Armani sharkskin suit and Gucci wingtips."

"Fellowes," I said for Forest's benefit.

"Well, he was with Sylvia. They walked together to the corner and disappeared. I expected you to follow her, Agent Dullard—"

"Agent Asshole," Forest corrected.

That was me, all right. Agent Asshole of the sphincter patrol. "Say, Roy, you didn't happen to mention to the Lieutenant here that I'm on a top-secret mission."

"We all know that was a joke," he said. But he gave me a broad wink.

I wasn't sure where Roy Fishman stood. He was like one of

those kids who don't believe in Santa Claus but leave cookies and milk . . . just in case.

"Anyway," Fishman continued. "You didn't leave the bar. That's when I suspected something might be wrong. I telephoned the police and was referred to Lieutenant Forest."

He glanced at Forest with big, round, puppy-dog eyes. If Roy had a tail, it would have been wagging, waiting for Forest's approval, but the Lieutenant said nothing. He stared through the windshield and refused to toss poor Fishman a bone.

Fishman refocused his gaze on me, trying to initiate a good cop/bad cop scenario, but unsure of which part he was supposed to play. "What happened in the bar?"

"I met a guy with a baseball bat. A genuine Louisville Slugger." There wasn't much point in reporting the assault to Forest. As he said before, he was only interested in homicide.

"What else?" Fishman urged. "How'd you end up in the water?"

I remembered a fantasy about sailboats and tidal waves, but I'd been far too drunk to have anything but a fuzzy-edged impression. I was still far too drunk. "Here's what's important," I said. "Sylvia was collecting stuff from the hotel. She'd package it up in an envelope, labeled with room numbers and deliver it here to the bartender at the Turk's Head for a pick-up by Guy Fellowes."

"Stuff?" Forest said. Though he didn't want to admit that I might have actually discovered something, he was reluctantly interested. "What do you mean, stuff?"

"Toothbrushes and combs and bits of tissue."

"Jesus, McCleet, are you telling me you think the murders are related to petty theft. Toothbrushes, my ass. That's the dumbest piece of shit news I've heard in a month, and believe me, I've heard some dumb shit."

"There was something about the Aztecs," I said. "Cutting out a person's still-beating heart and holding it up to the sun."

"Who said that?" Forest demanded.

"Guy Fellowes."

"Shit."

Vaguely aware that I was progressing from asshole to sublimely ridiculous, I added, "Voodoo cults use hair and toenails to make those dolls that they stick pins into. Maybe that's what Sylvia was up to."

"Shit," Forest repeated.

With the blanket wrapped around me and the heater going full blast, I had warmed up enough to feel human again. And I was tired. My eyelids weighed about a hundred pounds each, but I knew if I allowed them to close, they wouldn't open again until morning. I pressed my forehead against the windowpane, hoping the cold would keep me awake, and stared at the Turk's Head.

Fishman asked, "Was Sylvia stealing the complimentary toiletries from the hotel?"

"Afraid so, Roy."

"She'll have to be severely reprimanded," he said. "That sort of thing just isn't done."

"What happens to that stuff?" I mused. "Every time I stay in a hotel, I wonder what happens to all that free stuff the hotel sets out for guests. You know, the stuff they don't take when they leave."

"Anything still in the wrapper is left for the next guest," Roy explained. "Otherwise, it's disposed of, even if it looks as if it hadn't been used. For sanitary reasons . . ."

His explanation was infinitely fascinating. I gazed out the rear window of Forest's car, trying to remember what question Fishman was answering. A large, bald, familiar shape of the Turk's Head bartender walked into my field of view. He lumbered down the street and got into the driver's side of an ancient El Dorado. "That's the guy," I yelled.

"What fuckin' guy?"

"The bartender who clubbed me and got me drunk and dumped me into the canal."

"He's with Sylvia," Fishman added.

Both Fishman and I were ready to bolt from the car and grab the evil-doers. All Forest said was, "Fasten your fuckin' seat belts."

His first move was to whip a U-turn in front of the Turk's Head, then he proceeded at a sedate pace behind the suspects. He clicked on his police radio and ordered the dispatcher to run an immediate check on license plate EIE-100.

Fishman bounced up and down on his seat. "Aren't you going to pull them over? Aren't you going to arrest them?"

"Shut up, Smeltman."

"Fishman, doggone it. My name is Roy Fishman."

"Whatever."

I was lulled by their bickering. When I leaned back to rest my head on the seat, I felt a painful tenderness at the base of my skull. I maneuvered until I found a spot below my left ear that felt free from abrasion. Sometime in the future, I would have to look in a mirror, but it wasn't an event I was anticipating. Not because of vanity. A couple more lumps and bruises wouldn't be that much of a change. But I knew that once I saw the blood, it would hurt more. Until then, I could only guess at the extent of my injuries.

I allowed my eyelids to slam shut.

The next thing I knew, my shoulder was being shaken by Roy Fishman. "Wake up, we're here."

"Where?" I was groggy. My drunken stupor was turning into the mother of all hangovers.

"Back at the Roosevelt. Can you believe it? Sylvia had the nerve to come back here."

"Hey," Forest barked. "They're going inside. Let's get with it, Frogman. You're supposed to show me how your fuckin' security can track these assholes through the hotel."

Still draped in the army blanket, I staggered numbly behind Forest and Fishman through the lobby. Looking like this, like something that had been dredged from the sound, I had a taste of how the Elephant Man must have felt. The first thing I noticed was how rapidly the other people in the lobby moved away from me. The second thing I noticed was Alison Brooks.

She sat primly in one of the overstuffed wingchairs. Her neat ankles were crossed and her back was perfectly straight. She looked like the perfect lady she was, though the thigh-high slit in her skirt somewhat ruined the appearance of innocence.

Gracefully, she unfolded from the chair and came toward me. Her green eyes were murky, dark and angry. "My God, Adam, what happened?"

"I slipped on my rubber ducky."

"You look like hell."

"And you, my angel, look like heaven."

"Don't even think about kissing me," she said as I lunged toward her in a Quasimoto shuffle. "You're drunk."

"McCleet," Forest summoned. "Get your ass in here."

I escorted Alison into Fishman's command central. He'd already isolated the camera that followed the bartender and Sylvia. They were on the fourth floor. Unless I missed my guess, they were going to my room.

Sylvia used her passkey and they slipped inside.

"Definite grounds for dismissal," Fishman muttered. "Sylvia Erthpouch is history at this hotel."

When he started to rise from his chair and suit the action to the words, Forest clamped a meaty hand on his shoulder. "Hold up, Fishbreath."

"But this behavior cannot be allowed. Not for a minute."

"Think about it."

"About what?"

"Why the hell do you think they're up there? My guess is that McCleet hasn't got shit worth stealing. So?"

"So what?" Roy Fishman was truly puzzled. His one-track mind had fixated on the fact that Sylvia was breaking one of his precious rules and he couldn't see anything else.

I envied him. It would have been nice to view the world as

one-dimensional, direct and smooth. My own vision seemed shot through a prism, shimmering from one plane to another until I found something that made sense.

"What?" Roy repeated. "Why are they up there?"

I explained, "They're up in my room, waiting for me to get back. The bartender must have figured out that I escaped, and he's come back here to finish the job." I pulled Alison forward. "Lieutenant Forest, Roy Fishman, I'd like you to meet Alison Brooks."

Fishman looked up and nodded briefly, Forest did the same. Then he paused. His spine stiffened, and his cigar stuck straight out in his mouth. He turned gallantly toward Alison and, for the first time, I saw Forest smile.

"Pleased to meet you," he said. "Welcome to Seattle."

Alison often had an amazing effect on people. With one bat of her luxurious eyelashes, she could soothe the savage breast and reduce strong men to quivering puddles of Jello. With one such glance, she had performed the miracle of making Forest courteous.

"I've heard so much about you, Lieutenant."

"From Nick Gabreski?" he asked.

"Yes, and Adam has spoken highly of you."

Forest tossed a dubious look my way and said, "Has he?"

Fishman interrupted this tender moment. "What do I do now?"

"You stay here. Watch the monitor and tell me if those two make a move. I'll be in the cocktail lounge with Ms. Brooks."

"Please," she said, "call me Alison."

Forest offered his arm and she took it. The woman was fickle. She didn't even glance over her shoulder to see if I'd collapsed in the corner. "Hey," I called after them. "Can I come, too?"

Alison's tone was icy. "Maybe you ought to tidy up, Adam?"

"Normally, I would agree with you. But there are people in my room, and I think they want to kill me."

"Stop whining," Forest said. "Alison, shall we?"

I stumbled along behind the two of them like the village idiot. I even developed a limp when I tripped over the bedraggled edge of the blanket and twisted my ankle. It was my guess that Forest used this blanket for changing the oil in the slobmobile. In addition to my colorful array of body bruises and wet clothes, I now smelled like Prince William Sound.

We sat at a table for three. Actually, Alison and Forest sat, and I hunched over like the raw, beat-up creature that I was. My ribs ached where Fellowes had kicked me, and my butt felt raw, causing me to wonder vaguely if it was possible to have frostbite on my ass. Would they have to amputate? The only good thing about these injuries were that they distracted from the giant, throbbing hurt in my head.

A little sympathy from Alison would have been welcome, a tender stroking of the brow and a few gentle kisses while she ministered to my injuries and nursed me back to health. But she barely glanced in my direction as she ordered her dry white wine. Forest wanted a beer, and I croaked out a pathetic request for ten aspirin and black coffee.

The Roosevelt cocktail waitress, an attractive woman with a wide smile who wore a khaki blouse, a miniskirt and a Rough Rider bush hat leaned over me and whispered, "You look like shit, sugar."

Shit and sugar. There was a mental image for me to ponder, but it was an appropriate description for Forest and Alison who seemed to be hitting it off famously.

"An art gallery," he said with a slightly paternal chuckle. "You own an art gallery?"

As she glanced across the table at him, her eyes narrowed a fraction of an inch. There wasn't much that annoyed Alison more than being patronized. She didn't like being called cute, and she hated comments about how a pretty young thing like herself couldn't possibly run anything more complicated than a cosmetics counter. I knew for a fact that last year Alison's net profits had gone well into the high six figures. With her tense facial expression—which was, nonetheless, sexy as hell—she was shooting Forest a warning: Don't be condescending with me.

I hoped he'd miss the signals because it would be great entertainment to watch Alison slice and dice, castrate and eviscerate Forest's ego.

But the Lieutenant was smarter than I'd given him credit for. He leaned toward Alison and said, "I'd be interested in hearing about your gallery. I like art."

"Really?" Alison said, coolly. "What type of art are you most interested in, Lieutenant?"

Though I was sure that Forest's art interest fell somewhere between nudie tool calendars and black velvet paintings of matadors, I knew better than to gloat, or egg him on. This was Alison's confrontation, and she was capable of handling herself.

"Never got caught up by performance art," Forest said. "And a lot of the moderns, like Kandinsky, are too abstract for my taste. Andrew Wyeth," he said. "I enjoy the pure honesty of a Wyeth painting."

Not a bad answer from the guy who probably draws all those butt pictures on men's room walls.

"I own one," he said.

"What?" In spite of my aches and pains, I almost leapt across the table and down his throat. He owned a Wyeth? The guy who'd been riding me ever since he learned that I called myself a sculptor? This was the same hard-ass who had bestowed upon me the sensitive and meaningful nickname of "asshole?"

"A seascape. Just a little one." He grinned winningly at Alison. "I saved almost a year to be able to afford it. My wife said I should have bought a new car, but that painting gives me a hell of—excuse me, ma'am—a heck of a lot more pleasure than tight shocks and a smooth ride."

Alison beamed her approval. Forest had, unknowingly, described himself as her favorite kind of client. Though she cultivated wealthy collectors, the clients she felt most warmly toward were average people who were so touched by the beauty of art that they had to make it part of their everyday lives.

The waitress arrived with our drinks and two raggedy aspirin tablets she'd found in the bottom of her purse for me. I sucked them down and watched, dazed, while Alison discussed several fine local artists who emulated the style of Wyeth.

Forest listened and commented intelligently.

I slumped in my chair. The whole thing had become too surreal for me to comprehend. Sugary Alison and shitty Forest were chatting about the merits of acrylic versus oil. I'd been bludgeoned by a baseball bat and tossed out to sea on the orders of somebody named Guy Fellowes who was probably responsible for the mutilations of several yuppies and the death of Stuart Hall. There were important clues to be acted upon. How could these two be talking about art?

"Adam," I heard her saying, "you never told me that Ed had such an interesting perspective."

"Gosh, how could I have been so blind?" How could I have overlooked Forest's raging sensitivity when he was sticking my face into the gaping wounds of a bloated body on the beach?

Fishman bustled into the lounge, moving with such high velocity that he caused the cocktail napkins on the bar to flap in his wake. In a whisper loud enough to be heard on Guam, he said, "The man is leaving. Taking the stairs and not the elevator."

"I'm on it." Forest nodded to Alison. "I've enjoyed our conversation. Next time I'm in Portland, I'll visit your gallery."

"I'll look forward to it," she said, and she sounded absolutely sincere.

To me, he added, "Stay put. I don't want the guy to see you."

Neither did I. "What if he's coming down here for a drink?"

"Good point," Fishman said. "Better come back to security with me."

Alison accompanied me and Fishman as we hurried across the lobby and disappeared into Roy Fishman's den of surveillance monitors. I shed my blanket and straightened my damp clothes.

"You really are a mess," Alison said.

"Want to help me clean up?"

"Not really. I've never been sweet on stupidity, Adam."

"Then why did you come to Seattle?"

"That, my sweet, is none of your business."

If not for me, then what? This would require some further thinking, but first I needed to get cleaned up. I turned to Fishman who was, once again, jockeying around the floors with his video controls. "Hey, Roy, is my room available now?"

"As far as I can tell, Sylvia hasn't left." He brightened as he regarded one of the images on his screen. "But there goes the big bald man. He's heading out through the lobby. I hope Forest won't let him get away."

Of course, I cared about apprehending the bartender. But I figured that sooner or later the guy was going to have to return to his bar. And I had other things on my mind: a shower, a dry shirt and a pair of pants that weren't soggy in the crotch. If the only thing standing between me and warm water and fresh clothes was Sylvia Erthpouch, I'd take my chances. "I'm going up to my room."

"I wouldn't," Fishman warned. "Not before you check with Lieutenant Forest."

Though tempted to say, "Fuck Forest," such a comment would have been less than noble, especially now that Alison regarded the overweight jackal as the hero of the common man. Instead, I said, "I'm going to my room to change."

Alison followed me from the security room. On the elevator, she said, "I think you should wait for Forest."

She was right. Waiting for backup would have been a smart thing to do, but I hadn't been smart all night and I was still alive. Barely alive, but still drawing breath.

"Please, Adam. I don't want you to be hurt again."

"You're right," I told her when we reached the fourth floor. "You go back down and get Forest, and I'll wait here."

"Come with me, Adam."

"Too tired," I claimed. Besides, if I asked Forest to come up to my room and chase big, bad Sylvia away, he'd laugh, and I wasn't in the mood for more abuse. "I'll sit here, on this nifty bench beside the elevator, and wait."

The instant she got back on the elevator and the door closed, I was on my feet and marching down the hall to my room. I used my key, shoved open the door and dodged out of the way in case Sylvia had taken it into her head to shoot first and ask questions later.

There was no sound from the room, not even the whisper of breathing. The bedside lamp was lit, which seemed to indicate that Sylvia wasn't planning to leap out and surprise me in the dark.

The minute I stepped inside, I was hit by an odor with which I was entirely too familiar, the ferrous smell of death.

Sylvia lay across the bed. She was fully clothed, but her shirt was pushed up and her belly had been sliced open.

Chapter
Twelve

There was no reason for me to mourn Sylvia Erthpouch. She was a stranger who had made her own unfortunate choice of companions long before I was aware of her existence, and, considering the habits and habitats of those companions, it seemed likely that stealing toothbrushes was not the worst of her crimes. And yet, I remembered, earlier this afternoon, when she left the Roosevelt, she'd looked up at the sky, checking for rain-clouds. I was sorry the woman was dead.

"Oh, my God, Adam."

Alison's wide green eyes were full of questions I couldn't answer, and her hands trembled when she raised them to her throat, almost in an attitude of prayer. She looked like she wanted to speak, but no words issued from her lips.

Though it was too late to keep her from coming into the room, I stepped in front of her, shielding her from the grisly view. When I touched her shoulder, she didn't react. Her body was stiff, frozen.

"Come on, Alison. Let's get out of here."

"We can't leave her here alone. We have to call Forest."

Standard operating procedure. The rote, mechanical duties could be a comfort. "We'll call the police. But not on the phone in this room. We shouldn't touch anything."

She had unbent enough to allow me to place my arm around her waist and ease her toward the hallway. Her gait was stiff-legged. Alison usually moved like a dream, but now she'd fallen into a nightmare. "I'm sorry," I said.

"This is your world, Adam. Isn't it?" She was tense, but poised. "You can walk into a hotel room and find . . ."

"Let's go downstairs. We'll find Forest and tell him what happened here."

"Is that the correct procedure?"

"Not really. Technically, one of us should stay here and the other should call 911."

"Then, that's what we'll do. I'll stay."

I wasn't comfortable with the idea of leaving her alone in the hallway. However, we needed to report Sylvia's murder and didn't have a phone. Then I remembered the security camera in the hallway. Surely, Fishman was glued to his monitor downstairs. The problem was that the cameras didn't have audio pickup, and I would have to pantomime the message.

I gazed up into the nearest fisheye lens and mouthed the words: "Call nine-one-one." Then I made the motion for holding a telephone to my ear and held up nine fingers, then one finger, then one finger.

"Adam? What are you doing?"

"Fishman," I said. "I'm giving him the message."

When I looked back at her, her eyes were cold as the November winds across the San Juans, and her words came uneasily, almost in a stutter. "I knew you shouldn't have come back here. It's dangerous."

"But it's necessary."

"Why? You're a sculptor."

Now was probably not the best time to remind Alison that I'd been in Force Recon in Vietnam, and I'd seen enough dead bodies to fill one panel of the Memorial Wall in Washington. For fourteen years, I'd been a cop.

She searched my face, looking for something that she did not find. "I don't know you, Adam. I don't know you at all."

The elevator at the end of the hall burst open and a cloud of blue cigar smoke pungently announced the arrival of Lieutenant Forest. Fishman was with him, and his hogleg of a gun was drawn.

"I know there's trouble," Fishman said. "They were signaling me over the monitor."

"Shut up, Frogman."

"Fishman. It's Fishman, dammit."

"Whatever."

Forest remembered to give Alison a pleasant nod before he turned to me. "What now, McCleet?"

I gestured toward the room. "Sylvia is dead."

There was a flicker of surprise in his eyes. He stepped around me and blundered into room 427.

"Fuck!" He was back in the hall in a second, shouting orders to Fishman. "Call the precinct and tell them we've got a murder here, and I'm already on the scene."

"Yes, sir." Fishman darted back to the elevator.

"Hey," Forest called after him.

"What?" He whirled around so fast that he almost went in a complete circle.

"Put the gun away, Fishman. I don't want you to accidentally shoot off your foot."

He saluted and disappeared into the elevator.

When Forest returned his attention to me, I could see that he was more tense and cantankerous than usual, which was kind of like saying the military had dropped more bombs than usual during the Persian Gulf War. "How did you stumble into this mess, McCleet?"

"I came to my room to change clothes, used my key to open the door. The light was on, and that's the way I found her."

"Didn't I tell you not to come up here?"

"Not that I recall." Not that it made a difference. Sylvia was already dead when I came into the room. There was something out of sync with Forest's line of bluster, and I guessed at the cause. "What happened with the bartender? I thought you were following him."

"Lost the son of a bitch."

"You lost him?" Now I knew why Forest was pissed. While he'd been downstairs in the lounge, chatting about the techniques of post-modernist art with Alison, a murder had been committed. It was an affront. The killing had happened right under Forest's nose. Then, with all the skill of a rookie, he'd lost the murderer's trail. "How the hell could you lose him? The guy's eight feet tall and has a bald head the size of the Kingdome."

"It's none of your business how I lost him."

Forest took a giant step forward. He looked like he wanted to take a swing at me. That would have been okay; I was ready to punch something. "A dentist in a toothmobile wouldn't have lost him."

"Shut up, McCleet."

He gave a little shove on my shoulder. In spite of all my aches and pains, I didn't budge an inch. I shoved back. "Are you going to make me shut up, Forest?"

"Don't tempt me."

"Go ahead. Take a shot."

"Stop it." Alison stepped between us. "Both of you, stop it right now."

When Forest reached around her to tap me on the shoulder again, Alison centered her hands on my chest and pushed me away. Her anger encompassed both of us. "There's a dead woman in that room, and you two are acting like a couple of schoolboys. Show a little respect!"

Forest bit down so hard on his cigar that he nearly amputated the end. I could hear police sirens in the distance, approaching the Roosevelt. Alison glared at Forest. "Will you be needing us for anything else, Lieutenant?"

He shook his head.

"Then, Adam, I suggest we find another room."

I started back toward the room where Sylvia lay dead.

"Where do you think you're going?" Forest demanded.

"I need to get my suitcase."

His grin was pure evil. "Sorry, McCleet. Nobody touches anything in that room until the forensics crew has been over it."

"Yeah? Like it's some big mystery who killed her. We watched her go in there with the bartender. Fishman monitored the room. Nobody else went in. Nobody else came out. What do you think, Forest? Think the bartender did it?"

"Adam!" Alison was holding the elevator. "Let's go."

We rode down in silence. She was angry, and there was nothing I could say to make it better. I wouldn't score any maturity points by telling her that Forest started it.

At the front desk, I confronted a tall skinny clerk with hair that stuck up in front like a woodpecker. He darted his head around me to watch the first wave of cops arriving in response to Fishman's call.

"I need to change rooms," I said.

When he looked at me, his nostrils twitched. I smelled like a combination of harbor water, rotgut vodka and oil from Forest's army blanket. "I beg your pardon?"

"A room. I need a different one."

"And why, may I ask, is your current room unsatisfactory?"

"There's a dead body in it."

Alison yanked me aside. "You'll have to excuse my friend," she said. "He's not himself."

Then who was I? Did I get to pick? I'd always wanted to be Clint Eastwood, a silent tough guy squinting into the horizon. Nobody messed with a guy like Clint.

"I'd like a room for tonight," Alison said.

"I'm sorry, Miss, but we're full up. If you'd like, I could try the Puget Madrona."

She gave him her name and said, "That will be fine."

Resting her elbows on the countertop, she avoided looking at me, and I couldn't blame her. I was not a pretty sight.

The clerk leaned away from the telephone and asked her, "A single or double?"

"Single," she said.

I frowned. She took a single room. This didn't sound good.

When she crossed the ornate lobby of the Roosevelt, the heels of her pumps clicked on the marble floor. Clint would have let her walk away. He would have watched until she was out of sight, then made some terse, wise comment and blown away seventy bad guys with his Magnum. I wasn't that cool.

I caught up with her on the other side of the revolving door that was spewing cops into the Roosevelt. It wasn't raining yet, but the mist was so thick and heavy that it drenched me all over again. The circular drive leading up to the hotel entrance was jammed with cop cars with police radios squawking and red and blue lights spinning.

"Alison," I said.

When she turned toward me, her cheeks were damp with tears. "I'm sorry," I said, though I had no clue as to what I was sorry for.

"It doesn't do any good to apologize. I can't ask you to be something you're not."

"What are you saying? You think I like this? You think I like being beat up and thrown off a wharf?"

"It's a high, isn't it? Some kind of ridiculous, macho, selfish, adrenaline thing."

"Selfish? I got into this whole thing because I was trying to help my sister and Phil."

"That's how it started. But helping Margot isn't what's keeping you here."

I caught her arm before she could take off walking again.

"Come on, Alison. Talk to me. Isn't that why you came up here?"

"I came here for Trevor," she said.

An ice-cold dagger stabbed into my gut. I'd forgotten all about Trevor. "Is he all right?"

"He's hanging on. But he desperately wants this procedure he keeps talking about, and the doctor is planning to leave this area for an indefinite period of time. Trevor can't wait."

"How do we reach this doctor?"

"I've arranged for an appointment with Dr. Moorcroft tomorrow morning."

"I'll come with you."

"Not a chance, Adam. Apparently, this procedure isn't approved by the AMA or the FDA."

"What the hell are they doing?" I didn't like the sound of this at all. "What kind of procedure is this?"

"Trevor believes in it. Whatever they're doing, they have a seventy-percent success rate."

"You shouldn't go alone. It doesn't sound safe."

She regarded me coldly. "I can handle this by myself."

The hell of it was, she could. I wanted her to need me, but the bottom line was that Alison was a capable woman. It was one of the things that drew me to her in the first place.

As she crossed the open stretch between the hotel marquee and the underground parking, I followed like a puppy dog at the end of an invisible leash. It seemed important to keep her within sight as long as possible. She covered the distance briskly with shoulders thrown back and her head held high, not looking back.

In the garage, she went to her rental car, fitted the key in the door and opened it. I sensed that she was walking out of my life, and there wasn't a damn thing I could do to stop her. "Alison," I whispered.

She paused, rotated slightly so I could see her elegant profile. I thought I heard her say, "Good-bye, Adam."

My own rental car was still parked outside the Turk's Head,

so I couldn't follow her, but I wasn't going to let her get away. I knew where she was headed, and I could walk to the Puget Madrona. The clammy night wrapped around me like a shroud, and long blocks stretched wetly in front of me. I'd almost given up any hope of ever being warm and dry again.

The desk clerk at the Madrona was just as snotty as the guy at the Roosevelt. Obviously, I wasn't the clientele that any hotel aspired to. But when I flipped my credit card across the counter and said that I wanted a room, he responded as I knew he would—this is America, damn it, and any derelict with a gold card can get service wherever he wants.

In my hotel room, I undertook a task I'd been dreading. Though it felt amazingly good to peel off my soggy clothes, I knew it wasn't going to be fun to look in the mirror and take inventory of my injuries. My face had taken the worst of the beating. There was a raw abrasion on my forehead, almost at the hairline, and the wound had swelled so much that my left eye was half-closed. My jaw was lumpy. A strip of skin had been torn from my nose. I could only feel the goose egg on the back of my skull.

The rest of my body wasn't too bad, except that my skin looked as white and waxen as the statue of Jack the Ripper at Madame Toussaud's. A couple of bruises colored my arms and ribcage. The left cheek of my butt was black and blue.

In the final analysis, I decided that I'd live. So, I turned the shower to scalding and stepped under it. A medical person would probably have told me that the better treatment for swelling and contusion was ice water, but I wanted to be hot, to counteract the aching cold that I'd been feeling all night.

A good part of that chill came from Alison. We'd never had a major fight before, and I wasn't sure how to make it better. This hurt might be too deep to be healed.

I crawled into the bed, dragged the covers up to my neck and put in a wake-up call for five in the morning. Then I closed my eyes.

It seemed like only a few minutes later that I heard the phone ring. I picked up the receiver, mumbled and hung up. Then there was a hammering on the door. These people really took wake-up calls seriously.

Before I could open it, Forest charged through, followed by someone I could only guess was the security officer for the Puget Madrona. At this rate, I'd be the poster boy for hotel security all over Seattle.

Forest had been thoughtful enough to retrieve my suitcase from the Roosevelt. He dropped it in the middle of my chest. "Get up, McCleet."

"No, thanks."

"You've got to come with me and identify it."

It? I remembered that Forest had the habit of referring to corpses with the neutral pronoun. "Sylvia? Why do you need me to identify Sylvia?"

"Not her. We got another stiff."

Chapter
Thirteen

The bartender had been killed more neatly than Sylvia. The gaping slash across his throat wasn't surgical, but the wound showed a certain degree of efficiency. I sensed the fine hand of Guy Fellowes, performing an Aztec ritual with an obsidian blade.

But we weren't standing at a sacrificial altar. The bartender had been sliced in the alley behind the Turk's Head bar. He was still behind the wheel of his El Dorado, and wearing his seat belt. His blood stained the dashboard.

"That's the guy," I said to Forest.

He looked at me and bobbed his head once, not screaming obscenities and making demands on the cops at the scene. It was four in the morning, and somewhere in the night, Forest had lost his top dog bark. The Lieutenant had screwed up. Instead of apprehending them, he'd decided to just keep an eye on Sylvia and the bartender. His mistake in judgment had resulted in two homicides.

"When was the last time you saw this man alive," he said, following procedure.

"You know when that was. You were with me. We saw him on the video monitor at the Roosevelt."

"And before that?"

"In the street outside the Turk's Head." I repeated, "You were with me."

"And before that?"

"This is going to take a while," I warned. "If you want a statement, I'd better start at the beginning."

"I don't want the fuckin' story of your life, McCleet. I just want to know what happened. People are getting whacked all over my beat, and you're in the middle of it."

"Two words." I held up two fingers. "Guy Fellowes."

Forest rumbled before he said, "I know there's somebody running this show—somebody big—and it could very well be this Guy Fellowes character, but—goddamn it, McCleet—I need more than an alias to find him."

"Running what show?"

Forest exhaled a huge, earth-shaking sigh and gestured for me to follow him. He went to the slobmobile and I got into the passenger seat.

"Here's what we know," he said. "The forensic people and the pathologists have had a field day with these ripper victims."

"Like Phil," I put in.

"Your brother-in-law doesn't count," he said. "Because he didn't die."

"I'll be sure to tell him. Phil will be heartbroken."

"You know what I mean, McCleet. The coroner's crew didn't have their chance to put him under a microscope."

Forest slumped back against his seat and pulled in his chin, causing a ripple effect under his jaw that looked like a turkey wattle.

Though I was dead certain he'd been up all night, I didn't waste much effort feeling sorry for him. I was too busy regretting my own aches and pains. The hot shower that had felt so good had resulted in a surge of discomfort. Every time I moved, my muscles squealed like the off-key twang of a tuneless riff. The giant bruise on my butt pounded with stiff drumbeats. If pain was music, I'd have been a freaking symphony.

But I was grateful that Forest had gotten me out of the bed, especially glad that he'd taken me to the Turk's Head where I could pick up my rental car and be ready to follow Alison. I had figured six o'clock would be a good time to start waiting for her to come out of the hotel. She was meeting a doctor, after all, and I couldn't imagine any physician, even one who was on the lamm from the FDA, getting up any earlier than that.

"Tell you what, Forest, this explanation is going to take a while." I checked my watch, which had stopped sometime last night, probably after I got dumped off the wharf. "I don't know about you, but I need some food and a bottle of aspirin."

"Fine. Headache medicine is in the glove box."

He fired up the slobmobile engine and eased away from the curb. This time, he was driving like a sane person.

When I opened the glove box, a Smith and Wesson .44 revolver with an eight-inch barrel fell out onto my lap. "My head doesn't hurt that bad," I said.

"Keep digging."

I found an ancient rusting aspirin tin, knocked four into my hand and swallowed dry. Three of them went down, and the last one dissolved in my mouth.

"Forensics," Forest said, "tells me that all the victims have been surgically prepped. There have been traces of some kind of weird anesthetic in the lungs and bloodstream and the wounds have been antiseptically prepared before organ removal."

Seemed like a lot of trouble for a voodoo cult. "Why?"

"The organs, asshole. Somebody is doing transplants. We're talking black-market body parts."

Though he pulled up gently at a stoplight, my brain slammed around in my skull. "I don't get it."

"Okay, McCleet, I'll explain in terms that even you can understand. Remember Frankenstein?"

"I understand that part." My aching brain flashed on lightning and the mad surgeon cackling hysterically. *It's alive. It's alive.* "Transplants."

"Corneas and kidneys are the most common. But they're also doing hearts and spleens and livers. There are people all over the country who are waiting for healthy organs, people who are able to pay big bucks. And there aren't enough body parts to go around."

"But an organ transplant is a major operation. It's not the kind of thing that's done in the back of the Turk's Head."

"Jesus, McCleet. Didn't I just get done telling you that somebody big is behind this? It's a real fuckin' sophisticated deal."

When he parked in front of an all-night diner with half the bulbs broken on the light and fly spots on the windows, I stopped thinking about anything but food. The greasier, the better. I ordered a gallon of coffee, two burgers and home fries. While I was waiting, I asked for a slab of apple pie.

The first bite was sugar heaven. I forked down half of the pie before I spoke to Forest again. "I know there's a connection," I said, "between Sylvia Erthpouch and the bartender and your Yuppie Ripper."

"As fuckin' stupid as that sounds, you're right."

Surprised, I looked up with my fork poised halfway to my mouth. Forest had, without undue coercion on my part, admitted that my digging around last night had provided a clue. A sweet glop of apple pie splatted on the table.

Forest fixed the glop with a baleful eye. "Jesus, I can't believe you stumbled across anything useful."

Neither could I. As a cop I'd learned just how much legwork went into tracking down leads and finding hard evidence. When I'd been at the job long enough, I started to develop a kind of knack for stumbling into clues and turning up evidence. Intuition, that's what Nick called it. "It's the hotel," I said. "How many of the ripper victims were staying in hotels?"

"Only one of them was a local," he said, glumly. "The others were from out of town. Just tourists who came up here for vacations or conventions."

"And what about Sylvia? Was the Roosevelt the only place she worked?"

"No. She was a part-timer at a couple of different hotels. Two of the victims—three, if we include your brother-in-law—were staying at places where Sylvia worked." He drained the dregs of coffee from his cup and signaled the waitress for more. "We questioned the staff at the hotels, but nobody paid much attention to Sylvia. I should have done that, could have seen the pattern earlier."

When the waitress returned to fill Forest's cup, she brought my hamburgers which were at once charred and raw. "Anybody else work at both hotels? Maybe Sylvia wasn't the only one. And what was she doing with the toothbrushes?"

"Shut up, McCleet."

So much for intuition. I attacked my hamburgers.

"Here's the way it works," Forest said. "Last night, I talked to the coroner and told him how Sylvia was pilfering combs and toothbrushes out of the Roosevelt."

I continued to eat and listen.

"DNA," Forest said.

"Huh?" It was all I could manage with my mouth full of ground beef, lettuce, tomato, onion and bun. "How?"

"A lab only needs a speck. A drop of saliva. A piece of hair. A glob of snot off a used tissue. They can run tests and get a fuckin' picture of chromosome patterns and types." Forest quietly ran through a string of obscenities. "I should have known."

I chewed and swallowed, knowing why Forest was disgusted with himself for not guessing at this. Even before I quit the force six years ago, police work had taken on an incredible sophistication. While the regular cops were out on beat, getting shot and questioning dozens of dangerous characters to find a killer, there were white-coated guys in labs who ran tests and accurately identified rapists from a smudge of semen. They took fingerprints off corpses. Forest should have guessed what was going on as soon as I mentioned the toothbrushes. For that matter, I should have figured it out myself.

But the whole forensic thing was like laboratory voodoo to me. I couldn't fathom the scope of such a technology that could create a kind of as-built blueprint of the total person from a fingernail clipping.

Forest continued, "The coroner figured that Sylvia was providing the guy who's running this show with hair samples and saliva samples from the toothbrushes. A lab would run the tests and they'd find a good match for somebody who wanted a black-market organ. According to the coroner, these buyers are willing to pay millions."

"Millions?"

"Think about it, McCleet. If you had no hope for survival, how much would you pay for one more chance?"

"No more than I could afford and then only after I'd shopped around."

Of course, the ethics on this were a bit skewed. Survival of the fittest didn't give somebody else the right to yank a lesser person's spleen.

The irony was subtle but inescapable. The victims had been drawn from the ranks of the upwardly mobile because their DNA was most closely linked to that of the buyer. The killers and the dead were the same species of man, guys who belonged to the same country clubs, who drove BMW's and maybe even talked to each other on their car phones. One had to die so the other could live.

I could easily see the man who called himself Guy Fellowes as the engineer of this scheme. He had elevated himself to the status of an Aztec god, deciding who would live and who wouldn't.

"I got a good look at Fellowes," I said.

"So what?"

"I can identify him."

"From what, asshole? You think I have a book of mug shots for brilliant transplant surgeons who flipped out? He could be from anywhere? The fuckin' guy could be from fuckin' Tanzania."

"I can do a sketch," I offered. "In fact, I started one while I was waiting for Sylvia to make her move."

For an instant, Forest brightened. Then his face fell. "I thought you were a sculptor."

I didn't bother to tell him that I made dozens of sketches before I took one lick with my hammer on marble or any of the other expensive materials I worked with. Instead, I flipped over the paper placemat with a map of the northwestern United States on one side. The other side was blank. I asked the waitress for a pencil and started to draw.

In a few minutes, I had a fairly accurate scribble of Lieutenant Forest, complete with cigar stub and dirty glasses. I added a set of horns and slid it across the table to him.

"Damn. Look at the head on that fucker. That's Fellowes?"

I called over the waitress and showed the sketch to her. "Who's this?"

She yanked her thumb in Forest's direction. "Him."

"That's not me. Shit, I don't look anything like that."

"Are you sure you have an original Wyeth?"

I took another placemat and concentrated on my memories of Fellowes. The perspective was off because, at the time Fellowes and I were having our chat, he was standing and I was curled up on the floor in a fetal position having the shit kicked out of me. I finished my burger and the sketch at the same time. When I handed over the completed picture, I burped. "This is him."

"Do me another one."

Outside the fly-specked diner windows I could see the light beginning to thin. I needed to get back to the Puget Madrona to keep an eye on Alison, but I did another couple of sketches. When I turned them over to Forest, I had a nice sense of completion. In the grand scheme of police work, this was the most I could accomplish in avenging Phil's kidney and coming up with answers for myself.

If Forest sent out the sketches to doctors' organizations and medical schools, he would—sooner or later—know Guy Fellowes's real name. Even if Lieutenant Forest was never going to pat me on the back, I felt satisfied enough to ask for a favor. "Can you take me back to the Turk's Head so I can get my rental car?"

He made an affirmative grunt and stood up, bumping his gut against the edge of the table. I guessed that Forest wasn't going to give me a medal for my invaluable assistance on his case. He wasn't even going to pay for my food. I tossed a twenty on the tabletop and we left.

It was six o'clock in the morning when I got back to the Puget Madrona. On the off chance that Alison had softened toward me during the night, I went back to my room to call her before starting my stake-out. My body still felt like I'd been pulled apart and stuck back together. I would have liked nothing better than to sleep for a week.

I placed a call to her on the hotel phone.

"I'm sorry," the operator said. "That party has checked out."

"That's impossible."

"Sorry, sir, but Alison Brooks has already checked out."

Before dawn? What kind of doctor was up before the sun was at its zenith, shining down on grassy golf courses? I slammed my junk into the suitcase and went to the front desk where a fresh clerk informed me with a superior smile that Alison had, in fact, checked out.

I went back to my room to make a couple of phone calls. The first was to Alison's assistant, her right-hand man.

"Monte? It's me, Adam."

"Jesus, what am I? Command central? First, Alison calls. And now, you."

Bingo! I knew Alison would check in with Monte before undertaking any action. "What did Alison say?"

His voice was lilting. "Are you two having a spat? You know, Adam, I simply don't think it's right for me to get in the middle of your lover's quarrel. Because you're both going to end up getting mad at me and it's not my fault that you can't get along."

"Spare me the Ann Landers crap and tell me where she is."

"I really can't say."

The flamboyant little shit was stonewalling me. "Tell me, Monte."

"No can do. Alison said you might be calling, and she said that it was none of your business."

"She might be in danger," I lied.

"Alison?" He sounded distressed and suspicious at the same time. "Why do you think she's in danger?"

Unfortunately, Monte was bright enough to know that I wasn't really Agent Dullard on a mission to protect Dan Quayle. I decided to stick to the truth as I knew it. "She met with this Dr. Moorcroft and the guy isn't exactly Marcus Welby, M.D. His operation is being threatened by the Feds."

"I know all about Dr. Moorcroft."

"Yeah? Then what does he do?"

"Some kind of nuclear medicine, I think. The FDA doesn't like it, but then they don't like a lot of treatments. I have a friend who does homeopathic drugs, and you wouldn't believe how much trouble he gets into. You're such an alarmist, Adam."

"Tell me, Monte. Where the hell is Alison?"

"Well, I really don't know. All she said was that she wasn't going to be in for two or three days and she'd call me later with a phone number where she could be reached."

That was probably as much as Monte knew. My next call was the hospital where Trevor was staying. The duty nurse was adamant about not allowing me to talk to Mr. Ingersoll because he was resting quietly and he needed his sleep. I tried to tell her I was with the police, but apparently this nurse had heard it all. She hung up on me.

I would have paced around the room if movement had been

less difficult. Instead, I sat completely still. The greasy hamburger churned comfortably in my belly. It was entirely possible that I was making too much of Alison's meeting with Dr. Moorcroft. Since she'd told Monte she'd be out of touch for a few days, she must have convinced the doctor to take Trevor as a patient and be planning to escort him to the treatment center. This seemed like a good thing. I didn't want to interfere in something that might save Trevor's life.

If I was completely honest with myself, the urgency I felt had nothing to do with danger or trouble. I was hurting because Alison Brooks had whispered good-bye. If she didn't want to see me again, she wouldn't. It was that simple. Alison had met the brutal side of my personality, and she hated that I could take Sylvia's death in stride, that I was willing to get beat-up to solve a crime, that I was fully capable of all kinds of violence.

If I'd been as tough as all that, I would have kissed her off. But that wasn't the case. I wasn't a thug who wanted a dame. I was a sculptor who wanted Alison, and I wasn't ready to let her go.

When I tried to come up with a reasonable course of action, I was mildly surprised that my battered brain was able to perform logically. If Alison had convinced the doc, she must be on her way to pick up Trevor for his procedure. And, I knew, Trevor was still resting at the hospital. By the time she arrived at the hospital, I could be waiting. Unless Moorcroft had sent an ambulance for Trevor. But there would still be paperwork and doctor's permissions and all kind of delaying details. If I drove the speed limit, it would take every bit of three hours to get back to Portland. If I drove like a crazed lunatic, I could make it in two hours and fifty minutes.

I needed someone to stall Trevor's departure. My gravely-voiced pal on the Portland P.D., Nick Gabreski, couldn't do it. He was limited by police procedure. There was only one person I could think of who was capable of stopping an ambulance. She

could halt the launch of the space shuttle in the middle of count-
down. I dialed the number.

"Margot, this is Adam. I need a favor."

I expected her to cackle, and she did, emitting a low evil
sound that was more appropriate for a horror flick than sisterly
amusement. "You? Need a favor? From me?"

"That's right."

"Fat chance."

My lifetime of "taking care of Margot" apparently counted for
nothing. Though I could have stooped to Margot's own tactics of
whining, sobbing and dredging up ancient childhood promises,
I didn't think I could live with myself afterwards.

She continued, "You haven't even asked about Phil."

"How's Phil?"

"Doing very well—no thanks to you. He ought to be coming
home this afternoon."

"I'm glad. You might tell him that Lieutenant Forest of the
Seattle police department has pretty much figured out what hap-
pened to him and he expects to apprehend the person who took
Phil's kidney."

"While you stood around with your thumb up your nose.
Right, Adam?"

"Will you help me or not, Margot?"

"Maybe. But you're going to have to grovel nicely."

It was a measure of my devotion and caring for Alison that I
managed to squeeze out the word. "Please."

"Please what?"

"Please, Margot. Here's what I want. Go to the hospital where
Trevor Ingersoll is staying and don't let anyone take him until I
get there. Not even an ambulance. Even if Alison Brooks shows
up, don't let her take him."

"Stopping an ambulance," she said, considering. "Is that
legal? You know I would never do anything illegal because I
have great respect for the court system."

The court system had bizarrely awarded her enough money

in alimony payments to underwrite the national debt. "It's not illegal," I said.

"I have to get ready first. I'm not even dressed. And I do have to squeeze in a pedicure this morning."

"I need you to go now. I'll be at the hospital door in two-and-a-half hours."

"I'll do it." She cackled again. "You know, Adam, this means you owe me. You owe me really big."

That was a horrifying thought, but I would accept whatever feudal servitude Margot would, no doubt, insist upon.

I did the drive back to Portland at warp speed. Only once did I have a close call when a semi decided to get cute and change lanes while I was passing, but I careened along the shoulder and made it. After covering one-hundred-seventy miles in two hours and a half, I landed with an adrenaline crash at the door of the hospital. Outside, I saw an encouraging sign—Margot's Saab.

I dashed up the stairs and found Margot, shouting at three nurses who were at the front desk. She was wearing sandals and her toenails were a perfect, unchipped fuchsia color. She turned to me. "These idiots!" she said.

"You just got here, didn't you, Margot?"

"You have no concept of how difficult it is to get someone to do a pedicure," she said. "And I called ahead to these idiots and told them that Trevor Ingersoll was not to be moved. But would they listen to me? No!" She whipped back around. "Idiots!"

"Where's Trevor?" I asked her.

"He was picked up by a private helicopter."

"When?"

Margot didn't answer. She was too busy fuming. I looked to one of the nurses, a buxom young thing with a long blond braid that reached all the way to her buttocks. "When?" I repeated.

"About ten minutes ago."

"Where was Trevor taken?"

"We don't know," she said. "He signed himself out, and we can't keep a patient against his will."

Margot thrust herself in the young nurse's face. "You snippy little bimbo idiot! Didn't I tell you not to release him? Didn't I?"

"I'm sorry, Mrs. Stang, but you're not a relative and you don't have the authority to—"

"Forget it, Margot. It's too late."

Feeling empty and tired and sore, I turned slowly and walked away. Margot marched along beside me, muttering furiously about incompetence and lawsuits and repercussions that would make them wish they'd become hod carriers.

"It doesn't matter," I said. "Leave it alone. Give my best to Phil."

"What's wrong with you, Adam? You're not yourself."

"That's right. And I'm not Clint Eastwood, either." A glint of sunlight sparkled on Margot's pedicure as I drove away.

All things had probably turned out for the best. At least, Trevor would get the procedure he wanted, and that was really the most important thing. I silently wished him the best of luck. If anyone deserved a few more good years of living, it was him. These might be the years in which he created the finest master-pieces of his life or encouraged another young artist to stumble forward and take a chance. I had never known a more vital man than Trevor Ingersoll. He was a true leader, an innovator in the art world, who experienced every emotion to the fullest. I loved that fierce old man. In a way, he was more to me than my father who had died before I really got to know and appreciate him.

But what about Alison? I could only hope that she'd forgive me.

When I got back to my cottage, the rooms smelled musty and deserted. The best thing for me to do was to let in some air and crawl into bed.

After opening a window, I hit the flashing button on my answering machine to play back messages, then hobbled to the refrigerator and stood there, staring at a carton of milk that had probably gone south.

The seventh message gave me a jolt. I hit the replay button and listened carefully.

"Hello, Adam."

I knew that voice.

"Though we've only met briefly, you have caused me a great deal of inconvenience. Therefore, I am compelled to give you a small piece of information. Take this as a warning. I am with your friend, Alison Brooks, and we are on our way to pick up Trevor Ingersoll. If you value the lives of either of these individuals, don't interfere."

It was Guy Fellowes.

Chapter
Fourteen

The next phone message was from Monte.

"Adam, it's me. Alison dropped by the gallery and she said to tell you that everything was just fine. She'll be in touch in a couple of days. I really don't think she's mad at you, anymore. Bye-bye."

If I hadn't heard the Fellowes message first, I would have been elated. Now, Monte's blithe assurance that everything would be just fine struck the same cold, hollow chord as whistling in a cemetery.

I had a pretty good idea of how that had happened, but there wasn't time for reasoning. I raced out the door and leapt into the rental car which hadn't even had time to cool down from the Seattle sprint. While careening along Riverside Drive, I had time to think of other things. Like why I hadn't gotten pulled over for wantonly reckless driving. And why Forest's driving had impacted my bowels while my own screaming around buses and blasting over curbs didn't bother me at all. And why the hell had Margot—a woman who could halt the D-day invasion—failed to stop a simple helicopter. My opinion of Margot just might be tainted, I thought, as I squeaked through an opening between a delivery truck and a taxi. Perhaps I had overestimated the evil strength of my sister. Others might perceive her as just a simple, multi-divorced lady of the house with a reasonable concern for her hubby.

I squealed to a stop outside the Brooks Gallery. A couple of the staff people were crating my sculpture of Alison naked on the back of an orca, but I didn't bother to ask who had purchased the piece or to check if they'd received the full asking price. "Where's Monte?"

"In Alison's office," said the most responsible of Alison's secondary assistants. Her name was Diedre and she was quite literally a fair-haired girl, a student at Portland State. She touched my arm and bubbled, "Congratulations, Adam. You sold almost all the sculptures."

"That's wonderful." I couldn't match her enthusiasm.

Usually, I revel in compliments and hoard them up to replay on days when a slab of granite looks like a square rock. But today, there wasn't time. I was already in the back, charging through Alison's door. Monte sat behind the big antique cherrywood desk. He was working on numbers and he had costumed himself appropriately as a foppish banker with a green visor eyeshade.

He gushed when he saw me. "Adam, everybody loved your sea mammals. We're breaking down your exhibit and shipping out the pieces because so much is sold. Oh, my God, we're making so much—"

"Alison was here? This morning?"

"—so much money," he continued. "I just can't believe it, Adam. You're really a hit. Take my advice and stick to the sea-mammal stuff."

I reached across the desk and placed my hands firmly on his shoulders. "Was Alison here?"

"Don't get yourself in a snit." He slapped at my hands until I loosened my grip. "I won't say a single word when you're being so nasty."

I released him. "Talk."

"Alison stopped in. About an hour ago. And she said something about meeting a helicopter and I made a little joke about how she'd made so much money off your show that she was going to turn into a jet setter." He snickered cheerfully, utterly guileless and unsuspicious. "Oh yes, and she had that charming Dr. Moorcroft with her."

"Shit."

I sank into the chair opposite Monte, grabbed a receipt and scrawled a sketch of Guy Fellowes on the back.

"Adam, are you all right? You have a terrible bruise."

I stuck the sketch under Monte's nose. "Is this Dr. Moorcroft?"

He frowned as he assessed the sheet of paper. "Well, the nose is a little out of perspective, but overall I'd say that's him. So? You've met?"

"I'm intimately acquainted with the toe of his shoe."

I slouched back in the chair, closed my eyes and tried to think. Moorcroft was Fellowes. Fellowes was Moorcroft. And he was the mastermind of black-market organ sales, the Yuppie Ripper. It also seemed safe to assume that the "procedure" Trevor had wanted so adamantly was a transplant. Trevor Ingersoll would be the recipient of a fresh strong heart, surgically removed from the chest of another living soul, but only if I didn't interfere.

In a terrible way, everything was starting to make sense. Trevor, who had already had two bypass surgeries, was not a prime candidate for an organ transplant, but his only chance for prolonged survival was a new ticker. And he was wealthy enough to afford Moorcroft's procedure. Did he know what Moorcroft was doing? It pained me to think that the man I respected more than anyone else in the world knew that his last desperate grab at life would mean someone else's death.

I needed to notify Forest, to alert him to the plan that another yuppie was about to be ripped. But if I did, if Forest stepped up his investigation, if he actually got close to Moorcroft, Trevor and Alison would be trapped in the middle of some serious shit.

Moorcroft must have been delighted when Alison turned up on his doorstep this morning. He couldn't have known he'd taken the one hostage who could keep me from coming after him.

I knew he couldn't simply release Alison after she'd learned what he was doing. She'd be a witness. Moorcroft had had Sylvia and the bartender killed, probably for incompetence. What would he do to Alison? I had to find out where she was, and I had to get there before Forest.

"Jesus, Adam. You're so weird. What's wrong with you?"

"I want you to think, Monte. Do you have any idea where Alison was going?"

"Not really. She said she'd call after they arrived and give me her phone number."

I doubted it. Moorcroft wasn't going to allow Alison to have any contact with the outside world.

"How about correspondence?" I asked. "Has she been in communication with Moorcroft?"

"She doesn't tell me everything. I mean, I know that you two had some world-class sex the other night, but I don't do her personal correspondence."

I grabbed the "out" basket on Alison's desk and tore through the stack of paper, scattering the irrelevant sheets.

Monte protested, "You always make a mess in here, Adam. It's so eccentric."

I found a note on plain bond paper without a logo or return address. It was typed, even the signature, and it said: "Sorry, Ms. Brooks. I am unable to schedule the procedure for Mr. Ingersoll because of certain difficulties in our internal operations. Sincerely, A. Moorcroft."

I snapped at Monte, "Phone bill. Where's the phone bill?"

He folded his arms across his chest. "I'm not going to help you until you tell me what's going on. And that's final."

"This is life and death, Monte."

"I know that. Trevor's very ill."

"Alison's life," I said.

Monte's smirk slid off his face. His perpetual posing ceased in a heartbeat. His voice sounded a full octave deeper when he said, "Alison's in danger?"

"You got it. I have to find out where she went with Trevor, and go there."

Monte hurried toward a blue file cabinet in the corner of the room. In an instant, he'd located phone bills.

"Does the most recent one include long-distance calls made last week?" I said.

He glanced at the three sheets of paper and shook his head.

"Okay, I want you to call the phone company and get the numbers Alison called yesterday and the day before."

He was on the phone. All business. No matter what else I thought of Monte, Alison had hired him for very practical reasons. In the performance of his job, he was extremely efficient, and I guess "rescuing the boss lady" came under the auspices of work description because he had cut through the typical phone-company bullshit and transfer process in a matter of seconds.

He disconnected the phone and turned to me. "She made twelve long-distance phone calls, and I recognize ten of the numbers."

"The other two?"

"Friday Harbor," he said. "Both calls were to a diner called the Scrimshaw. The first call lasted two minutes and seventeen seconds. The second, exactly three hours later, went on for nine minutes and forty-seven seconds."

I guessed that she had a number to reach Moorcroft in an emergency. She'd called it, placed a message and was told to call back. Then she'd set the appointment.

Alison had met with Moorcroft in Seattle, I thought, continuing an elaborate mental reconstruction based on the scanty evidence of two long-distance phone calls. He'd agreed to work his magic on Trevor, picked him up via helicopter, and now, perhaps, they were somewhere near Friday Harbor, the larger of the two harbors on San Juan Island.

It made sense for Moorcroft to base his illegal operation in that area. The constant boating activity would serve to conceal the comings and goings of Moorcroft's patients. Also, the San Juan Islands were close enough to the border so he could easily jump across to Canada if things got too hot in the U.S.

"What time of day did she call?"

"Morning," Monte said. "And, you know, it must have been right after that when she made her plane reservations to Seattle."

Admirably, Monte had kept his cool, though the strain on him was obvious. He fidgeted with his tie and pulled at his cuffs as if his clothing had suddenly become restrictive.

"Call information," I said. "See if Moorcroft has a phone in the San Juans."

It was a long shot, and it didn't pay off. There wasn't even an unlisted number.

"What do we do now?" Monte asked.

"We? We don't do anything. I'm going up to Friday Harbor."

"Don't be a bitch, Adam. I can be very useful, and I can stay out of the way. If Alison really is in trouble . . ."

"She is."

"Then I'm coming."

Before I could object, he had bustled out of the office and into the gallery. When I dragged my sore butt out of the chair to follow, all my joints creaked like rusty hinges. Too much driving and tension had combined to slow me down. Maybe it wasn't such a bad idea to take Monte. At least he had full use of his arms and legs. I caught up with him as he found Diedre.

"Sweetie," he said, "you're going to be the boss today."

"Really?" Her long blond braid bounced enthusiastically.

Apparently, Monte considered his job done. He'd handed

over the reins and was already headed back to Alison's office. I was a little more concerned with the running of Alison's business.

"Diedre," I said. "Monte and I have a little problem, and we need your help."

"Okey-doke." She beamed. I knew she was well over the legal age of consent but she looked like an apple-cheeked sixteen-year-old.

"Alison might be calling," I said. "It's very important that you don't tell her Monte is gone. Especially that you don't tell her Monte has gone with me."

She nudged me in the ribs, and I winced. "Gotcha, Adam. You guys are playing hooky."

If only it were that simple. "Right," I said. "But be sure you copy down any phone number Alison might give you, and we'll check back with you for messages. Understand?"

"Gotcha," she repeated.

I felt like I was leaving Alison's precious gallery, not to mention the packing and handling of my own sculptures, in the hands of an adolescent prom queen with an extremely cute butt. Some men were turned on by young women, and I had to admit that there was something appealing about high firm breasts, shining waves of hair and flesh that still held the residual softness of baby fat. But I'd long ago lost patience with little girls who were likely to giggle during sex. I adored every tiny line on Alison's face. I admired her tenacity in working out to keep her incredible body firm. She was a grown-up woman, strong and capable and endlessly fascinating.

In contrast to my shimmering thoughts of her, I felt a gathering darkness in the back of my mind. I generally don't indulge myself in anger, but I could feel the cold, hard, unthinking presence of a dangerous rage. The first time I killed a man in Vietnam the rage had consumed me, directed my movements and probably saved my life. In those fire-lit jungles of camouflage green, anger had been my constant companion, my savior and my nemesis. I had fed on the beast and kept it close. And the beast fed on me.

As a cop, I had learned to exercise a tense control that had begun to manifest in ulcers before I quit the force. And now, after six years, I knew the rage was still there, dark and brooding. Trevor had recognized the potential for explosion in me; he'd urged me to use it in creating art. But that wouldn't have been safe for me or anyone around me.

And now, I felt it again, poised for action, waiting happily to be called upon. If anything had happened to Alison, if Moorcroft had touched one hair on her head, I would kill him.

"Adam?" Diedre crowed. "Are you okay?"

"Fine. Do you remember what I told you?"

"You bet. You and Monte have a fun time, okay?"

"Yeah. Fun."

I returned to the office where Monte chattered on the phone again. While on hold, he informed me that he'd checked departures and shuttles for commercial airline flights and had decided they weren't fast enough. He completed arrangements for a charter plane, hung up and bounced to his feet. "Let's go, Adam. My place is on the way to the airport, and we have just enough time for me to pick up a more appropriate outfit."

Monte's idea of the proper attire for rescuing a damsel in distress was not, fortunately, a suit of armor. He dressed conservatively in black jeans, black sweater, pea coat and a black knit watch-cap that made him look positively butch.

While we waited for takeoff, I laid out the ground rules. "I'm not going to babysit you, Monte. When we get there and find a lead to Moorcroft, your job—your only job—is to contact Lieutenant Ed Forest of the Seattle P.D. and tell him we've got the Yuppie Ripper. Then you give the location. Is that clear? You don't get in the way."

"Certainly not."

After we landed at the general aviation airport near Anacortez on Fildago Island, I inquired about helicopters. There were plenty of chopper services but none of them had ever heard of Guy Fellowes or Moorcroft or Sterling. Either Moorcroft had managed to keep his whole operation a secret or he'd paid enough to buy silence.

On the ferry to Friday Harbor, I stood moodily at the rail. At least, the weather was fairly decent. There were clouds and the threatening rain, but right at the moment, the sun was shining.

Monte took a position next to me and repeated the question he'd been asking since we left Portland, "When we get there, Adam, what do we do?"

"We go by intuition."

"Well, that might be just fine for you, but my gut doesn't usually talk to me, unless it says something like the quiche is too rich."

He wanted a plan, and that didn't seem like an outrageous request. But I didn't have a clue. We needed to find out where Moorcroft was, but we didn't want to spook him into thinking we were interfering in his grand scheme.

I came up with a first step. "We go to the Scrimshaw Cafe, and we try not to be too obvious."

That wouldn't be as difficult as fitting colorful Monte into the black-leather atmosphere of the Turk's Head bar. Friday Harbor encouraged tourism, which meant it was fairly full of strangers, many of whom were fairly strange. They browsed through a plethora of art galleries and craft shops that lined the streets of this homogenized fishing/tourist village. Though some shops offered excellent pieces, most of what actually sold was knock-off. I myself had had the dubious honor of having my sculptures copied and mass-produced. Friday Harbor was one of the few places on earth where I might be recognized as a celebrity.

The Scrimshaw Cafe featured a decor that was as weathered as Cape Cod and tacky as a garage sale. The fishing nets draped from the ceiling were knitted yarn. The totem pole and the anchor near the door were plastic reproductions. In a smudged, greasy glass case was a display of scrimshaw that stated clearly on a hand-lettered sign: Not Real Ivory. The artwork hung in cardboard frames could have been the product of one of those carnival spin-art machines.

Monte shuddered as we sat. "My God, do people actually live like this?"

"Maybe it's supposed to be satirical," I said.

"But that would imply that the proprietor had some concept of good taste and then decided to purposely go for campiness."

"It's possible."

He rolled his eyes. "I think not. Take a little peek at the man behind the cash register."

When I peeked, I experienced a shock of *déjà vu*. The man slumped on a stool at the door could have been the twin of the Turk's Head bartender who'd had his throat cut—except this Friday Harbor version was less bald and more flabby. His chins fell onto his chest and his gut spilled over his belt buckle, creating the effect of a huge mound of tallow that was slowly melting. He wore a black armband, and Monte was right. He did not look like a paragon of tastefulness.

The waitress who advanced on our table in a muscular fashion was obviously a member of the same broad-shouldered, tall family. The biceps that bulged under her pink uniform indicated a weight-lifter . . . or a cross dresser. Her voice, however, was a high-pitched female squeak.

I ordered coffee and a chicken-fried steak.

Monte took his diet more seriously. "On the salmon patties," he said. "Are those deep-fried or baked?"

"Deep-fried."

"Well, I can't have that, can I? It's way too much fat. Maybe I should stick to a fillet. Is it fresh? Are the fish caught around here?"

"Not today."

"What about the tartar sauce? Is it made with real cream?"

"Comes out of a bottle."

"Oh dear. I'll have a chef's salad without the ham and no

onions, please. And I would adore if you could put three or four black olives around the edges. Vinegar and oil on the side."

In other circumstances, I might have been annoyed with his nit-picking, but I figured we might be hanging out at the Scrimshaw for hours, waiting for something to happen. We ate, and I went to find the men's room. The public phones were hanging beside them, and I perused the graffitti on the wall. There were comments about the anatomy of someone named Trish, but nothing that vaguely resembled a clue, not a single notation that said for a good time, call Avery Moorcroft. I flipped through the phone books to see if there were any tell-tale scribbles. Nothing.

I proceeded down the hallway. When I first spied the tallow man at the cash register, I knew what I would do. It's been said that history repeats itself and a smart man learns from his first time around. But I was too desperate to be smart. At least that was what I told myself when I slipped through the door marked Private.

Assuming that the proprietor of the Scrimshaw and the bartender at the Turk's Head were related, I was surprised to find a tidy desk and file cabinets. Apparently, slovenliness did not run in the family. In less than five minutes, I had rifled through the desk drawers and impeccably ordered file cabinets. In the ledger book, I hit the mother lode. Under accounts receivable the initials A.M. were listed dozens of times, and the amounts were in the thousands. Avery Moorcroft was paying these people for something. But what? And why? And, most importantly, how? Did they know where he was?

I returned to the table where Monte was carrying on a perky conversation with the waitress. He had actually found a food he liked among the Scrimshaw's offerings. The blackberry cobbler. "Fabulous," he said. "Just the right flavoring of sugar and tart berries. And the crust is, well, it's perfect."

"I'll tell the cook," she said, almost smiling.

"The chef," Monte extolled. "Anyone who can make crust like that deserves to be called chef."

I stared at the proprietor, who hadn't moved a quarter of an inch since we'd entered, and I tried to gauge my chances of learning Moorcroft's location from him. If the black armband was, indeed, a symbol of mourning for the bartender and not a fashion statement, this big guy might be pissed enough at Moorcroft to want to cause him trouble. On the other hand, he might be another budding Babe Ruth with a Louisville Slugger hidden behind the Not Real Ivory artifacts in the smudged glass display case.

I looked up at the waitress who was really warming up to Monte. I said, "My friend wants to compliment the manager. Is that him?"

"That's him. That's Jake." She lowered her voice. "But I don't think you ought to talk to him. He's blue. I know he doesn't look it, but Jake's a sensitive person. He writes poetry."

"I love poetry," Monte said. "Why is he upset?"

"His cousin was killed in an accident yesterday."

Right, a knife had *accidentally* sliced open his carotid artery. Much as I hated to initiate an unpleasant relationship with a poet who made Sumo wrestlers look anorexic, time was wasting. Outside the Scrimshaw windows, the afternoon was fading.

I glanced at the muscular waitress. "Maybe my friend can cheer up Big Jake."

When we all craned our necks to look at the huge man and assess whether or not Monte's elfin charms would have a positive effect on his deep gloom, he moved. There was a surprising agility in his movements that worried me. I didn't want to get in a fight with this large poet. He thundered across the restaurant and stopped at our table.

He spoke softly, in almost melodic tones. "If the mountain will not come to Mohammed, Mohammed will come to the mountain. What do you want?"

"Nothing," the waitress twittered.

"You were staring." He directed his observation at me. "You scared?"

"A little."

"There's nothing to fear but fear itself," he advised. "What's the deal?"

We had met the cliché poet of Friday Harbor. I gestured to Monte. "My friend wanted to compliment you on the truly exceptional blackberry cobbler." I took a deep breath and plunged onward. "And I wanted to ask you where I might find Avery Moorcroft."

Monte visibly stiffened.

The waitress scuttled back toward the kitchen, probably to fetch Jake's baseball bat.

The mountainous man lowered himself into a chair. "You a cop?"

I shook my head.

"Then, why have you come here?"

"I knew your cousin," I said. "He was a hell of a baseball player. And I know Moorcroft caused his death."

"His death diminishes us all."

"You were both working for Moorcroft," I continued. "But the good doctor plans to skip town. I need to know where to find him."

He considered for a moment. "Blood is thicker than water." The cliché must have had some meaning for him, because his small dark eyes, tiny as watermelon seeds in the redness of his large face, filled with tears.

"Moorcroft has a friend of mine, and I want to get to her before he hurts her. I need your help. You can avenge your cousin." I threw out an old adage of my own, "An eye for an eye."

"Hey, hey. I'm not cutting off my nose to spite my face. You get the hell out of here."

He rose and lumbered back toward his perch. I was about to follow when Monte tapped my arm. "Don't bother, Adam. We've got a bimbo at two o'clock. Front window."

Though I appreciated Monte's heterosexual leanings as much as the next person, now was not the time. "Later."

"Not just any bimbo. *The* bimbo."

I followed his gaze in time to catch a tantalizing flash of tail as the blond call girl who had Maced me in front of the Puget Madrona sashayed down the street. Monte and I threw money on the table and headed out the door.

I paused at Jake's side. There was something decent inside this guy, and I needed to call upon it. "Don't tell Moorcroft we were here."

"I will not betray you. May God hold you in the palm of his hand."

Chapter
Fifteen

Our blond quarry strolled gracefully down the street, and we followed from about half a block away. In the pedestrian traffic of tourists and some colorful artiste locals who still hadn't heard that the sixties were over, she stood out like a beacon of healthy, sweet, Southern sensuality. Here in Friday Harbor, she hadn't bothered with the sexy attire she'd worn in Seattle. She didn't need to. Her butt-hugging jeans and a T-shirt were suggestive enough. When she dropped one of the packages she was carrying, Monte and I carefully observed her perfect, pear-shaped bottom as she leaned down.

She paused at the window of a store, and I held Monte back, hoping she wouldn't notice we were following her. She stood for half a minute, fluffed her hair in the window's reflection and shivered deliciously. The afternoon was turning chilly, and fog was rolling in.

Something about the way she handled herself gave me the definite impression that she knew we were behind her. She was the sort of woman who has radar. Her regular job for Moorcroft, I assumed, was pretending to be a hooker. Then she and her blond cohort would lure unsuspecting yuppies, guys less dominated by their wives than Phil, into his clutches. I didn't think luring was a kind of behavior that could be taught, and the blonde was a natural, a female who was always aware of male attentions and how to use them.

Quite possibly, Moorcroft was, once again, using the blonde as a bait. To catch me. It gave me a moment's satisfaction to realize how much I must have annoyed Moorcroft. After all, I was the one who got away, the poor fish that should have been in permanent cold storage in Davy Jones's locker. Instead, I was here and closing in fast. But maybe that was exactly what he wanted me to do. Checking up on Alison's long-distance phone calls was a pretty obvious move. He might expect me to follow the blonde, maybe even to approach her. And she would deliver me and Monte into his lair.

I was beginning to feel out-maneuvered. Moorcroft had all the advantages. He had Alison and Trevor. He was on his own turf.

We followed the blond woman to the marina where she climbed aboard a large motor launch, stowed her packages, putted to the docks and got into a line of other boats, waiting to get gas. I needed a boat to follow her, and I needed it fast.

"How are we going to follow her now?" Monte asked.

"I'll find a boat."

"Pardon *moi,* Adam, but do you know anything about boats? I'm not a good swimmer, and I hate what salt water does to my skin."

I went to the marina headquarters with Monte trailing behind me. The guy behind the counter told me that all the rentals were out. All he had left was a sea kayak. Though he warned me about the dangers in the fog, I took it.

"What about me?" Monte demanded when we were on the pier again. "I hope you don't expect me to ride shotgun on the back of your kayak."

"You go back to the Scrimshaw and talk to Poet Jake. Maybe

he'll tell you Moorcroft's location. In the meantime, call Lieutenant Forest and tell him what's going on."

Monte pulled his mouth into a tiny round circle. "Oh, dear. Oh my. If you're calling in the reinforcements, this sounds pretty hopeless."

"Just a back-up," I lied. I was feeling hopeless.

"May I remind you that Alison and Trevor are hostages?"

"You don't have to remind me of anything."

I had a clear picture of my chances on being able to perform a rescue mission all by myself. I had a better chance of getting struck by lightning. Not only had I been beaten thoroughly, the night before, not only was I an aging ex-Marine, ex-cop turned sculptor who hadn't gotten his knuckles bruised for years, but I didn't even have a weapon. But there was really no point in keeping score. I looked at the kayak and decided I'd probably drown in the fog before I ever got to Moorcroft's island.

"Adam, are you okay?"

"Never better. Just do what I said."

He stuck his hands on his hips and flounced down the pier.

I looked around the corner of the bait shack beside the fueling station. There were only two other boats in front of the blonde, one of which was loaded with teenagers who were having a struggle with the pumps. I approached a silent old man who sat watching. He had one of those faces that had weathered like an apple core, and he reminded me of my father, which I took as a good omen. When I noticed that his bright eyes were turned on the blonde, I sat beside him. "She's pretty, isn't she?"

"Yeah." His lips didn't move.

"Is she from around here."

"Yeah."

"Where?"

"Little island. Big house."

"You know the name of the island?"

He turned toward me, interrupting his ancient calm. "What's it to you?"

I took out my wallet, peeled off a twenty and handed it to him. He made a grunting noise and stuck the twenty in his pocket. "What island?" I repeated.

"Going to cost you a hundred bucks."

There was only one other boat in front of the blonde. I didn't have time to bargain. So I counted out the hundred. My last hundred.

"Eleanor," he said. "That's the island's name, not hers. She's Tamara."

I returned hopelessly to the kayak. No way was I going to be able to follow her with this thing. It would take all my concentration to keep from flipping the thing over. But now I knew the name of her island, Moorcroft's island. Tamara's Island. I could call Forest and do this right. We could storm the island with SWAT teams and frogmen. And then what? What would Moorcroft do to Alison for his revenge?

"Yoo-hoo, Adam."

Monte putted up beside me in a sadly abused, eighteen-foot day-sailer with a small, open cabin, cheerfully bouncing the hull off the wooden pier and bashing the power ski.

"Oh, my God," Monte said as he pulled up on the tiller as if he were setting the emergency brake in his car. "How do you stop this thing?"

He swung around and the bow of the sailboat aimed at the pristine white side of a yacht that would have cost two years of Monte's salary.

"Oh, my God!" He flung the tiller again and the bow struggled around in a one-hundred-and-eighty-degree turn. I noticed the name stenciled on the back of Monte's boat: *Hump Back*. "Don't just stand there, Adam."

Reluctantly, I hopped aboard and relieved Monte of the helm. In a few seconds, I'd pointed us in the right direction to follow the blonde. Catching her would be impossible. The ten-horsepower outboard motor on *Hump Back* was capable of maybe six knots, which was nowhere near the speed of Tamara's launch.

Still, the wind was good, and with the sails up, we might keep track of her.

"For future reference," I said. "The proper nautical greeting is, ahoy. Not, yoo-hoo."

"Isn't it, yoo-hoo-hoo and a bottle of rum?"

I shook my head while maneuvering our way out of the marina and into the open seas. "I take it you've never sailed before."

"Not unless you count a cruise to Nassau."

The little sloop handled smoothly, and we reached the mouth of the marina just as the blonde pulled away from the fuel dock. "How did you get this boat, Monte?"

"Well, I stole it, of course." He giggled, and I really hoped he was joking. "Actually, the captain was getting out and I could see that he'd been doing some serious drinking. I gave him a check for five hundred dollars and my American Express card. He gave me the keys."

"I'll bet he did." And the *Hump Back* pirate was probably right now, as we spoke, racing into Friday Harbor and charging the max. But that was Monte's concern. The first and foremost plan was to stay within sight of the blonde.

We were less than ten minutes into the journey when *Hump Back*'s motor sputtered and stalled. A few urgent yanks on the starter chord were futile. The greasy red gas can was empty.

Raising sails on the small craft required very little physical effort and the cold sea breezes were relieving some of the ache in my limbs. The pain of bruises was rapidly replaced with the numb pain of a deep chill as the fog began to gather in a thick, wet curtain.

A quarter mile ahead, I could see Tamara's boat well enough. She was headed south-southwest in the San Juan Channel.

After some uneasy luffing, I took the rudder and the sails went taut as I harnessed the wind and sliced across a fairly calm gray sea.

"Oh, my God!" Monte shrieked. "You're going too fast! I

really hate swimming. Really! You're not going to make this thing turn over, are you?"

"We won't capsize," I said. "Go below, Monte."

"And miss all the fun?"

"Go below or shut up. Voices carry on the fog."

Amazingly, we'd kept pace with the powerboat, and I decided my previous assumption about the blonde luring us into Moorcroft's grasp was probably correct. She was skillful enough to give the impression of speed while staying just within our sight. I had seen an expensive-looking radar antenna on Tamara's boat. She didn't need to proceed slowly into the thick, dark fog. I didn't have the advantage of radar and I didn't like sailing full speed into the opaque wall of gray mist.

When she reached the southern end of the channel, the blonde headed almost due south on a heading of one-nine-zero degrees, according to the cheap compass mounted on *Hump Back*'s transom.

The new heading went straight into the wind, which was dying. I had to tack like a madman to keep our speed up. Every time the mainsail came around, Monte looked up in shocked surprise and made a little shriek as he barely ducked out of the way. It was like sailing with one of the Three Stooges until he turned green.

"Oh, my God." While he grabbed his belly, the sail came around and whacked him on the neck. "Oh, my God, I'm going to die."

"No, you're not, Monte."

"I'm sick."

"Quit whining."

"Easy for you to say, Mr. Macho Sailor. I'm serious, Adam. I'm really sick. My tummy is all queasy. And I'm cold."

I concentrated on the sound of the motor, which was growing steadily more distant. But it didn't matter. I knew where she was headed. Eleanor Island. "Monte, go below and find a map."

"It'll be worse down there. We're bucking around and I feel like I'm going to throw up."

"Don't worry, Monte. We'll probably be dead from hypothermia before you really get sick."

He dove through the hatch into the small cabin.

If I'd been in the mood to be thankful for small favors, I would have noticed the fairly smooth seas. At least, we weren't stuck in a gale wind. The sea was, in fact, so becalmed that the sails hung slack. Helplessly, I listened as the sound of the speedboat faded entirely.

Being lost at sea was appropriate. I thought back on all the things I should have done, the plans I should have made, the answers I should have known. The fog grew darker, and I knew the night was closing around us. I kept the little sloop on its southerly heading. I hoped *Hump Back*'s battered compass was reasonably accurate.

Occasionally, the soupy mists lifted, and my hopes soared until I realized that all I could see was gray. Dark gray seas. Lighter skies. A monochrome view, textured with matte strokes. It seemed to clear, and my spirits lifted. Then I heard the thunder and felt the first splat of rain. I knew that very soon, the fog would be displaced by a nuclear wind and we'd be needing all hands on deck.

"Monte!" I yelled.

When he stuck his head out of the cabin, I noted that his skin tone had gone from green to the palest white, and I knew that he'd puked in the cabin. Without sympathy, I instructed, "Get out here."

"I think not."

"Get out here. I need you for ballast."

He slithered into the cockpit, moaning. I positioned him on the windward side of the boat. In an instant, I had the sails trimmed and ready for stronger winds. But in that scant time, the rains had begun to fall and the wind was starting to provide some lift.

When I sat beside Monte, he forced a smile and whispered, "Land, yoo-hoo."

"What?"

He pointed toward an outline of rocks and trees, and a bitter-sweet elation rose within me. It was about time for some luck, although I doubted that in the dozen or so miles since Friday Harbor we'd been fortunate enough to stumble upon the correct island. The presence of land meant that Monte and I might actually survive a rainy night in the San Juans, but we would make no progress toward finding Alison.

I pulled the helm hard over and we came around quickly, running the hull of *Hump Back* onto a shallow sand bar. I dropped sails and tossed out the anchor. "Let's go, Monte."

He didn't object.

We climbed through a stand of trees into a clearing. There were no roads—only a path. The rain slashed down upon us, and the sea behind us roiled and tossed like a roller coaster. Monte glanced back at it and moaned.

"I hate boats. I hate sailing. And I'm never going to do that again."

"You'll feel better in the morning," I said, confidently.

"Oh, no, Adam. This is a lifetime decision, thank you very much. You'll have to send a helicopter to get me."

I spotted a cabin. Unlit. Nobody home.

I hesitated, but Monte plunged ahead. He rapped lightly on the door. "Anybody home?"

A high wind screamed, but there was no other response.

Monte tried the doorknob, I took it as a sign of our improved good fortune that the door was unlocked. When Monte flicked the switch, the lights came on, and we stumbled into a hideaway so quaint that it might have come out of a fairy tale, like the story of the three bears.

The cabin had electricity. The propane heater came on when Monte touched the thermostatic control, and the kitchen was stocked with canned goods. The only amenity lacking was a telephone. We settled in and raided the pantry, warming our butts and filling our bellies.

Monte seemed blissfully satisfied. I felt like shit. I'd failed. Somewhere out there, in the midst of a gale, Moorcroft had Alison.

By now, she'd probably figured out that his operation wasn't exactly on the up and up. But she'd known that before. Trevor hadn't made a secret of the fact that his "procedure" was illegal. He had, however, led us to believe that the nefariousness of this medical operation was not much more than a technicality. He hadn't explained that other people would die for the sake of this procedure. I could only assume that Moorcroft hadn't told him, or that Trevor's desire to live was so intense that he was willing to sacrifice the life of another human being to save his own.

"Shit," I said. That summed up my feelings. "Shit."

I should have been tired, but I feared sleeping because I might dream, and my head was stuffed with nightmare material. Nonetheless, I stretched out on a plump sofa in the living room and closed my eyes. When I opened them again, I found myself covered with a wool afghan. The first word out of my mouth was, "Shit."

Monte chirped, "Really now, it won't do a smidge of good to fixate on defecation. Did you have a nice rest, Adam?"

"How long did you let me sleep?"

"It's only been an hour."

"Shit."

"Adam, please."

"Fuck." I varied my vocabulary.

"That's a more pleasant thought, but not terribly helpful." He tossed a sheaf of papers into my lap. "This might brighten you up. I found them in a drawer in the kitchen."

"Charts."

I spread the papers out on the floor and studied them. Since the owner of this cabin had thoughtfully labeled this island, it was simple to figure out bearings. We were on Manger Island. Due west, about five miles, was Eleanor.

In spite of my aches and pains, I bounded to my feet. The heaviness lifted from my shoulders. I was hopeful and I began to pace. The more I considered, the more I was sure the blonde had been sent to entice me into Moorcroft's lair. Even if she hadn't set out with that plan, she couldn't have helped noticing our pathetic sailboat attempt to keep pace with her.

Surely, she would report to Moorcroft that I'd been stupid enough to follow her into the fog, and Moorcroft would logically surmise that I'd been shipwrecked, turned back, or drowned. If I could get through the storm to his island tonight, I'd have the element of surprise in my favor.

"Jesus, Adam. Quite a mood swing."

I grabbed Monte by the ears and planted a kiss on his forehead. "You done good."

He rubbed furiously at the spot. "Don't ever do that again. I mean, I'm the last person in the world to be homophobic, but I really, really don't like to be kissed by guys."

I went to the window. "The wind's holding. Good."

"Excuse me? You're not thinking of going out in the storm, are you?"

"This is a plan, Monte. This is an actual strategic plan."

"I don't think I'm going to like it."

"We get back in the boat and sail to Eleanor, which is where Moorcroft has his hospital. It'll be an intense beam reach all the way. The whole trip will take less than an hour. It'll be dark when we get there, and he sure as hell won't be expecting us tonight. What do you think?"

"It's positively Rambo."

"Weapons," I said jubilantly. I needed to arm myself.

Moorcroft wouldn't be alone on the island. At the very least, he would need a staff of nurses to run his hospital. These people who came to him for their transplants couldn't very well hop out of bed the next day. They needed a recuperation time of weeks, maybe even months. Their care and feeding meant there had to be kitchens and equipment and lots of staff people.

If I was going to storm the island, I needed something I could use to defend myself.

Monte and I searched the cabin without finding anything more lethal than kitchen knives. I flopped into the center of the chintz bedspread. "This has got to be a woman's cabin."

"Or a tasteful man's," Monte said.

"A woman alone on a deserted island in the San Juans would have a gun," I reasoned. "But where would she hide it?"

"Underwear drawer?" Monte looked and shook his head.

During the few times Margot had lived alone, she'd had a gun. Of course, she kept it cocked and loaded on her nightstand, probably praying for a male intruder so—she could blow the jerk's balls off. But where would a sane female hide her gun?

I searched under the bed and in the bedroom closet. In the bottom shelf of the closet, behind a copy of _Vanity Fair,_ I discovered a Colt .45 automatic. It was unloaded, and Monte found the bullets in a jewelry box on the dresser.

I cleaned it and hefted it and decided I was ready. When I checked through the windows again, the rain had faded to a slight drizzle but the wind was holding. I stepped onto the porch, and allowed the chill to invigorate me. For the first time, I thought I might have a chance. My mission had changed from kamikaze mode to an actual possibility that I might rescue Alison.

"I'm going, Monte."

He whined, "Back on the boat? I don't want to go on the boat."

"You stay here. If there's any way you can get to a phone, call Forest and tell him that Moorcroft is at Eleanor Island."

"I can't let you do this, Adam. Alison will be so angry."

"She's got no room to be angry," I said. "Alison is an intelligent woman, but she's made some stupid moves."

Monte handed me a Navy cold-weather parka he'd found in

the cabin. I said, "Thanks," and started down the path to the sailboat.

"Bon voyage," Monte called after me.

Hump Back had disengaged herself from the sandbar and was bobbing eagerly. I stuffed the chart into the parka, waded to the boat and climbed in. Clouds concealed the stars but I didn't need them. I would sail a compass heading of two-five-zero all the way. I hauled in the anchor, set the sails and took off like a scalded cat.

Keeping the small boat upright in the fierce wind proved to be a challenge worthy of the saltiest of sailors. But I had sailed in worse weather with lesser boats. No sooner had I spotted a light on Eleanor when the wind died to a whisper. Dropping the sails, I ghosted into a small cove on the eastern side of the island.

Chapter
Sixteen

The feeling of urgency was nearly overwhelming. I had to find Alison and get her out of danger. Then I could contact Forest—if Monte hadn't already done so.

I had already wasted too much time and it was difficult to resist storming the island, commando style, shooting everything that moved and let the authorities sort them out. But I did resist. I had already exhausted my quota of screw-ups. This game was for all the marbles and losing was not an option. I decided to invest a little more time in checking out Eleanor Island.

I beached *Hump Back* in a small, rocky cove near the northeast corner of the island. Quickly crossing a narrow, sandy beach, I crouched in the shadows of a low cliff and reached into my parka for the chart.

On the small-scale chart of the northern San Juans, Eleanor Island was slightly smaller than my thumbnail. As best I could tell, by light of moon, the island was basically triangle shaped— about a half mile long on its sides. There was a larger cove, the kind suitable for seaplanes and large motor launches, a hundred yards or so to the south. I stared at the chart until I had memorized every important detail of the island. Ten seconds was more than adequate since the small map was never intended for more than identifying places you shouldn't bump into with your boat.

I needed to learn everything I could about Eleanor Island in an extremely short period of time. The large cove to the south seemed as good a place as any to begin gathering intelligence. I climbed the low cliff and paused at the top, in the cover of a twisted Pacific Pine. The night was clear and calm and, except for the occasional cry of a loon, quiet. The three-quarter, waxing moon would provide enough light for me to move quickly through the trees and underbrush without announcing to the world that I was less than graceful.

It felt good to get the .45 automatic out of my pants. I pulled back the slide, chambered a round and started to return the gun to my belt, but decided to hang on to it instead. It may have been Douglas MacArthur who said, "Never stick a loaded gun in your pants." With weapon at the ready, I headed directly inland, moving cautiously. After a short distance, not more than fifty feet, I came upon a narrow footpath, which appeared, more or less, to skirt the entire island. A quarter mile to the west, I could see the lights of a house, situated in a hollow between two small hills. The house would be my objective but I'd had enough experience in Vietnam with surrounding myself with the enemy and fighting my way out. I needed to be holding as many aces as possible when I confronted Moorcroft. Allowing someone to get the drop on me because I hadn't properly secured the island would be unforgivable, not to mention fatal.

I moved south on the trail, only pausing once to get stuck in the eye with a low-hanging branch and fall down. After five or ten minutes, I emerged from the trees on the southern side of a short peninsula. The larger cove was a bite at the southeast corner of the island about five hundred feet wide and fifteen hundred feet long. An outcrop of jagged rocks on the east side of the cove extended a couple of hundred feet to the north, obscuring the narrow entrance from the outside.

On the west side of the cove, there was a floating dock with a small shed on one corner. A gangway covered with an awning led from the dock to a large gazebo on the shore. There was no sign of activity in the cove. I moved quietly yet quickly to the gazebo, down the ramp and onto the dock. A single-engine float plane was tied off on the outside edge of the dock. The large launch that Tamara, the blonde, used to lead me halfway here was secured at the north end. On the southern end of the dock a small aluminum fishing boat was tied next to a four-man, inflatable raft.

I was about to leave the dock and continue the reconnaissance when it occurred to me, since my back could not be more against the proverbial wall than it already was, a good way to keep anyone from following when I sailed off with Alison in _Hump Back_ would be to remove all other means of escape from the island.

It could never be as easy as slipping the spring lines and watching the vessels drift away in the tide. The tide was coming in. The plane and boats would just drift to the south end of the cove and gently ground themselves on the sandy bottom near the shore. Not exactly a devastating effect. I had to get the transportation outside the mouth of the cove.

I tied the vessels in a train with the raft in front. The aluminum rowboat was next, followed by the launch and finally the plane. I was about to start the outboard on the _Avon_ when I heard a noise. A door opened and closed at the boat shed located on shore, immediately south of the gazebo. I remained motionless and listened to the muffled voices of a man and a woman.

The couple walked to the parking area adjacent to the marina then stopped to engage in chatty conversation for several minutes. I was working on ideas of how to take them both out when I heard them say good-night. The woman was obviously headed for the house, but the man stayed. The guy was, no doubt, the security for the marina. He had only taken time out to grab a quickie in the boat shed. He was probably feeling pretty good about himself, but somehow I just knew he was going to shit when he saw all the marine hardware on the island tied up in a row.

I slipped out of the rubber raft and on to the dock. Crouching beside the small shed at the bottom of the gangway, I waited for Romeo to recognize the obvious. It didn't take long. I could hear the wheel of his lighter striking the flint. I could see the loom of the flame when he stood at the top of the ramp and lit his cigarette. His words echoed in the darkness when he uttered, "What the fuck?"

My spine stiffened as he started down the ramp. I was ready to pounce on him when he reached the bottom. I tested what little spring I had left in my knees as his pace quickened. The security guard was less than ten feet away and running when I felt the rush of adrenaline I needed to dispatch him stealthily. As he rushed passed my hiding place, I stood and reached for his neck, but I was too late. I couldn't stop him from running, head first, into the wing tip of the airplane, which was now parked where he never expected it to be. The sound of a human skull slamming against reinforced aluminum is like no other. The big man stumbled backward. It was all I could do to get out of the way before he fell on me. Oblivious to my presence, he grasped his forehead and doubled over, cursing. I delivered a quick blow to the back of his head with the butt of the .45, which served to turn his mild concussion into deep sleep.

The guard offered little resistance as I took the Glock 9mm from his shoulder holster and stashed it in my belt. It never hurts to have a spare weapon when you're attempting to overrun an island of people who cut the organs out of perfectly serviceable yuppies. With a pen from his jacket pocket, I scribbled a note on the back of the map I'd marked with directions to Eleanor Island. *This man is dangerous. He is an accomplice in the yuppie mutilations. Treat him as a prisoner and deliver him to Lt. Forest of the Seattle P.D.* I scrawled my name at the bottom and stuffed the map into the rope which bound his wrists behind his back. I thought I had enough credibility with Forest so he would take the note seriously when he saw my name. I hoped that whoever picked up the bad guy would read the note before untying the knots. Maybe they'd call the Coast Guard.

With the sentry bound, gagged, and resting peacefully on the floorboard of the aluminum rowboat, I felt more comfortable about starting the outboard on the raft. I was reasonably certain he was working solo. Otherwise, he wouldn't have been playing hide the banana in the boat shed. It took ten minutes to get the Eleanor Island fleet clear of the cove entrance and set each craft adrift.

I motored back to the dock, climbed out of the _Avon_ and opened the air-valves to all of its chambers. There was no need to hang around and watch it sink. I knew it would.

Less than half an hour had passed since I'd landed, but I couldn't help feeling like I was moving too slow. Exploring the remainder of the southern third of the island at a run revealed more trees and little else. Returning to the parking area in front of the gazebo, I followed a single-lane paved road which led northwest, toward the lights of the house.

The most cautious approach would have been to stay off the road, keep to the trees and long shadows, but that would take too much time. I stayed on the pavement and kept the fastest pace I could without getting winded. It wouldn't do to be panting like a Great Dane in heat when it came time to sneak up on someone.

I had only been walking at a brisk pace for about a minute when I came to a junction. A gravel road, about the same width as the paved road, wound into the trees to the west. I was compelled to maintain the integrity of my original plan—secure the entire island before taking the house or hospital or whatever it was.

The unimproved road led up a small hill. At the top of the hill, nestled amongst the gnarled trunks of madrona trees, was a neglected tennis court, enclosed by a twelve-foot-high chainlink fence. The court was less than a hundred yards from the main house. A half-dozen yards to the west, I peeked through the dusty windows of a large maintenance shed. It was too dark to make out much, but I thought I could see a tractor inside.

I was rattling the lock on the double doors of the shed when a dog started barking near the house. I froze in place as I imagined the powerful jaws of a German shepherd sinking into the soft tissue of my scrotum.

"Bummer!" a woman yelled. And the dog stopped barking. "Shut up and go pee," she demanded in a Southern accent. Then a door slammed and Bummer resumed barking.

I wondered what kind of dog allowed himself to be called Bummer. Probably some old lapdog who runs around sniffing and barking when he's outside because he can't pee on anything but a sculptured pile carpet. However harmless the dog may have been, he was still a noisy problem. His barking would eventually attract attention and someone would come to investigate.

Sub-plan A, I thought, would be to attract the attention of one individual from whom I could gain intelligence without wasting more precious time sneaking around the island. And, if my newest plan worked, Bummer could be very useful.

I rattled the lock again and the barking grew louder and rapidly closer. I moved into the open so Bummer wouldn't have any trouble finding me. I didn't see him right away, but when the barking seemed like about twenty feet away, I ran like a maniac toward the gate to the fenced tennis court. I could feel the dog snot in my shoes when I leaped high onto the court's gate, gripped the steel mesh with the tips of my fingers and lifted my legs from the path of Bummer's jaws as they slammed shut. The gate swung in with a rusty creak and a crash. The black Labrador retriever, who was the size of a small mountain and no less angry because he missed me, charged into the enclosure, snarling. In the instant it took for the beast to turn himself around and readjust his aim, I jumped off the gate, pulled it shut and latched it.

I was on the outside with all my body parts still attached and Bummer the Wonder Dog was contained. Now, if I was patient, his barking would bring me someone to talk to.

It wouldn't take long for someone to come see what it was all about. Bummer barked and yelped incessantly as I took up position in the trees about halfway between the tennis court and the main house. Several minutes had passed and I was beginning to think sub-plan A wasn't going to work when I heard the woman's voice again. "Bummer," she yelled, "come here, boy." The dog continued barking.

The porch light came on and I saw Tamara the Blonde, dressed in hospital whites, step into the yard. She yelled for the dog again and, after a moment, started walking up the hill in the direction of the tennis court.

Tamara passed within a few feet of my hiding place. She looked as good in the nurse's uniform as she did in the hooker costume. I waited for her to get far enough up the trail so I could creep out of the brush without her hearing me, then quickly stepped up behind her. I clapped my left hand over her mouth and slipped my right arm across her chest, pinning her arms. At first her body tensed and I braced for a struggle. But then she relaxed and seductively snuggled her butt against the gun in the front of my pants. I whispered, "Don't scream and you won't get hurt." She nodded and I slowly removed my hand from her mouth.

"Oh, baby," she said in a breathy whisper, "is that a gun in your pocket or are you just happy to see me?"

Her reaction caught me by surprise. "What?"

"I'd love to play some more but I've got surgery, darlin'. Besides, I thought you got enough in the boat shed. Have you been at the gas again?"

She had obviously mistaken me for the man who was by now floating blissfully in the Strait of Juan De Fuca. "Where's Moorcroft?"

She tensed again when she realized I was not who she

thought I was. Then, she purred, "Why, Mr. McCleet. What took you so long? We'd given you up for lost."

"You were expecting me?"

"Of course. Dr. Moorcroft knew you'd have to come after your girlfriend." She wiggled against my gun. "You didn't really think I was dumb enough to let you see me in Friday Harbor and then wait around to get gas so's you could follow."

"You were setting a trap," I said.

"And I guess it worked. Because here you are."

Her logic was inescapable. I had marched right into Moorcroft's trap. It was time to play one of the aces I had up my sleeve. "I arranged for back-up. The cops will be here when the sun comes up."

Her sexy little wiggles ceased immediately. "The police?"

"Hundreds of them. Storming the island. If you don't get killed in the shoot-out, you'll get to go to prison. The question is, for how long?"

Her heartbeat accelerated. I could feel it. Somehow, her incredible body turned cold. "What would it take, Mr. McCleet, for you to let me go?"

"Cooperation. I want to know what else is on the island, how many people are in the house? Where's Alison?"

"Then you'll let me go?"

"Sure, I promise." Why not? There wasn't anyplace she could go. The boats were gone. Her boyfriend was on his way to the Pacific Ocean. I started with an easy question, "How many people are on the island?"

"Eleven. Men and women. That's not counting the patients. Or your girlfriend. Or Dr. Moorcroft and Dr. Sterling."

"How many are armed?"

"I'm sure I don't know."

"Guess."

"Maybe half of them."

"Where are they?" I asked, hoping they were all contained in a small room where I could lock the door and go about my business of rescuing Alison without further interruption.

"Most everybody's sleeping," she said vaguely. "Of course, we are preparing for another surgery."

Of course. So there was another individual on the island she had not mentioned. A nameless yuppie bastard who was about to ride that great Beamer in the sky so Trevor Ingersoll, genius artist, might have another few years of life. And I was going to pull the plug on his operation.

Aware that Bummer's barking might attract even more attention, I repeated, "Where's Alison?"

"Second floor bedroom. On the northwest corner of the house. Can't miss it. There's a balcony and steps leading up from the swimming pool." She inhaled deeply and her breasts expanded against my arm. "Please let me go, Mr. McCleet."

She seemed innocent enough, this female who had Maced me in Seattle and had led me and Monte through a storm to Moorcroft's doorstep. If I could have seen her baby blue eyes, I'm sure she would have batted her lashes.

"Please," she repeated. Her voice was as sultry as wind through the faraway magnolias of the deep South. "I won't tell anybody."

If I let her go and if she believed my statement that the cavalry was on the way, her most rational course would be to scamper down to the docks, grab her boyfriend and take off. I loosened my grasp.

She slipped out from under my arm, whirled and did, in fact, flutter her eyelashes. "Thanks, darlin'. You won't forget to tell the police how I helped, will you now?"

When she went down to the dock, when she found the boats and her boyfriend gone . . .

"Will you?"

This woman could cause a lot of trouble for me.

"I'm eternally grateful, Mr. McCleet."

I couldn't take the chance. "Come here, there's one more thing I need to know."

She stepped toward me. "What's that, darlin'?"

"Who killed Stuart Hall?"

"Who?"

"The little dentist that got tossed off the roof of the Puget Madrona."

"Oh. That was Wolfgang."

"Is he on the island?"

"Yep. You can't miss him. He's guarding your girlfriend."

I thanked Tamara with one quick punch to the side of her head, a sucker punch. I took care not to break her nose or jaw. She hit the ground like a sack of sugar.

I flung her over my shoulder, carried her to the tennis courts and wedged her through the gate. Bummer calmed immediately, lay down beside her and began salivating on her limp upturned palm. It was a particularly touching picture, and I felt like shit for knocking a woman unconscious. I promised myself that in two or three weeks, when Alison was safe, I would feel guilty.

The swimming pool around back was lit fluorescent blue. I spotted the bedroom that must be Alison's. A faint pinkish light shone through the French windows. As the unconscious Tamara had described, there was a flight of stairs leading to a balcony. I crept up the steps as silently as possible. It seemed unlikely that Moorcroft would leave Alison in a room with an outdoor access without a guard.

I peered around the edge of the window frame and saw Alison lying flat on a hospital bed. Her wrists were fastened to the side rails with restraints, and I guessed from her position that her ankles were similarly secured. Her head turned toward the window, and her eyes widened a fraction of an inch when she saw me. Immediately, she nodded toward the foot of her bed where there was a white sofa. On the sofa was a giant body-builder type with a shoulder holster. He thumbed through a back issue of _Screw_ magazine. Wolfgang, the guy who'd snuffed Stuart, was the same behemoth who had attacked me in the parking garage when I was looking for Phil's car.

Alison cleared her throat. "I'd like a drink of water."

Muscles did not respond.

"If you don't mind," she said after a moment. "I want some damn water."

He dragged himself upright with all the grace of a wrecking crane. He was tall enough to touch the ceiling with his knuckles when he stretched and yawned. Slowly, he ambled from the room into an adjoining bathroom where I heard him running water into a glass.

I twisted the doorknob in my hand. It was a pleasant surprise to find it open. Apparently, security hadn't been much of an issue on Eleanor Island. I stepped inside and crouched behind an elegantly upholstered wing chair.

Returning to Alison's bedside, the guard stood with his back toward me and held out the water. "Here."

Alison's hands in the restraints balled into small fists. "I can't hold it. Maybe you could unfasten one of these restraints."

"Not a chance." He bent at the waist and slipped one hand beneath her hair to prop up her head. When he held the water glass to her lips, I figured he was pretty much preoccupied. I would have been.

I was in no mood to play slap and tickle with a murderous walking muscle. In two strides, I was behind him. I wrapped my forearm around his throat, grabbed my own wrist with my free hand and yanked. He made a wheezing noise as he tried to inhale but couldn't. His struggle was minimal, then he slumped to the ground.

"Is he dead?" Alison was propped up on her elbows. Water dripped from her face.

I worked at unfastening the restraints on her wrists. I didn't want to answer her question.

"God, Adam, I was so wrong. I'm so glad to see you. Is he dead?"

"No, Alison. He's just sleeping." In fact, the ogre who killed Stuart Hall was dead. Crushed windpipes are generally fatal, but I figured Alison had been through enough. She didn't need a dead guard on her conscience.

As soon as her hands were unfastened, she threw her arms around my neck. "I'm so sorry. Can you forgive me?"

Being on the receiving end of an apology was always nice, but we really didn't have time for a relationship talk. "We need to get out of here, Alison."

"Absolutely." She flopped back on the bed and allowed me to untie the restraints on her ankles. "We need to get out of here. After we find Trevor."

"Fuck Trevor," I heard myself saying. "You and me. We. Us. Two of us. We need to get off this island. Now."

She curled her feet up under her and pushed her wet hair off her forehead. "I'm not going without Trevor."

Somewhere, in the pit of my heart, I knew she was right about this. If I left Trevor in the clutches of Moorcroft or allowed him to be picked up by Forest for questioning, I would regret it. His selfishness had gotten us into this mess but he hadn't intended Alison or me to be hurt. Still, there was a logistical problem. "Can he travel?"

"Not for any distance."

"Then we can't take him. I only have a small sailboat to get off the island."

"What about the helicopter?"

I blinked stupidly. "The helicopter?"

"You can fly it. It's just like the one you took me for a ride in."

My surveillance of the island had not extended far enough. Time for a change in plan. "Okay, let's find Trevor."

I grabbed her hand and shepherded her toward the French doors. Just as Alison stepped onto the balcony, I heard the door behind me open with a crash. Moorcroft stood there, silhouetted in the light of the hallway.

He got off the first shot.

My lower leg exploded in pain.

Chapter
Seventeen

Time slowed to a halt. My mind saw the bullet tear through the lower leg of my jeans before it actually happened. A second explosion meant that the shot which I had intended for Moorcroft, was on its way. From my vantage point on the floor, I saw Moorcroft drop his gun as he fell. I saw a lot of other things too: my father and grandfather, a collection of all-too-familiar faces from Vietnam, the first girl I had sex with, a mutilated dead man on Alki beach, and scores of other images both pleasant and profane.

By the time I got around to thinking about my leg again, Alison was at my side, trying to get me on my feet. "Adam, can you walk?" she asked urgently.

The panic in her voice brought my reality back into real-time. Suddenly my total being was consumed with pain. She was pulling on my right arm and, since Moorcroft's bullet had opened a tunnel a few inches below my right knee, it was impossible for me to move in that direction. "Don't pull," I groaned. "Lift."

Alison bent down and I put my right arm over her shoulder.

"We'll stand up together," she said. Her jogging and healthy eating were paying off. Alison supported a tremendous amount of weight as I worked my left leg into position and pulled myself up. "Oh, my God, Adam. You're not going to die, are you?"

I wasn't completely sure. "Not yet," I said through gritted teeth. "Let's move."

Using a small female as a substitute for a leg is an awkward proposition. Our first step together sent us both sprawling. Our second attempt was more successful. Negotiating the stairs was dicey, but by the time we hit level ground, we were moving like the Radio City Rockettes.

At the south end of the house, a small set of concrete steps led to the double doors of a garden-level basement. "This has got to be the hospital," I proclaimed.

I checked the Glock to make sure the safety was off before we stumbled down the steps and crashed into the steel doors. They were locked. I was about to shoot the lock when Alison said, "Wait."

She pushed a button beside the door and I could hear a faint ringing. We waited less than a minute for a man's voice on the other side to say, "Who is it?"

"Avon," Alison said in a cheerful, salesperson's voice.

"Who?"

"Domino's," I said.

The door swung open and a large young man in whites greeted us with a large gun. I shot him.

Alison was astonished. "You shot him."

"I know. Good thing he works in a hospital."

What looked like a basement from the outside was a full-blown surgical hospital. Expensive equipment lined the hall. The ceramic tile floor sparkled. On the left side of the hall was another pair of doors, bearing a piece of masking tape with Lab written on it. A glance through the round window at the top of the door revealed more expensive equipment but no people.

A large, single stainless steel door on the opposite side of the hall had no window but it did have a similar piece of tape marked Surgery. I tested the latch. The door was not locked. I pushed it open and Alison and I hobbled into the room.

We were greeted by a tall man with long, stringy gray hair. I recognized the beard and granny glasses. "Mr. McCleet?" he said with an appropriate degree of surprise in his inflection.

"Sterling."

He stepped toward us but stopped as soon as I resteadied my aim. "I'm Dr. Lionel Sterling, chief surgeon."

Alison looked at Sterling with tears welling in the corners of her endlessly green eyes. "Can you fix his leg, Doctor?"

"Well, of course I can fix his leg, you adorable creature. I can take his heart out and put it back in time for him to join us for breakfast."

This did not sound like a good idea to me. "Alison, I'm okay. Let's just get Trevor and get the hell out of here."

"You're losing a tremendous amount of blood," Sterling said. He was talking to me but he was looking longingly at Alison. "I could do such a wonderful job on your friend's leg, and I would love you to see me work."

"Adam, please. At least let him stop the bleeding. How can you fly the helicopter if you're bleeding to death?"

"I'm not bleeding to death, Alison. I feel just fucking fantastic."

"Euphoria," Sterling chirped. "You, sir, are most definitely bleeding to death."

"Oh, God, Adam, please," Alison pleaded. "I'm scared."

"Scared is a proper attitude. Do I have to remind you that this joker kills people?"

"I also save people," Sterling said. The sincerity in his voice was unmistakable. "I need you significantly more than you need me." He was no longer looking at Alison. Instead, his narrow-set eyes were fixed on me.

I didn't understand why Sterling thought he needed me, but the logic of Alison's argument did not escape me. I understood that I was bleeding more than either of us would have liked. But, the idea of putting my life directly into the hands of Dr. Demento stunk, out loud. "How long would it take?" I asked Sterling.

The doctor's eyebrows lowered as he stroked his beard. "Well," he began to mumble, "we'll get some blood started. Of course I'll need x-rays, a bone graft may be indicated, they usually are in these types of injuries. Then there's the cast and recovery and rehab and—"

"How long?" I demanded as I aimed the Glock at his furrowed brow.

"With my highly advanced techniques, I can have you in a walking-cast in about a week."

I started to laugh, then felt as if I was going to the bathroom on myself. I knew I was blacking out and there seemed to be very little I could do about it. Alison knew from the additional weight I was applying to her frail shoulders that I was going to collapse. She tried to move me toward a vacant gurney. I started to go with her but my feet didn't follow. Sterling stepped forward and—

It felt good to be lying down, until I realized that I had blacked out. I wondered for how long. Resisting a slight urge to panic, I slowly opened my eyes.

A plastic bag, a third full of something that reminded me of pigeon blood, hung from an I.V. stand beside my head. A tube, full of the crimson liquid, ran from the stand to a piece of adhesive tape on my right forearm. At the foot of the gurney, Alison stood holding the gun. The barrel of the 9mm trembled in her two-fisted, white-knuckled grip. Her aim was in the general direction of Sterling, who was smiling and humming the theme song to *M.A.S.H.* as he worked over my leg. An annoying absence of pain made me wonder for an instant if I was dead.

As reality settled back in to my thought process, I remembered the reason I didn't want this wing-nut working on me in the first place. I also remembered the discomfort in my lower abdomen, caused by the barrel of the extra gun, which I had stashed in the waist of my trousers, pressing against my pelvis.

The draw, cock, and aim, skillfully executed in one quick and deadly motion which I had visualized did not come off as smoothly as I might have preferred. My fertile imagination had failed to compensate for the difficulty of using my left hand to draw a weapon which had been holstered from the right. When I finally struggled to get the gun from under my belt, the grip was up-side-down in my hand. Cocking the thing was a physical impossibility. I had to lay the .45 on my chest to get a proper grip on it. By the time I had taken aim on Sterling, he was waiting for me to stop jerking around.

"What are you doing to my leg?" I demanded.

"I'm saving it," Sterling said. "And, if you can just hold still for a few more minutes, you'll be able to fly us all off this island."

I propped myself up on one elbow and got a good look at the purple and yellow flesh around an angry red hole which, I was certain, went through my shin bone and out the back of my leg. Sterling was sewing stuff back together. "I'm not flying you any-where." I returned to the prone position. "You're going to wait here for the police."

Sterling continued sewing. "As I was explaining to Alison, I am not the dangerous person you both think I am. I'm a scientist, not unlike Louis Pasteur or Jonas Salk. Through my research here, I have developed organ-transplant techniques that will blow the socks off of the medical community. Not to mention an anesthetic which all but eliminates surgical trauma and acceler-ates recovery time exponentialy."

"Would that anesthetic be a gas that makes you feel like a teenager and gives a man a twenty-four hour erection?" Alison asked.

"Yes. It's not completely without side effects."

"You've got something with the gas," I said, "but your so-called research has cost the lives of at least fifty percent of your patients. I wouldn't hold my breath waiting for the Nobel prize if I were you."

"How'd you get into this business in the first place?" Alison asked.

"It wasn't as difficult as you might think," Sterling said. "Avery Moorcroft and I worked together at a hospital in Denver, Colorado. He was the chief of staff and I was the chief surgeon. Avery took money to pull the plug on an otherwise-healthy coma patient, with a decent chance of recovery, so I could put a young heart into an aging and sinfully over-indulgent movie producer from Aspen. We did it. Someone found out and we were both fired and barred from practicing medicine. The only reason we didn't go to prison then was because the hospital wanted to keep a low profile for fear of being sued by the family of the coma patient.

"When Avery proposed the idea for this enterprise, it seemed to make such perfect sense for both of us. He could make all the money he ever dreamed of and I could continue my research." Sterling became indignant. "What are the lives of a few tedious, pathetic, hopelessly plastic people when compared to the thousands that will be saved by what I've learned from them?"

A reality check seemed to be in order. "You don't get it yet, do you, Doc? You blew it. You're going to jail, they might even hang you—they still do that in Washington. You can't possibly believe that anyone is going to listen to the medical ravings of a convicted, multiple murderer. At best, you'll be sterilizing specimen bottles in a prison infirmary for the rest of your twisted life. Now finish up because Alison and I are getting out of here."

"And Trevor," Alison said.

"Sure," I continued. "But you, Doctor—"

"And him," she interrupted, pointing to the unconscious stranger who lay on a gurney a few feet from the operating table. "We can't leave him here."

"Okay, but," I had to draw the line somewhere, "the doc, here, stays. And he can tell the cops all about his brilliant research." Considering the fact that my lower leg had been reduced to a bag of broken glass, I couldn't have been less diplomatic to the man who held it in his hands.

"It is you who don't get it, Mr. McCleet. If you leave me here, Avery Moorcroft, or one of his men, will kill me long before the authorities arrive."

"Why would Moorcroft want to kill you?" Alison asked.

"You're his meal ticket," I added, lifting my head to check his progress.

Sterling was wrapping a bale of cotton over the wound. "I'm afraid Avery doesn't see it that way. You see, greed has driven him quite mad. You can't imagine the amounts of money involved in a simple cornea transplant."

I watched as Sterling surrounded the cotton with a layer of bubble-wrap from my ankle to mid-thigh. "For a guy who likes his job so much, he seems to run a pretty sloppy ship. Leaving bodies lying around for the cops to find is not exactly the best way to avoid getting caught."

"I left the bodies where people would find them," Sterling said. "One of Avery's many mistakes was to trust me, a man who wanted to be caught. I was trying to leave a trail."

Sterling had somehow confused dead people with bread crumbs. "If you wanted to be caught so bad, you could have turned yourself in to the cops instead of visiting my hotel room."

"I was on my way to do precisely that. But first I had to know if Dr. Stang survived. I never would have operated on a medical professional if I had known."

"Before you could get out of my room, Moorcroft's people found you and dragged you back to this island."

"Correct," Sterling said. "When Avery discovered what I was up to, he promised to kill me if I endangered his business again. He meant it. He was already in the process of eliminating everyone involved."

Like Sylvia. And the owner of the Turk's Head who had his throat slit from ear to ear, and Stuart. Moorcroft was purging his organization, eliminating the employees who could not be trusted. Killing them was probably easier than paying unemployment compensation. But Sterling was a fairly essential ingredient in his scheme. "Without you, he's got nothing," I said. "There can't be many surgeons who do organ transplants."

"Unfortunately, I've worked myself out of a job," he said, sounding almost reasonable. "Avery was actually planning to franchise. My techniques have been so carefully documented that I already trained two nurses. If they follow the procedures I've taught them, they can manage the most intricate of operations quite nicely."

"And nobody who pays for an illegal transplant is going to file a malpractice suit."

"Avery Moorcroft is not a fool, Mr. McCleet. He won't make the same mistakes when he opens shop in another country. He'll stop at nothing."

"He'll stop at a bullet," I said.

"You would shoot him?" Sterling asked.

"I already did."

"You shot him? Is he dead?"

I didn't really know if Moorcroft was dead or alive. I hadn't bothered to go back and check his vitals when he went down. "I'm not sure. At the very least, he's wounded. And he's not getting off this island."

With a portable gas bottle, similar to the one I remember from my hotel room, Sterling inflated the bubble-wrap. "Done," he announced. "Wiggle your toes please."

I obeyed. Even though I couldn't feel them very well, all five of my toes functioned to Sterling's satisfaction.

"This will only get you to the nearest hospital," Sterling cautioned, "if we don't waste any more time."

I sat up and swung my legs off the gurney. The bandaged limb stuck out parallel to the floor and felt like it belonged to someone else. The trek to the helicopter was going to be tricky. I hopped down.

"Don't put your weight on it," Sterling advised.

"Whose weight would you suggest I put on it?" I took a step. Not pretty, but functional. I could move.

Nodding to Alison, I said, "Let's go."

"You hold the guns," she responded. "I'll wheel Trevor to the helicopter, then I'll come back and get—"

"Whoa, Alison. Time out. I want to get off this island before Christmas."

She shrugged. "Then we'll have to take Dr. Sterling so he can handle the other gurney."

"Okay. He can help. Then we'll say good-bye at the helipad."

Alison and Sterling were already in position behind their respective gurneys. I opened the surgery door and led the parade. Our progress was as subtle as a platoon of Shriner clowns on squeaky tricycles. But since the gunshots hadn't drawn any attention, I doubted that our little parade would wake anyone.

"Where is everybody?" Alison asked.

"Sleeping soundly or having sex," Sterling said. "The off-duty staff likes my gas."

The path leading from surgery to the helicopter pad was paved to provide a smooth ride for the patients who had paid big bucks to have their faulty organs replaced. Patients like Trevor. What the hell had he been thinking? I really hoped that he had deluded himself into believing that this was some mysterious process that would not hurt anyone. I hated to believe that my old mentor would be willing to take another person's life so he could overindulge himself for a few more years.

I'd been wrong about someone noticing. Along the path, about ten yards ahead of us, I caught sight of a baseball cap dodging behind a shrub. It was too dark to identify the team logo, and the fact that I cared was an indication that my brain was not functioning up to speed. My lack of sensibility was further evident when I looked toward Alison, Sterling and two men on gurneys and said, "Duck."

Instead, they froze. Alison repeated, "Duck, Adam?"

Before I could explain, the baseball hat came charging along the path. The man wearing it aimed a rake at my chest like a knight with a lance. What we had here was an overprotective gardener. It would have been easier if he were a cold-blooded thug I could shoot in the chest without straining my conscience too badly. But I couldn't gun down a man who was armed only with a rake, especially not since he was wearing a University of Oregon Ducks baseball cap. The Fighting Ducks were my favorite team.

I pivoted on my good leg and avoided the avenging rake. The guy went down, but bounced right back up. I showed him the gun. "Drop it."

He paused. "Who are you?"

Sterling actually made a useful statement. "It's only me, Armando. We're taking these patients to another facility."

"I don't think so. Dr. Avery says you don't go nowhere near the transportations or he shoots everybody."

Sterling ignored him and proceeded along the path. Alison followed.

"You better not," Armando warned. "Dr. Avery is going to be real mad."

"You like the Ducks?" I asked conversationally. Sooner or later, I was going to have to take the guy out. But I didn't have a clue as to what method I would use.

He was thinking faster than I was. He swiped with his rake and whacked the cast on my leg. Though I was still carrying enough anesthetic to put a yeti to sleep, I felt the jolt from the nerve endings in my teeth to the farthest extremities of my body. If I'd been fully aware, the pain would have killed me.

"Look, Armando, I don't want to shoot you, but if you do that again, I will be forced to open a causeway through your chest with this big gun."

But Armando wasn't listening. He was dancing around with the rake, feinting and jabbing like a crazed ninja. His next assault was a full swing. He hit my good leg.

There was nothing wrong with my reflexes. I was barely

aware that my right arm had grabbed Armando by the shirt front and lifted the little man off his feet. His face was inches from mine. "Go away, Armando."

I threw him backwards and pivoted on my formerly good leg, heading toward the helipad.

With a kamikaze yell, Armando raced toward me. He'd been planning to leap onto my back, but I bent down and the little man flew over my shoulders.

"Armando, I'm starting to wonder if our relationship is really going anywhere."

Alison came running down the path. "Adam, what are you doing? Let's get out of here."

I really couldn't take the time to explain the code of ethics that made it wrong for me to kill an overzealous gardener, no matter how tedious Armando had become. It was a guy thing.

And it didn't bother Alison in the least. She darted around Armando, took the gun from my hand and aimed it in the general direction of his chest.

The gardener's eyes were the size of Volkswagen hubcaps when the 9mm slug went through his foot. Without further ado, Armando passed out.

I snatched the gun from Alison's hands. "Don't do that!"

She took my arm over her shoulder to displace some of the weight from my bum leg and helped me limp toward the helicopter. I decided to save the lecture about shooting unarmed men for another time.

The helicopter, a Jet-Ranger, was custom equipped as an air ambulance. Two seats in front for the flight crew and two jump seats in the back for the medical crew. The cargo door on the starboard side was open and I could see Sterling crouched in the back with his two patients on collapsed gurneys. Alison helped me to the other side and climbed into the right seat.

I pulled myself into the pilot seat and lifted the useless leg in with both hands. "This is where we say good-bye, Dr. Sterling,"

I said as I turned on the battery and scanned the instruments for the first time. "Get out. And close the door behind you."

Cold steel pressed against the back of my neck and a voice behind me said, "Dr. Sterling was unavoidably detained. I promised to say good-bye for him, after you've flown me to Canada."

Alison looked over her left shoulder. "Moorcroft," she gasped.

"Are you sure?" I said. "I thought I killed him."

"If your aim had been a few inches lower, Mr. McCleet," Moorcroft said, "You would have. Instead, you just splintered my collarbone. It is most painful, but I can assure you that I will survive. Now, start this thing and head toward Victoria."

Reasoning that Moorcroft would be less likely to shoot me if I was actually engaged in the act of piloting his escape vehicle, I did as I was told, after a fashion. I headed the Ranger toward the west long enough to convince anyone with a sense of direction that we were headed for Victoria. After a few minutes, I started a slow, almost imperceptible, turn to the right. I was counting heavily on Moorcroft not knowing how to read the directional gyro. If he didn't, I'd have him in the middle of downtown Friday Harbor in no time.

I felt the gun barrel press harder against my neck. "The heading will be two-eight-zero, McCleet," Moorcroft yelled over the noise of the engine and wind rushing into the cabin through the cargo door. "Are you lost?"

So much for sub-plan B. Moorcroft had traveled this route before. "Why don't you put the gun away? You're not going to shoot me as long as I'm flying this thing."

I felt the pressure release from the back of my neck and heard Moorcroft say, "You're correct, of course. How about if I shoot your lady instead?"

The sight of the gun barrel pressed against Alison's delicate skin was profane. The light was too dim for me to see her eyes but I knew she must have been terrified. I stomped on the left rudder pedal and the tail of the helicopter jerked violently to the right.

The move could have been fatal for Alison but the fact that Moorcroft had no intention of letting any of us live was inescapable. The gamble paid off. Moorcroft slammed against the port bulkhead with a groan. Before he could recover, I pulled into a steep climb, just long enough to add a few pounds of gravity to his weight, then pushed the nose over. The maneuver was everything I hoped it would be. When I looked over my shoulder, Moorcroft was floating around the aft cabin like a balloon and he no longer held the gun. His weightlessness however, was only a temporary state. When I pulled the stick back again, he slammed to the cabin floor. I heard a moan from Trevor, or his donor. Bouncing Moorcroft around the inside of the chopper was fun, but I wasn't going to be able to keep it up. The other passengers were suffering.

One more carefully timed maneuver was all I needed. The next time I looked aft, Moorcroft was getting to his feet. He appeared to be in a great deal of pain. In billiards, positioning is everything. I allowed him to stumble forward a couple of steps then pulled the stick back again. Moorcroft was held in place by the additional gravity. I pushed the Ranger into a steeply descending right turn then pulled up hard. Moorcroft screamed as he went out the cargo door.

Alison screamed, "Oh, my God, he fell out."

He should have buckled up.

Alison looked at me with waves of tears staining her cheeks. "Is it over?" she asked in a trembling hysterical kind of voice.

"Almost. Do you think you can climb in back and check on Trevor? Maybe you can get that door closed while your back there."

Alison nodded, unfastened her seat belt and climbed aft. I turned to a new heading—one that would take us to safety. The sun's first rays loomed across the mainland and I could see several craft headed toward Eleanor Island. Monte had done his job. The timing left something to be desired but at least they could round up the remaining bad guys and Sterling, if there was anything left of him.

The next order of business was to set the chopper down at the nearest hospital. I was about to ask Alison to look around for an aviation chart when I heard her scream. My immediate thought was that she had fallen out the door while trying to close it. When I looked aft, she had fallen on the floor and was clinging desperately to an iron pipe which extended through the nylon webbing in the port side jump seat. Her feet were nearly out the door and the fingers of a man's left hand dug into her ankle. Moorcroft had managed to hang on somehow and was now either trying to pull Alison out, or himself in.

Fancy flying wasn't going to solve this problem. Anything I did was likely to loosen Alison's grip on the seat and send her plunging to a certain death. With my own mobility restricted by the stiff cast on my leg, there seemed to be nothing I could do. "Hang on," I yelled.

My mind raced, sifting through and discarding possible options as quickly as they occurred. We were more than a thousand feet above the icy water of the Puget Sound. A fall from that altitude would certainly kill her. If I could descend low enough in time, she might survive. It wasn't much, but it was all I could think of. I pushed the stick forward until we were headed down at a rate of five hundred feet per minute. I tried to get hold of Alison but she was just out of reach. I had never felt more useless. Alison's grip was slipping and I couldn't help her.

My attention was split between keeping the chopper right-side-up and trying to see what was going on in the back. When I looked back, Trevor, who I thought was unconscious, was trying to turn over. The jostling I'd given him had probably been painful.

Just as Alison's grip failed, Trevor reached out from his gurney and grabbed Moorcroft's wrist. Trevor's expression was one of total determination. The veins of his muscular hand bulged.

When he was in good health, Trevor's grip was like the talons of an eagle. No matter how hard he squeezed, he always had a little more strength in reserve. I only hoped he had some reserve now.

Finally, the old man's strength prevailed. Moorcroft released his grip on Alison's leg. Trevor's hand trembled violently. For a moment, it looked as if he was going to drag Moorcroft back into the helicopter. Instead, he lifted him up until he could see the pain and terror in Moorcroft's eyes, then smiled contemptuously and released his grip. Moorcroft's fingertips caught the doorway and clung there for an instant, then slipped out of sight.

"What have you two been doing, rearranging the furniture?" Monte asked as Alison and I exited her office, marked PRIVATE.

"A gentleman doesn't discuss such things," I said, tucking in my shirt.

"Monte, is everyone here?" Alison asked.

"Everyone except Margot. She got tired of waiting and left for a sale at Gucci."

That was fine with me. I wasn't particularly eager to hear my sister's critique of my latest work. The three of us walked into the gallery with Monte leading the way. We paused as he introduced me with a grand flourish. "People," he announced, "the Brooks Gallery takes great pleasure in presenting one of the premier artistic, investigative adventurers of our time, A. A. McCleet."

An overly enthusiastic round of applause rose from the small, private gathering of friends and family. They had come by invitation for the unveiling of a sculpture I'd been working on since Trevor's funeral.

Trevor had been unconscious when we set down at Bellingham. By the time he was transferred to Seattle by air ambulance, he was D.O.A. We never had the opportunity to speak to each other again. After several months of confusion and doubt, I finally chose to believe my old friend didn't know that Moorcroft and Sterling were hurting other people.

I nodded graciously and moved into the crowd with Alison on my arm. Phil Stang was the first to greet me with a wide orthodontist smile. He looked none the worse for a man who'd lost a kidney only four months earlier. "How's the leg, Adam?" Phil asked.

"Good, Phil. The cast comes off in a couple of weeks." The doctors were astounded at how fast I recovered. I actually encouraged them to meet with Sterling—who was being held for trial without bail—and listen to what he had to say. The man was twisted, but he definitely knew his medicine.

"Now," Phil said, "when we get together, we can talk about our operations."

"You can talk about anything you want with me, Phil."

Phil was misty eyed. "You'll never have to worry about your teeth as long as I'm around."

So I had that going for me. Phil's overt demonstration of his affection was touching, but I decided to slip away before we moved into the hugging phase. "Phil, would you excuse me?" I asked, resting a hand on his shoulder. "I see a gaggle of obscure cousins starting to clump in the corner over there. We're trying to encourage them to date outside the family, you know."

We exchanged smiles and handshakes and I moved on with Alison to repeat the process with as many of the people there as possible. It felt good to be out and among friends again. I had spent enough time with my memories and I had come to a kind of peace with them. Now, what I needed most of all was close contact with sensitive, caring, intelligent, supportive, gentle human beings. When I saw Nick Gabreski and Ed Forest working their way across the room toward me like a pair of linebackers, I estimated they possessed, between the two of them, at least three of those qualities, if you count being human as two. Nonetheless, I was glad to see them both.

"So, Adam," Nick said as we shook hands. "What's this new statue—another naked lady on a fish?"

"Not this time, Nick. This time it's something completely different." I turned my attention to Forest, who was already engaged in conversation with Alison. "Glad you could make it, Lieutenant." I extended my hand and he grasped it firmly.

Alison and I had spent a great deal of time with Nick and Forest over the previous months, answering, explaining, helping to tie up loose ends. It was Forest who kept me from being hung by the Coast Guard and the Washington Bureau of Investigations and the F.A.A. and countless other agencies, large and small, for my involvement in what they had come to refer to as, "the Eleanor Island incident."

"Is it an abstract?" Forest asked. "I'm cultivating an appreciation for the abstract."

Nick interpreted. "He's trying not to hate the shit."

"You'll all see soon enough," I said as I stepped toward the large lump of red satin, which occupied the space of honor in the center of the gallery. "Friends," I announced, "thank you for coming. I wanted all of you to be the first to see this piece, which is dedicated to the memory of Trevor Ingersoll, friend and teacher." I grasped the satin drape and pulled it away with a flourish. First there was silence. I had taken the room by surprise. The silence turned into a collective mumble and crescendoed into applause and finally cheers.

"It's kind of abstract," Nick remarked. "But I do like it."

"It's no more abstract than life itself, Nickster," I said. He and the others liked how it looked. But I liked what it meant and how it felt. The piece was made of black granite and depicted two strong arms rising from a block of clay. There was no way the viewers could know that the left arm was Trevor's and the right was mine. A human heart balanced delicately on the fingertips of the two powerful hands.

"What do you call it, McCleet?" Forest asked.

"No. I'm McCleet. This piece is called *Spare Parts*."